DEADTIME

As Glyndower came around the curve in the corridor, he was met by a stream of bullets. Someone down there was using a fixed-mount gun instead of the little portable stuff they had been using earlier. He waded into the bullets, pushing harder and harder as he neared the gun. It was one of those weapons that fired six hundred slugs a second, with a large shield behind it to keep an attacker from picking off the person doing the firing.

I must be getting close to something good, he thought . . .

SPACE COPS
KILL STATION

DIANE DUANE & PETER MORWOOD

AVONOVA

AVON BOOKS • NEW YORK

SPACE COPS: KILL STATION is an original publication of Avon Books. This work has never before appeared in book form. This work is a novel. Any similarity to actual persons or events is purely coincidental.

AVON BOOKS
A division of
The Hearst Corporation
1350 Avenue of the Americas
New York, New York 10019

Copyright © 1992 by Bill Fawcett & Associates
Cover art by Dorian Vallejo
Published by arrangement with Bill Fawcett & Associates
Library of Congress Catalog Card Number: 91-92089
ISBN: 0-380-75854-7

First AvoNova Printing: January 1992

AVONOVA TRADEMARK REG. U.S. PAT. OFF. AND IN OTHER COUNTRIES, MARCA REGISTRADA, HECHO EN U.S.A.

Printed in the U.S.A.

RA 10 9 8 7 6 5 4 3 2 1

"Laws are like cobwebs, which may catch small flies, but let wasps and hornets break through."

Swift, *A Critical Essay upon the Faculties of the Mind*

"I beg cold comfort."

Shakespeare, *King John*, v. vii. 42

ONE

☆

THEY WERE TWO HOURS PAST JUPITER AND heading for the Outer Belt, and Evan was eating Spaghetti Bolognese, his own recipe, and reading the message from their supervisor. It was a moot point which of them would give him indigestion first.

"For pity's sake," Joss said, "don't put that stuff there! You'll ruin the upholstery."

Or perhaps there was a third candidate—Evan's shipmate. "You worry too much. It's just spaghetti."

"And the tomato sauce is acid. You'll ruin the leather."

"Ah, then," Evan said, sighing and moving the bowl off the right-hand seat and onto the instrument panel between them, "my mother would love you, you know that?"

"Not there, either!!"

The interior of the ship was indeed very neat and clean, but it could hardly help being so, for Joss had cleaned it about six times since they left Earth. Evan was having some difficulty dealing with his partner's frightful tidiness. But then, what could you expect of a new sop, almost still wet behind the ears, who had just been given his first patrol vehicle?

"It wants dirtying up a little," Evan said, grumbling on purpose as he turned away from Joss's fussing. "You may want anyone who sees us to think we're just new out of Earth and crazy eager, but by the good God, *I* don't. Too much shine attracts attention."

1

Joss came and leaned over Evan's seat, very pointedly removing the flat plastic spaghetti bowl from the console between the two front seats. "Who was it, then," he said, "that I saw mooning over the last sealer coat, oohing and aahing and telling them where to put the shield? Hypocrite."

"Come back here with that!" Evan shouted after Joss and the spaghetti, but there was no point in it. They *were* close to their destination, and Joss was already into the ship's little galley, tidying again.

Evan sat back and sighed once more, looking out through the plex at the seemingly unchanging view of blackness and stars. It was true enough that having their own ship, so soon in their partnership, was a bit of a plum. Nor was it a bad craft at all—not the usual two-man patrol "crib", but a ship with separate staterooms, with its own tiny detention facility, and with a computer core worth having. It was just as well: they would need the computer core where they were going. Even hyperboosted data signals couldn't go faster than light, and once past Mars they were a good two and a half light-hours from the computer facilities in the Solar Patrol HQ on the Moon. A daily back-and-forth dump from their core to the SP master reference would be the best they could afford. It was a little hard to get used to. The familiar voice of their online facilitator, Telya, was missing from their inner ears for the first time in months.

As senior partner of the team, and with both of them being in good odor from their last job, Evan had gotten away with insisting on the addition of some armaments that many sops didn't get to see put into their ships. Money had not changed hands—nothing so sordid—but Evan had used the old Glyndower charm, and had called in some favors among the people in Shipfitting at Solar Patrol headquarters, and his and Joss's supervisor, Lucretia, had pointedly looked the other way during the proceedings.

Well, mostly.

"POINT THREE," said the communication that was

presently showing on Evan's pad. *"Expenses.* While I understand that your business on *Freedom* required a great deal of capital outlay, the Commissioner has told me to impress on you that inappropriate professional largesse, such as the habitual spending of almost your entire year's salary in the pursuit of one drug manufacturer, is not to be further encouraged. This job is going to be a considerably lower-outlay sort of procedure. You are not to construe your being given a ship as meaning that you are free to mistreat it, damage it, or use it for unnecessary jaunting about. It simply seemed likely to transmit the wrong message if we sent two officers out to the Asteroids on a mere scheduled carrier—schedules being what they are, or mostly, what they aren't . . ."

Evan shook his head and stroked one of the pad's control surfaces with a fingertip, making it scroll back up the message. It was a long one: Lucretia had been too busy to see them before they left the Moon on this run. She was in charge of security for the opening of the new HighLands L5—a big deal, very much a symbol of the United Planets' intercooperation, billions of credits of joint investment, thousands of scientists and researchers all working together with the newest and most advanced equipment for the betterment of humanity, blah, blah, blah. . . . The publicity hacks had been trumpeting the thing all over the media for months now. Evan had been heartily sick of the whole business even before it began becoming a major distraction for their supervisor, making her even more hurried and perfectionist than usual. He wished that, after the *Freedom* business, Lucretia might have had a few words of praise to spare for them. But no such luck, as Joss would say. Lucretia had her hands full; and even if she *had* had time, Evan suspected she would simply have asked them coolly what they wanted—to be made a big deal of because they did their jobs? He sighed and went on with his reading.

"I don't know what you put in that sauce," said the voice from behind him, "but it's impossible to get the dishes clean. You should market the stuff as a universal adhesive. Going over the Bill of Rights?'' Joss asked, plunking himself down in the other seat.

"Precious few rights here,'' Evan muttered, and glanced over at his partner. Joss O'Bannion was shorter than the usual run of sops, but Evan, being a powered-suit operator, had for a long time known better than to judge anyone's ability at anything whatever by their size. Under his short dark hair, Joss had something that was a great advantage—a bland sort of face that didn't stand out or impress one as being anything special: Oriental in cast, but with some of the usual Euro-mixture added, Finnish and French and heaven knew what else. Joss was well-built without being blatant about it, was in good training, and was quick on his feet and with his gun when he needed to be. All these qualities Evan valued. But more than these, he valued Joss's cleverness with machines, computers especially, and his ability to reason his way through the messiest tangles of evidence and illogic.

It was almost enough to make Evan forgive him for being so bloody *neat*.

He glanced at Joss with what was meant to be good-natured scorn. "Don't you ever take your uniform off,'' he said, "even when you cook?''

"What? And get my civvies dirty?''

Evan snorted. "Cleaning is going to be expensive where we're going.''

"So what won't?'' Joss leaned back in his own seat and reached down beside it for his pad, idly bringing up the same message that Evan had been looking at. "A little restrictive about money,'' he said. "The Commissioner didn't get that pay increase, I guess.''

"It's always feast or famine with that one, from what I hear,'' said Evan.

"Mmf. Well, we'll try to keep it under control. I can't see why people would need as much bribing on this job,'' said Joss. "Drugs are a problem in that there's too much money in it: the stakes are too big, and people expect bigger payoffs. But in the asteroids there's no fast money. Only the long haul.''

"Or the Glory Rock," Evan said. There were always tales of the one big hit on an asteroid that was something really precious—gems, sometimes even gold. Such things had been found. But what was left of them after the miner in question had paid his debts to the local suppliers, or the tax men, often took the glory off the rock in short order. If some other miner didn't take the Rock itself first.

"Hmf," Joss said. "Think that's what we're after this time? Somebody ripping off a few billion credits' worth of palladium from a passing miner?"

Evan laughed at him. "You've been watching your daft vids again," he said. "Miners with donkeys. Little old men with long beards and foolish accents. What was that one? *Death Valley Tales?*"

"*Death Valley Days.*"

Evan grunted again and pretended to become absorbed in what was showing on his pad, before Joss could once again tell him that preposterous story about the old vidshow's presenter going into politics, and actually getting elected for something. When business was involved, Joss was strictly truthful, and would as soon lose a whole body of evidence as misrepresent one fact; but when it came to his collection of ancient vids, he was inclined to draw the long bow. "In all this space," Evan said, "I think we have something more going on than mere claim-jumping. Not that it doesn't happen."

"No, you're right about that."

Evan glanced up at the top of the communication. The Belts were an odd place, not quite like any of the other spaces that man had begun to tame. In all of those, according to the old rule, law on the planet surface—or inside the habitat—was administered by the local government. That law stopped at atmosphere, as the saying (and the legality) went, the point where the sky went black, and the Solar Patrol took over.

But in the belts there was no atmosphere, except inside

the domes of the older settlements, or inside the dug-out cubic of the newer ones. And the governments were not the familiar names of the inner system. No member of the loose confederation of habitats and worlds that was the United Planets had ever tried to lay specific territorial claims to even one asteroid. That was sensible, because distance and expense would have made it impossible for any one nation or multinational to police. It was damn near impossible to police *generally.* The Solar Patrol had numerous small stations scattered around the Belts, on or in the biggest of the asteroid colonies or concatenations. But their policy was largely laissez-faire, simply because there was no way it could manage not to be—not if the whole sop force had been posted out that way, with a sop on every thousandth rock.

Law was an iffy proposition in the Belts. Any law that a local asteroidal government made was binding locally: as far as the surface of the asteroid, or the top of its tallest dome. After that, no law until the next asteroid, two or twenty or two thousand klicks away. The Solar Patrol was law everywhere in between, and theoretically had the cooperation of all local law enforcement groups— theoretically. After all, no one wanted to be declared a "black spot," a place where the sops would not work if they were needed. But cooperation came in a lot of shades, and a sop learned to work by himself and not depend too heavily on assistance from the locals.

Should real trouble arrive, the sop was again mostly on his or her own. There was a Space Forces base on Mars, another in orbit around Jupiter, but planetary orbits being what they were, neither of those would necessarily be in a position to reach any part of the Belts in better than a week or so. The Belts were therefore both a place of opportunity—for there were steady livings to be made out that way—and occasionally of extreme danger.

As the communication made plain.

"SITUATION: SPHQ has been receiving numerous reports of disappearances of citizens and personnel in the

Belts. Over the past three standard months, these reports have exceeded the mean expected number by some twenty-nine percent, a number which SP statisticians find not specifically suspicious, but unusual even for a statistical fluke. The possibility of such a fluke remains, since the past three years have had a much lower than projected number of such unaccountable disappearances. However, Statistics has had recourse to chaos/ordinate analysis of these figures, and their feeling is that the present jump in occurrences is of a pattern that does not agree closely with any predictable pattern of fluke increase.

"DISCUSSION: The attached map shows areas where disappearances have been reported. Approximately eighty percent of them have been reported or have occurred in an area approximately centered on Willans Station/Ceres Minor. Case specifics are attached in the appendix. Space Forces patrols operating in this area have reported no new dangers to navigation or other known physical causes for disappearances."

"Huh," Evan said softly. He had an opinion of the Space Forces that was not entirely complimentary: he felt they were soft, overpaid, underworked, and a drag on society. He knew for a fact that they certainly felt the same about sops. But he did not let this bother him. He was, in any case, confident in SF's inability to find a pig in a sack, even when they were tied in the sack with it, and handcuffed to it as well.

"What?" Joss said, from the other seat. "Our friends in blue?"

"Dangers to navigation," Evan said scornfully. "As if they care about anything they can't blow up. Or as if they'd notice any rock that *was* small enough for them to blow. Ah, never mind them."

"Just as well," Joss said cheerfully, "because they surely won't pay any mind to *us*. We're well on our own out here."

"And a good thing, I say."

"And as for you," Joss said, "you're just jealous of

them, because they have full military suits, and you don't.''

That bit close, but was probably true, so Evan said nothing. In his police work on Earth, in the part of the world that had once been the United Kingdom and was now just another part of the Confederation, he had been Armed Enforcement Department, and had been trained in the best mobile suit made anywhere—a properly armed piece of walking armor, a suit that let you wade confidently through a brick wall, or into a troop of less well-armored infantry, or into the middle of a bank robbery, with no worries except how you would carry the perpetrators back to the station afterwards—under your arm, or in dustpans. But when he had left the AED—something about enjoying his work a little too much, being too good at it, carrying home what that week's superior officer thought was one corpse too many—the army had stripped his suit down. A sop was a peacekeeper, not a warrior, they had said; and besides, much of the armament he was carrying was classified, Defense secret, sorry Evan old chap. . . . He had said some rude things in Welsh, but he had put up with it, and then gone up to the Moon and done his sop training. His suit was the best police suit you could hope for, better than most; well cared for, smooth-running, mean-looking (which was half the battle sometimes). But he still felt naked when he thought about the arms that were in its ports these days when trouble started, and he still missed the plasma cannon, and the helium-acid lasers, and the nuke. Especially the nuke. He had never had to use it. But it had been a reassuring weight in the small of his back.

''That's as may be,'' Evan said.

''They don't know what to do with them anyway,'' Joss said kindly. ''No brains.''

''Mmf,'' Evan said, feeling that to agree too vehemently would give more away than he wanted to.

''ASSIGNMENT: You are directed to proceed to the marked area and conduct investigations to determine the proximate cause for these disappearances, or whether there is any non-statistical cause. Reasonable requests for materiel and additional personnel will be considered. Optimum desired duration of assignment: one standard month."

"They're out of their bleedin' minds," Joss said, mild-voiced, shaking his head.

Evan looked at him. "Tchah. Language!"

"Look at it," Joss said. "They've tagged our expense account to one month's time out. How are we even supposed to *eat* on that?"

"Your mistake," Evan said. "You shouldn't have been so eager to provision this thing before we left. We could have eaten out all the time."

"No point in it," Joss said. "No good restaurants out here."

"That's not what the Michelin Guide says," said Evan.

Joss burst out laughing. "You're so full of it, your eyes should be brown, you know that? Your idea of good food is toasted cheese."

"Can't help that," Evan said. "The ugly ghost of nationalism. Won't lie down and be still."

"Neither will your Welsh Rabbit."

"Oh? And what about your stir-fry, you thumb-fingered Cordon Bleu reject? I had to use the pulse-laser on the last wok to clean it, it was so—"

"—well-seasoned, you gun-happy Taff! It took me nearly six months to get that wok into a state worth cooking in, and then along you come with your goddamn hopped-up can opener, and burn off a perfectly good layer of—"

An alarm on the front console began to go off, making a noisy hooting like a loon stuck in a bucket. "Oh jeez, that can't be Willans proximity already," said Joss, swinging round to the console. "Then again, yes it can."

Evan looked at the console suspiciously. "Shouldn't you be doing something about that?"

"No, it's all automatic," Joss said. He hadn't pulled

the control array and yoke over, but he was leaning forward in the seat and watching the readings on the instrument panel with some interest. "I'll keep an eye on it. Meanwhile, we should be able to see something shortly."

Evan peered out the plex, but could see nothing: no spark of light anywhere but the stars, all seeming to swing gently in the same direction. That was another of the odd things about working this far out in space, away from any planet, where there was always something largish to orient by. Out here there was no seeing a body until you were practically on top of it—and, you hoped, not running right into it. Even though the asteroids were nowhere near as close together as popular myth still painted them, there were accidents. Failures of guidance systems, sudden changes of asteroid trajectory or orbit, ephemeris errors, pilot errors.

Though certainly *some* accidents might be disguised as more innocent ones. That was one possibility they were going to be looking at closely.

"There's their docking system's acknowledgement," Joss said. "Let's see how they do."

"Run in tandem with it, for heaven's sake," Evan said. "I've no desire to be a pancake just yet."

For a good while they both gazed out the plex, but saw nothing. The swinging of the stars stopped, though, and they steadied into one heading. "You were out here at one point, weren't you?" Joss said.

"A couple of years ago, before my desk work on the Moon. But it was the other side of the Belt, over by Highlight station, and the Crux. Bigger settlements, mostly. This was hicktown to those people. No big money, they said."

"Possibly we should be grateful."

"You mean if we're shot at," Evan said, "it'll be for something besides money."

Joss looked bemused at that, but said nothing for a little while. "There," he said finally. "See it?"

Evan peered out the plex. "No."

"Sort of the lower left-hand corner."

He peered for a few moments more. "Is that a red light on it?"

"That's it."

"Should be green, shouldn't it? If it's the approach beacon."

Joss pulled over the augments and peered through their oculars. "Looks like the approach beacon is burnt out. The actual docking facility is on the far side."

"Wonderful," Evan said, leaning back and feeling for the restraints. "Do you want to give them a ticket, or shall I?"

"I wouldn't," Joss said, "not till we've had our on-site briefing, anyway." He fumbled around for his own restraints and started fastening them up, the cross-belts first.

Willan Station started to grow larger in the front window, and Evan began to understand why the miners and holders over on the other side of the Belts might not have had a very high opinion of it. The asteroid was big enough to have been dug for cubic—it was about eight kilometers long and five wide, a lumpy potato-shape—but its surface was pocked all over with domes as if with a bad skin condition. And the domes—some clear, some opaque— were the old, unstable ribbed variety rather than the reinforced Fuller design that had supplanted the first kind almost as soon as people had begun settling out this way. Willans Station was *old,* from the looks of it—and no one had made any great attempt at modernization. Possibly understandable: materials were expensive out here, labor hard to find, or to keep—at least, good labor. But in this environment, your life depended on the integrity of your dome.

"They never mined here," Evan said, glancing over at Joss.

"No," Joss said, "there was no point. According to the ephemeris, this asteroid's nothing but conglomerate and stone—worthless. There's a fair amount of nickel iron found around here, though. Enough for it to work pretty well as a trading base and credit center.''

''Independently owned and operated, I take it,'' Evan said, looking at the central dome as the station data system spoke to their ship's and brought it around and over toward the docking area. The dome was patched, and not very well. In places, laminate patches overlapped composite plastic patches in a way that caused Evan concern about the level of maintenance of things here.

''It started out as a franchise operation from ConBelt,'' Joss said, peering through the augments again. There was an abstracted sound to his voice that Evan had heard before: it meant Joss was getting nervous about something. ''It earned out about twenty years later, and the family who were titleholders at that point started running it on their own.''

''They broke even, did they?'' Evan said, very hopefully, as the attitude thrusters fired again. Well off to one side of the central dome, attached to a smaller dome—opaque, but similarly patched—was a round set of bulkhead doors divided down the middle, the generic opening to a docking bay. There was only one problem: it wasn't open. And Evan watched them starting to get very close to that docking bay, very fast.

Joss looked annoyed and reached out to a toggle. ''Willans control, Willans control,'' he said, ''this is Solar Patrol vessel CDZ 8064 incoming, please check your autoapproach computer, over.''

Nothing but the hiss of empty air. Evan looked at him.

''Willans control, Willans control—'' Joss looked bemused, did something to the console, said again: ''Willans control, this is Solar Patrol vessel CDZ 8064, reply please.''

Nothing.

Joss said something under his breath that Evan didn't catch, yanked the yoke and control array around in front of him, and started hammering on the controls that would do things to the attitude jets, very quickly indeed. Evan clenched his teeth, then loosened up, remembering that clenching was exactly the wrong thing to do. He would have closed his eyes, but there seemed no point in dying if you didn't know how it had happened. So he watched the ugly round slitted bulk of the docking doors swim closer and closer outside the plex, slowing only slightly—

"Oh, come on, dammit," Joss said, "come *on,* you idiots!" He was practically hammering on the console now. Evan sweated, wondering whether Joss was hollering at the people on the asteroid, or the ship's equipment. In any case, there was nothing he could do to help; flying the ship was Joss's speciality. Those doors were closer, and closer. The soft hiss of firing rockets, all that could be heard of the attitudinals from inside the ship, went on and on—

"If you people make me crash my new ship," Joss was muttering, "you're all meat, that's all. Just hamburger, and I'll feed you to the first dog I see." He locked all the attitude thrusters into one configuration and sat there, gripping the console. There was nothing else he could do, from the looks of him.

" 'Your' ship?" Evan said, watching the docking bay doors draw near, and wondering why his life wasn't flashing before his eyes.

"Good God," Joss said then. "It's working."

"It is?" Evan said, but at that moment he realized that the ship was in fact slowing, slowing a little faster every moment, so that those doors, surely no more than five hundred meters away now, came toward them a little more slowly, a bit more slowly still.

"Are we going to be able to stop?"

"Good question," Joss said. Evan broke right out in a cold sweat.

They slowed, they slowed—and the doors were four hundred meters away, three, two— " 'Our' ship, I should think," Evan said, trying desperately to sound conversational.

"Sure," said Joss. "Come on, you idiots, come to! Isn't anybody home?"

—and they slowed and slowed, no more than fifteen meters a second now, ten meters a second—Evan watched the passive meter on the console read down, digit by digit. But ten meters per second could still kill you quite dead if your shell breached and the atmosphere got out. Not to mention the simple shock, and the results of hitting, say, a dome, and being in the way of an explosive decompression equivalent to a thousand tons per square inch of released pressure—

Joss was cursing actively now as they came down past five meters per second, and the bay doors were seventy meters away. Four meters, three—the meter hovered there for what seemed like a little lifetime. Why did deceleration seem to take *longer* near the end? Evan wondered. Two meters per second, one and a half—

—and the doors were right in front of them, right in front of the plex, and the rounded front of the ship hit the doors, neatly on target. For a horrible fraction of a second everything seemed to stand still while the physics of the situation sorted itself out. Evan visualized several physical laws standing there in that moment, playing scissors-paper-stone with one another, and he listened with all of him for the sound of the groaning hull that in a moment would be a single bang, and then no sound at all—

And then they started going backward at half a meter per second, and accelerating, because of the attitudinals' setting. Joss cursed harder and started hammering on his board again.

"There, how about that?" he nearly shouted. "The doorbell didn't work. Isn't knocking enough? Wake up in there!"

Evan wiped his forehead. In front of them, slowly, the docking bay doors started to open.

It took another five minutes to drop their backward acceleration, and to pull forward again into the bay. The docking bay proper was little more than a metal box fifty meters on a side, fitted inside the dome to cut down on the loss of air. It was a dark box; half its lights were out completely, and the rest seemed to be running at half or one-third power. They were in any case quite dim, and the dimness only served to point up the occasional fractured and welded sideplate. Apparently some of the pilots had not been as careful as Joss at getting into the bay.

While the back doors were closing behind them, and Joss was setting the ship down onto its vectored jets, Evan said, "If that's typical of what happens when you try to get in here, it's no wonder people leave and don't come back."

Joss nodded, and said, "The question is, was that an accident?"

Evan put his eyebrows up. "Now why would anyone here want us to come to harm?" he said. The question was meant ironically: no matter where you went, there was always *somebody* who didn't care for sops. "And how would they have been able to react so quickly, if they did?"

"They wouldn't have needed voice transmission to know us," Joss said. "Our black box transponder will have been talking to their radar computer for the past hour and a half, maybe more."

"That would narrow down the list of suspects somewhat," Evan said. "The people in the station radar room. You'd think they would find a better way to off us without attracting attention to themselves."

Joss sighed and said, "We're starting out on our paranoia a little early, aren't we?"

"I hate to get caught in the rush," Evan muttered.

"And we really have to find something to call this ship," Joss said, as the front doors of the bay began to open before them.

" 'Hey, you'?" Evan asked.

Joss very carefully brought the ship up on its bottom jets, but he refused to vector them back until the doors were fully open, showing them a well-lighted circular floor space about two hundred meters in diameter. Lines of smaller craft were parked off around the circumference, and there were blister junctions where other smaller domes, probably used for storage, met this one. "No good," Joss said. "It has to be a proper name, so we can swear at it."

"You didn't sound like you needed any help."

"Oh, it's not the same." Joss nudged the ship forward and out into the light. "Really good swearing has to be personal."

"Here comes your chance," Evan said, looking across the hangar dome. There were several people hurrying in from a side dome, two men and a woman, dressed in the insulated skinsuits that were popular in places like this, where central heating couldn't exactly be found in every room and corridor.

"No rush, no rush," Joss said, setting the ship down with what should have been insulting precision in the very middle of the hangar circle. Evan was very glad to feel the slight jar as the skids came down on the floor; and then things in the cabin began to quiet down as Joss killed the final attitude jet and shut down the engines.

"We secure?" Evan said.

"Oh, yes. You want to put your uniform on before we go out?"

"I'll put mine on and be out in a second. I think you have things you want to be looking at," Evan said, as Joss hurried past him toward the airlock.

"Idiots," Joss remarked *en passant*, and was through the inner door and had it sealed a second later. Evan smiled to himself.

He headed into his stateroom, reached into the cupboard where his tunic was, and slipped it on. Fine-looking as the black and silver uniform was, it was not what he would have preferred to go out in, the first time. Evan looked lovingly over at the gunmetal grey shape of his suit in its clamps off to one side of the stateroom. It usually made a most favorable impression the first time an officer wearing a suit strolled into an area he had come to patrol.

There was no harm in reminding the people you were assigned to protect that here was someone who could see clearly across half a mile of smoke or fog or darkness, or all of them together, using the vision augmentation equipment built into the helm; someone who could pick up a ton unassisted, or walk through a wall, let alone shoot or blast through it. And as for what the people you were assigned to catch thought of it—why, the more cautious it made them, the better, Evan had always thought. Frightened perpetrators made the best mistakes.

For the moment, though, he merely touched the seams of the tunic closed, made sure his SP shield was on tight, and took down his Winchester beamer. It was a useful thing. Not as useful, perhaps, as the Heckler & Koch beamer he had used in the AED: that could have burned right through the outside airlock in a matter of seconds. And his other favorite, the custom-built Holland and Holland projectile gun that had cost him two months' pay and was well worth all of it, was no good to him here, in a pressure-sensitive environment. But the Winchester looked mean—an advantage for the gun, as for the suit—and was light and dependable. Interior walls wouldn't give it trouble, and as for human beings. . . . He smiled slightly and settled it in its holster, then headed for the airlock himself.

As he stepped out of the ship, two of the three people he had seen coming into the dome went past him in what seemed a hurry. The man, in his late thirties, with a badly heat-scarred face, tall and thin, and the woman, in her forties perhaps, slightly overweight, blonde going grey—merely looked at him and didn't stop. "Excuse me," Evan said.

"We don't work here," said the man, and the woman added, "And will you move that thing out of the middle so people can get in and out?" And they hurried past him without another word.

"Hmm," Evan said, and walked around to the front of the ship, where Joss was standing and running his hands over the rounded nose with a very aggrieved expression.

"Brand new," he was saying. "The mothers! That coating was *hours* old! Look at this!"

Evan looked and saw a slight dent in the nose, and a wrinkled place where the paint had been cracked away. "It looks to me as if we were lucky not to have smashed like an eggshell," he said. "A little paint won't matter. We'll tell everyone we rammed someone broadside."

Joss snorted, then looked over his shoulder as the third person, a man in his early twenties, very small and slight, went past them after the first two. "Excuse me," Joss said, "but would you please tell us if—"

The young man took one look at them, spat immediately and copiously on the floor, and just kept going. Joss looked distastefully at the floor, then at Evan.

"Not the welcoming committee, I take it," he said.

"And they say you should move the ship out of the way," said Evan.

"Like hell," said Joss. But he looked after the young man with a calculating expression. "Then again," he added, "no point in antagonizing the locals."

"Yet," said Evan.

It took a few minutes to get the ship moved. The ship belonging to the three people who had come in started to rise up on its jets as soon as Joss had finished moving. Their ship was typical of many others sitting around in the hangar, and was everything the patrol vessel wasn't: ugly, blocky, scarred, a sort of conglomeration of bolted-together metal boxes with an ancient nonreflective black coating on it. How nonreflective it was at all was in question, since the coating had flaked or been scraped or banged off in who knew what collisions with small asteroids or, for all Evan knew, other craft. The thing had crude jets on it, not vectorable, just fastened on at any angle; and there was what looked like a secondhand ion driver assembly at the rear end, held on with metal straps and probably prayer.

Evan raised his eyebrows as he turned away. He might have been teasing Joss about old grizzled miners with donkeys, but it struck him that those old men from the vids were probably safer in their environment than these people were—if they were in fact miners. Quite a few people who were not came to live out this way. They might like the freedom of the Belts, the way there was little of the control of the inner worlds. No one asked you for ID every five seconds; there was no need of the ID itself. People couldn't care less if you had a banking history, or a credit history, or whether it was a good history or not. In fact, there were always people who preferred that the histories of those they dealt with should not be *too* good. . . .

Joss came back in a few moments, and stood with Evan to look after the ship that was leaving. "I built one like that in the back yard when I was six," he remarked. "But the boxes were cardboard. And it flew better."

"It flew?"

"Oh, yes," Joss said, as they walked off toward the largest of the blisters leading to the next dome over. "Once we pushed it off the garage roof."

"I take it the pilot survived."

"Sure. But ever since then I've been twitchy about any large object coming at me fast. Like the ground, or a set of landing bay doors."

Evan smiled slightly as they walked through the airlock into the next dome. The airlock doors neither opened before them nor shut behind them, having been jammed open. Joss looked at the control panel, which had been sabotaged with a power tool of some kind, to judge by the cracks in its front, and said, "These people don't look too worried about losing atmosphere, do they?"

Evan shook his head. It was an almost unbelievable level of carelessness, unless you had just been through the docking they had, in which case belief became a lot more accessible. "Seems that way."

"And no welcoming committee at all, it looks like. Not even from the people who almost crashed us into the bay doors at too damned many mips. A bit unfriendly."

Evan shrugged. "I'd like to see those people myself

. . . and I will, sooner or later. But as regards anything formal, it's not something you're likely to see. Places like these aren't as regimented as inner-system stations. No customs, no immigration—as a rule—or it's handled differently from any way you expect. Some places, records aren't even kept on computers . . . on purpose. I know some places on the other side of the Belts that don't care where you've come from, or what you've done, as long as you're willing to give them all your money. There are lots of people who think that's a good deal.''

Evan saw Joss make a wry face. He knew that Joss was no fool about such things. The man had been partnered with him, he suspected, specifically because his mind was so quick and his knowledge even of things outside of his experience was so considerable. Such a man was a natural choice to partner with a powersuited officer. But Evan suspected that the basic untidiness of an environment like this would annoy Joss mightily, once he actually got into it himself. He had been raised in order, on the Moon, in an environment where things were controlled and kept rigorously correct. The sloppiness of the Asteroids would be trying for him. Evan was committed to making sure that this wasn't too much of a problem for Joss, but at the same time he had never promised not to be amused by it.

The small dome into which they had walked was indeed a storage area for vehicles, and a service area as well. More ships, most of them one- or two-man vessels, were sitting or lying about in various states of repair. Some were little more than stripped-down chassis; others showed signs of having pieces of five or six different vessels bolted together, the matings often looking rather crude, and occasionally positively unsafe. It was the spacecraft manufacturers themselves who had made this possible, in the days when the Belts were first starting to open up. Most people going out had very little venture capital to work with, and the shipmakers had decided that if they were going to get any of this eager money at all, they had better come up with something cheap, simple, and easily replaceable and repairable. So VW and Skoda and Lada had decided to cut most of their potential losses. They and the other major marques had pooled their r&d money, largely duplicated one another's designs, and brought out ships that could be put together in pieces, suiting the needs of individual spacers: heavy hauling vehicles, ships with lots of extra storage, or bigger engines, or better power arrays that could manage more tools inside and outside the ship.

Naturally, when you sold your ship on, the person who bought it secondhand might find it wasn't *exactly* what he had in mind—though it was close. So he would detach the module that didn't work, or just chop it off if he had to, and add another bit that did, possibly bought from the same dealer. Within brands, of course, the module parts and their fit worked perfectly. But if you had a VW body and wanted a Lada cargo module, which was bigger than the VW's, what to do? *You* naturally had no intention of staying with all VW parts—though that had certainly been VW's intention. The pooling of designs had not been *that* complete. So you went to see your local mechanic, and for the right price, he made the Lada rear end work with the VW front.

At least, you hoped he did. Naturally, none of this work ever came under the warranty, and the person who did the repairs tended to be a long way away if something went wrong. For the first twenty years or so of the opening up of the Belts, as many spacecraft mechanics died as miners did, usually at the hands of the miners' friends or relatives. After that, most of the survivors had gotten the hang of making the customizations work, and had in turn trained replacements who knew how, too.

Joss was looking around at the handiwork of the station's mechanics with some concern. "Not sure I want anyone from this place touching our ship," he muttered.

"You and me both, boyo," said Evan. "You locked it up, did you?"

"Hell, yes. It's on voiceprint."

Evan smiled. "Just make sure you don't say anything that sounds like the opening code."

Joss laughed. "Are you kidding? It's not that kind of voiceprint reader. Ours wants to hear your pulse and see your EEG as well."

Evan was impressed. "You've been tinkering again."

"Two weeks from Earth, what was I supposed to be doing? Watching old vids?"

"Ouch," Evan said, for he knew a gentle dig when he felt one. "Never mind that. How close do we need to be for all this hocus-pocus? Is the ship going to be able to make out details like this if we're heading for her at a run?"

"Absolutely—that's her business. You can check her later. Meanwhile, I guess we should find out the local time."

"It's twenty hundred," Evan said. "I saw two of the chronos on those people that just went by me."

"You just hope they're not keeping personal time," Joss said, "and it's actually three in the afternoon. Or eight in the morning."

Evan merely smiled and pointed up over the door into the next bubble. It said 2002.

"Smartass," said Joss: but he said it cheerfully. "Well, there'll be someone in the radar room; we can still go pay them a visit."

"I was looking forward to it," Evan said, with feeling.

"But it's too late to go to the station police office and get our onsite briefing. That'll just have to wait till morning."

"So it would seem."

"So after we go see the people in Radar, we'll just have to go out to get something to eat."

"Indeed."

"And something to drink!" Joss said with relish. Their ship, like all SP patrol vehicles, was dry.

"Heavens, what a concept," said Evan.

They headed out through the airlock to the next dome, which was also jammed open.

Behind them, a tall lean figure stood up from behind one of the craft under repair, and stared, fingering the gun at its belt.

THEY DID NOT GO STRAIGHT FOR THE FOOD and drink, of course. There was first the matter of the radar installation. When they got there, Joss had been just about ready to kill someone, but they had found only a lone technician, gangly, painfully young, and terrified at the sight of them. He had been left on his own by the older technicians and told not to touch anything, since the autodocking system was in the middle of being repaired. Indeed, its parts were all over the floor when they arrived. The other technicians were off on their dinner break. They had told him just to keep an eye on the place and not to worry, since no one was expected in for several days. He had heard Joss's call, but hadn't touched anything, and didn't know what to touch anyway.

Between them, Joss and Evan had managed to calm the poor boy down. There had been no point in waiting for the techs to come back. But the two of them had promised to stop by tomorrow. Joss suspected that he would dream of that final approach as soon as he dropped off tonight. He felt pretty sure of being able to adequately communicate his feelings on the subject to the techs in the morning.

Then there was the matter of finding a place to stay. The station itself was not supplying accommodation; that wasn't their business, they had apparently told SPHQ when the initial arrangements for the investigation had been made. Any accommodation in the place would accept the visitor's chit or voucher, of course, but it was unheard of to take bookings in advance: the policy was strictly first come, first served.

The young tech, once he got over his initial terror of

two men in SP uniform, one of them unusually large and
fierce-looking, had been able to recommend a couple of
places where they should be able to stay. There were not
hotels as such; there were never that many visitors to Willans. The closest equivalents were domes or parts of domes
that had been sectioned up as "rooming houses." The
youngster had given them directions, and they had set off
into the depths of the station, though Joss had had some
misgivings about the whole thing. The directions had been
issued at high speed, and were of the "third left, fourth
right, turn south at Murphy's Bar" sort that assume you
know your way around better than you actually do.

It had turned into a long walk through domes and corridors that to Joss's mind were ill-lit, ill-kept, and dirty.
He kept reminding himself that little outposts like this
could hardly afford to have sweepers coming through every
thirty seconds: that even mechanized labor was expensive
(though having seen the way the domes were patched, he
had his doubts whether the maintenance available here was
sufficient to keep any cleaning robot working for long),
and that people were busy making enough money to keep
body and soul together. But at the same time, the place
looked grimier than it needed to. There was litter in the
halls—stuff that should have been picked up and recycled—and dirt that should have been swept up months
back. Worse, in all this mess there were no graffiti, a sure
sign of a sick place. Everywhere else Joss had been where
there had been dirt like this, there had been scrawls on
walls and doors, expressions of outrage or despair. It was
as if no one here could get up the energy to complain—or
worse, as if no one cared.

The people they met tended to look furtive and nervous.
Joss suspected that was probably due to the formidable
uniforms he and Evan wore. Even their smile got no response from anyone. People slipped hurriedly away around
a corner, or through a doorway, whether they seemed to
belong there or not, and vanished. "Oh, well," Joss said
after about twenty minutes of this, when they were finally

approaching the rooming house they had been heading for. "They'll get used to us soon enough."

"Mmf," Evan said. He had been paying more attention to the people than their surroundings, but that was often his way: after a day of it, he always compared notes with Joss, and the details he picked up were sometimes surprising. It was one of the things about Evan that had most delighted Joss when they were first partnered: the acute observation, and the compassion, in this big hard-looking man with the chilly blue eyes. Most people who saw Evan immediately pigeonholed him as a thug, and probably a stupid one, equipped with big guns and too much inclination to use them. That misprision had cost various people very lucrative criminal incomes. It had cost some of them their lives, but not because Evan had encouraged them to throw them away. People *will* shoot at a suited officer, Joss thought, and then be surprised when he shoots back—and doesn't miss. . . .

They came to the door of the rooming house, a small dome off one of the minor corridors. Just inside that door was a desk, and at the desk was a small, balding man with a pinched, narrow face and an expression that Joss would have sworn came right out of an eighteenth century woodcut of some grasping, greedy moneylender. He looked at Joss and Evan as if they were some new and interesting kind of bug: ones with money that he might manage to get before swatting them.

"Help you?" he asked, in a tone of voice that made it plain helping them was the last thing on his mind.

"Yes," Joss said pleasantly. "We'd like two rooms, please."

"How long?"

"Hard to say," Evan said. "We're on assignment, and it may take a while. Two weeks?"

"Eighteen hundred creds."

Joss looked at Evan incredulously. It was even worse than he had expected. Strangers could expect to be taken for three or four times the usual fee. But five was pushing it a bit. "Fifteen hundred."

"You're on account," said the man, "and y'won't do any better anywhere else." And the glint in his eye said, *because I'll be on the comm to every other flophouse in this place within minutes.*

"Eighteen, then," Evan said.

"Plus utilities."

"Fair enough."

"And air."

"Now, wait a moment," Joss said mildly. "We pay the O2 charge with our landing taxes."

"Haven't paid for it yet," the man snarled. "Don't know if I'll get reimbursed, do I?"

The question, "How do you know we haven't paid for it yet?" didn't even bother coming out. In a place this small, it was plain that news traveled faster than an ion-driver gone critical.

"Fine," Joss aid at last, knowing when he was beaten. "Let's see the rooms."

Scowling, the man led them through a curtained door-way behind his desk. The doorway gave onto a corridor lined with more doors. The man opened one, then the one next to it. Joss stepped in and noted the equipment: one plastic-seated, tube-metal chair, rickety, one single bed made up with dingy grey linens, and extra *un*-firm—the mattress sagged as though it had been used by a herd of elephants—one sink and 'fresher unit, the water meter mounted prominently nearby (where they would have to stare at it while they were shaving); one desk, composite-topped and cigarette-burnt, its legs well kicked.

Joss glanced at Evan, who had been looking at his own room. Evan shrugged, the *yes, what choice do we have at the moment?* shrug.

"All right," Joss said. "The keys, please?"

The man gave them over with ill grace. They were stan-dard reprogrammable cards, of the kind that had been common for a hundred years now. Joss thanked him, pocketing his.

"Is breakfast included?" Evan asked sweetly.

The landlord gave Evan a look that had an infestation of swearing swarming underneath it, the way a rock has centipedes. "That's all right," Evan said. "We'll manage our own. Be back later." He turned and went out.

Joss nodded politely at the landlord, bought another cuss-laden look for his trouble, and headed out after Evan. When they were a safe distance down the hall—not that there were safe distances in a place like this; doubtless the neighbors would run to inform on them in seconds if they overheard something juicy—Joss asked, "Breakfast?"

"Where I come from," Evan said, "people who let out rooms for a living know how to make a proper breakfast, as a matter of course. But they wouldn't do that here, I suppose." His eyes glinted a little over the innocent smile. Joss thought he heard a rustling in the walls as they passed. Surely not mice . . .

Evan entertained him for a while with tales of Cumberland sausage and Chester sweet cream butter, and *bara brack* all hot from the oven, while they wove and twisted their way through the dirty corridors and in and out of the occasional dome, where numerous corridors would meet near some living area. Eventually, Joss, his stomach growling, said, "For a man trying to pick a fight, you do it in some funny ways."

"Oh?"

"Making fun of their breakfast? Come *on.*"

"I am just a traveling groundhog," Evan said in a mild voice, but with a sidelong look that had a sly touch to it, "and if that's how they see me, so much the better. Meanwhile, here's a bar."

They went in. It was in another small dome, not quite as big as the one where their rooming house was. The bar proper was circular, in the center of the room. At least, what they could see of it was, for the lighting in the bar was almost nonexistent. There were faint gleams from lights on the tables, and a few around the walls; and there were people sitting, leaning, standing here and there. Other details were hard to make out for someone standing outside in the bright corridor. A sour smell of spilled beer, cheap gin, and homemade potato vodka came floating out to meet them, along with more savory cooking smells.

Joss walked in first, because his night sight was slightly better than Evan's, and because he hated people to think he was sending Evan in ahead to take the brunt of first looks and assessments. As his eyes started to accustom themselves to the dimness, Joss found himself wishing they hadn't. The place began to get quiet, like bars in old western vids when the sheriff walks into the Dry Gulch Saloon. Every eye in the place was turned on them and their black and silver uniforms. People stopped moving, except very slightly—toward weapons, Joss suspected.

He and Evan made their way to the bar in silence. The barkeeper was a young woman with long dark hair and a long somber face, pretty but serious-looking. Joss found himself wondering what she was doing in a place like this, then began to take himself to task for thinking in clichés.

"Beer, please," he said softly. Evan echoed the order, handing over his credit chit to be run through the bar's accounting system. The barkeeper nodded and went off to the other side of the bar, where the taps were, to see about it. The men stood there in the middle of the thick silence, until Joss said conversationally, "So how about those Mets, then?"

Evan looked at him as if he had lost his mind.

Around them, conversation began to start again, though at nothing like its original volume. "You know," Evan said, "they don't have a chance this year. Tokyo will win."

"No way. Not after those last three trades."

Their beer arrived, and Evan's chit with it. "The annoying thing is," Joss said, when he thought the noise level had increased enough, "we don't have hats to take off."

Evan smiled at that. In his part of the world, it had been traditional for an off-duty cop to remove his hat or helmet when entering a bar to have a pint on his lunch hour. A cop who came into a bar with his hat on was on business, probably to ask someone uncomfortable questions, and the sign of unremoved hats tended to ruin the patrons' enjoyment of their drinks. "Perhaps if we had lighted signs for our shields," Evan said, "that said 'HERE TO GET DRUNK'. . . ."

They drank, and Joss looked around him with increasing misgiving. Forms hunched over tables stared at them; eyes glittered in the dimness, though there were no sudden movements. "When we have to start asking questions," he said softly, "these people aren't going to be a lot of help to us."

"Ah now, don't be so pessimistic," Evan said. "We've only just got here, and they haven't a clue what we're about. Surely no one's going to object to us trying to find their missing mates."

"Not unless some of them engineered their being missing."

Evan drank again, put his pint down and reached down the bar for a bowl of what in this light looked like some kind of salted crisps. He pulled it over, then stared at it. *"Cara dhu,"* he said, picking up one of the things and looking at it, "what are these?"

Joss pulled the bowl over, gazed into it, broke into a smile of recognition, and reached into it. "Now will you look at that," he said, and bit into what he was holding. "Pig tails."

Evan looked at him bemusedly. "Pigtails? Is that some kind of cracker?"

"Pig tails. Tails of pigs, broiled. Look, here's an ear."

Evan was incredulous. "Pigs' *ears?* And you're *eating* them?"

"Watch me. You're from pork country, way back when— haven't you ever had pig tails? Poor man. Last time I had these was in Provence, a few years ago. Must be someone

French here. Watch out, though, they're salty. It's a good way to get people to drink."

Evan smiled, apparently understanding that quite well. "You can't be serious about the Mets, anyway," he said.

Joss glanced up from his crunching to note Evan's look over his shoulder. He turned slowly, making it look casual.

Most of what he saw at first was beard. To judge by what skin he could make out, the man was no older than his forties: but the big ginger-colored beard covered almost everything from his chest to his eyebrows, except for a bit to either side of the nose, which was small and pug. He wore a loose, soft shirt, white but stained, over a dark one-piece skinsuit, one of the quilted kind that were intended to go under a pressure rig. His eyes were narrow and wary, their color impossible to tell in this light, except that they were pale. The man was at least two meters tall, so that Joss had to look up at him a bit.

"Evening," he said, and offered the man the bowl of tails and crackling. "Have some?"

The man took the bowl, but shook his head and grinned at Joss. Joss wasn't entirely sure he liked the grin, but he reserved judgment. "Seems a bit like canibalin' to me," the man said, in a slow, grating voice.

Joss glanced down at the pig tails, then up at the man again. He smiled—very slightly.

"Don't see many of you people around here as a rule," the man said. There was a movement in the shadows behind him. Joss didn't stir. Evan was with him; for the moment, that would do.

"Business," Joss said. "But that's not till tomorrow morning."

"What kind of business?"

"Some people working in this area have been disappearing," Evan said. "A few too many. We want to find out why. But as my partner says, it can wait till tomorrow. Mr.—"

"Smith," said the man. There was soft laughter from further down the bar at this witticism.

"Smith," Evan said, the soul of courtesy. Without missing a beat, he made it perfectly plain how likely it seemed to him that "Smith" was the man's real name. "Glyndower. My partner, O'Bannion." Joss nodded amiably at the man. "What are you having, sir?"

"Not that piss," said Smith, turning away from them both with an expression that looked mostly like a sudden wrinkle in his beard. "Bash, gimme a Stoly."

Joss leaned forward over the bar, took another pig tail, and chewed on it slowly, glancing at Evan. Evan's expression was resigned; he drank his beer and said, between drinks, "I still think you bet wrong."

"How did you know I bet?" Joss said, slightly scandalized.

"Oh, come on! You may have been programming and so forth *sometimes* on the way out here, but I knew you would be getting your bets in before we left."

"Someone's been ratting on me," Joss muttered.

Evan grinned. "Telya's in your betting pool."

"Why, that little—!"

Smith's drink arrived. No matter what he had called it, the vodka in the glass had never been any closer to Moskva than this asteroid's perihelion, while it was still a potato. He tipped his head back and drank about half of it without stopping, then put the glass down and belched emphatically. Joss chewed on his pig tail and refrained from comment.

"You bet on horses?" said "Smith" suddenly to Joss.

"No," Joss said, rather surprised. "Never got the feel for it. Baseball, mostly."

"Smith" smiled again, the same not-very-nice smile. He began to chuckle. "That's a slit's bet," he said, to himself at first, then to the bar in general. "A slit's bet. We got a right one here, people. Mister sop here bets like a slit!"

Joss held his expression as it had been. "What do you bet on then?" he said.

"Horses," "Smith" said. "Fights. Who comes back."

Joss nodded. He knew, as the miners did, that there was always a certain percentage per year of people who didn't return. He knew that there was betting on those whom people at a given station thought the more likely suspects. But at the moment, it seemed like poor taste to mention it. However, nothing ventured—"Any luck?" he said softly.

The man's eyes narrowed. "Now, that's a nasty question," "Smith" said. "A man might have lost friends. A man might be sensitive."

"He might," Joss said, in a tone of utter unconcern. "He might hate losing a bet."

From the other side, Evan nudged Joss gently. Joss nudged back, acknowledgement that he knew perfectly well what he was up to . . . he hoped.

"Smith" laughed in his beard. "Might. Won a few times. It's not hard."

"No, it wouldn't be," Joss said. "Dumb people tend not to make it in space."

"Smith" looked over to his left at someone else who had come up to the bar, a tall skinny man with a face so literally like a hatchet that Joss was momentarily fascinated by it. He hardly had eyes at all, they were so close to his nose, and that nose was about half an inch thin all the way down, and hooked. Joss wondered if it bumped into the faceplate of his helmet, or if he'd needed to have one made especially to cope with it. "You hear that, Den?" said "Smith." "Dumb people tend not to make it in space, says mister sop here. Guess that makes us all pretty smart."

Den said nothing, just looked at Joss with an expression of total malice. Joss blinked. Why did he have the feeling that there was at least one person in the bar who had mistaken an ironic delivery for insult?

"Smith" turned back to Joss, his lips twisted in an evil

smile. "Guess all of us must be pretty smart, to be out here in space all by ourselves, with a shiny ship and lots of credits and all," he said.

Or maybe two people, Joss thought. He said nothing as a third man materialized just behind him, a looming presence, bigger even than Evan. He didn't turn to look at him. It seemed unwise at the moment to do anything but keep his eyes on "Smith" and his tall thin friend.

It was just as well, because suddenly that man's fist came straight at Joss's face. There was a moment of shock reaction—*it's not fair!*—and then reflex took over and ducked Joss sideways. Unfortunately, it ducked him into the man behind him, the big one, who promptly wrapped his arms around Josh, pinning him.

"Smith" braced himself against the bar to kick Joss in the gut—not the friendly kind of kick meant to incapacitate the victim for further beating, but the kind meant to go through and come out on the other side of the backbone. Joss shifted his balance, found the sweet spot, and heaved the big man who was pinning him neatly over his head and into "Smith": they crashed together against the bar, most satisfactorily, and slid to the ground.

Unfortunately, at that point everybody in the place leaped up and rushed the bar.

It had been some years since Joss had been in a brawl, a real brawl with chairs smashing and so forth. But it was surprising how quickly he remembered the lessons he had learned the last time: break all glasses and bottles within reach as quickly as possible by knocking them to the floor—preferably with human bodies, so that they will be useless as weapons; stay away from tubular steel chairs, which won't break anything but your head when they hit you; try to avoid smashing the mirror behind the bar, since it can give you valuable hints about who might be coming up from behind you; don't allow yourself to be pushed into a booth, where five or six people can easily pile in on top of you and make your life more difficult than it needs to be; watch out for unbroken half-full glasses, as their contents may wind up in your eyes.

It was surprising, too, how many of those rules he suddenly found it impossible to keep. Joss knew perfectly well that he dare not touch his sidearm. It wasn't only that he'd feel unprofessional later on for not having been able to handle the situation with wits and bare hands. Using a gun in a situation like this would also make any later questioning of these people impossible. Sure, the gun would have made matters a lot simpler; but he had no time to think that more than once, as another body hurtled at him and he sidestepped—right into a punch. Sidehand blocks had never been his strong suit, as his unarmed combat instructor had told him again and again: Apparently, the guy had been right, Joss thought as he reeled away. Something flew across his field of vision—another of the bar's patrons, Joss saw, pitched tidily across by Evan. *He makes it look so easy,* Joss thought wistfully, as another patron threw a punch at him. This time Joss was annoyed, his ears still ringing from the last one, and he blocked it so hard he heard bones snap; then another fist came out of nowhere, a wild swing, missing him.

"Tsk," Joss said, as he swiped the man's legs out from under him with a leg sweep and knocked a table over on top of him, just to give the guy something to think about for a few minutes.

He paused a moment to see what Evan was doing. Evan was doing just fine. He had "Smith" in one hand, and another man in the other, and he was banging their heads together. The resultant sound was not altogether musical. *Didn't hit him hard enough,* Joss thought with mild regret that he had made extra work for Evan. As someone grabbed his right shoulder from behind, Joss spun around the other way and put a punch just to the left of where the right shoulder had been. The woman who was standing in that spot, with her fist cocked and ready, went down. "Oh, crap," said Joss, and then three people jumped him from three sides. He went down, and one of them sat on his head.

It was a bad moment. Joss lashed straight out with one fist at the last target he saw before his vision was obscured. It was a focused strike, maybe a little too focused, but it made sure that at least one of the men would have to give recreational sex a miss for a good while. The peculiar hooting screech he immediately heard confirmed that. His only remaining business at this point was to shift his own lower body as fast as he could, to keep anyone from doing anything similar to him.

A moment later the weight came off his head and was flung away to one side, to judge by the thump and screech that followed. "Come on, old son," he heard Evan say, and a hand the side of a ham closed on his upper arm and hauled him to his feet.

"Wait a minute; I don't think we should leave this unfinished," Joss sad, looking around him hurriedly. "There are only—" He did a hasty headcount of the crowd closing in. "Uh, there are only thirty of them—"

Evan backed toward the door, and Joss went with him. He didn't have much choice, any more than did most human beings or other heavy objects Evan picked up and threw over his shoulder. "Why do you start these things when I don't have my suit on?" Evan asked.

"Whaddaya mean, *I* started it?"

"I could have wiped this whole place up," Evan said ruefully, but not too loudly, since about fifteen of the thirty people were pacing them toward the door, though at a safe distance. "Now we're getting thrown out of a bar. This is not going to do my reputation any good."

"Thrown—You can't throw us out," Joss shouted. "We're leaving!"

"Aah, shut your cakehole," Evan said in good-natured disgust. "At least there's this: everybody on the station is going to want to talk to us now, to see if they can get us into a fight. It's an ill wind, and so forth. Come on, let's go clean up and get some dinner."

TWO

☆

THE WILLANS POLICE STATION WAS IN A DOME.
Evan was scandalized; the place should have been properly
dug into the asteroid, for security's sake if not for the
safety of the staff who worked there. It was not the first
time that morning he had been scandalized, and he was
getting unhappily used to it.

When they had emerged that morning—Evan after a
prolonged battle with his 'fresher unit, which was defec-
tive, and needed more than the usual picking out with a
pin that he found himself doing to shower heads and
'fresher fixtures all over Sol system—the landlord, that
shrunken-souled creature, had tried to hit them for several
new charges that they had not agreed to the evening before, including a blanket O2 charge which did not exist.
Evan had leaned over him, at his chipped, stained little
desk, and glowered. This was normally a technique Evan
was too proud to use. His size was an accident; the good
God had decided to make him two point one meters tall.
He hated to make capital of it, but this man was a walking
excuse for intimidation—and not by some blackmailing
lywdllych thug of a miner, but by someone with the law
on his side. Evan stood there, therefore, eyes narrowed,
expression darkening, leaning closer and closer to the man,
and quoted the station's housing law to him, chapter and
verse. He did this before he had brushed his teeth, which
was simple enough, because the 'fresher had broken down
between the haircut and the shave. The man had winced

and gone scowling off into his own quarters, muttering about changes in the law and calling the station. He hadn't come back.

Evan was satisfied. So was Joss, who had left Evan to deal with the guy at the desk and had gone about the morning's first errand: that postponed discussion with the people in the approach control. "Maybe the guy heard about last night," Joss said to Evan as they headed out together for the station police office.

Evan laughed. "I doubt there's anyone within a light-hour's circumference who hasn't heard," he said. "There's nothing to do out here but work and gossip. And which would *you* rather do?"

Joss grunted.

"And how was your interview with the radar techs?"

Joss rolled his eyes. "Pretty pitiful. None of them had anyone's demise in mind, I'm sure of *that* much. It looks like they're understaffed, and they're working with the kind of equipment I haven't seen since my high school science fair. I yelled at them some, but my heart wasn't in it. They'll be more careful, maybe, but how much good is it likely to do when you're working with machines that have vacuum tubes in them?" He grimaced.

The look was unusually pained. "Your head bothering you?" Evan said.

"No, I'm fine. It just seems—" Joss shrugged. "Maybe it's just me, but everything looks dirtier this morning."

"Oddly enough, I know what you mean," Evan said, and there was truth to that, as he thought back to what he had found in the 'fresher head, and how long it had taken him to remove it before anything would flow freely again. "You were right. People do seem awfully preoccupied here, at first glance, much more so than normal. Even the bare minimum of cleaning doesn't seem to be done."

"Or other things," Joss said. "I had a closer look at the rock this morning."

"Trust you to do that," Evan said, only partly banter-ing. Among various other hobbies, Joss was an amateur geologist and spelunker, when he could find a cave worth crawling into. "What did you do, pull up the flooring?"

"Not much to pull up. We're on raw rock here, cut flat. The dome seals are direct, just aged silicon clathrates."

"*Diw,*" Evan said softly. 'How cheap can you get?" Such seals were little better than sticking a dome to the rock of the asteroid with rubber cement.

"That cheap, at least. Evan, the rock's not as bad as the reports made it out to be. It's straight conglomerate with iron and iron oxides. Even without my kit, I make it out at about one percent iron. It's hardly high-grade ore for these parts, though, and even if they had slagged the asteroid out when they first came here, I'm not sure they could have made their settlement expenses back. It's too bad."

Evan shook his head. It all fit together in a veritable panorama of tackiness. The patched domes, the dirt, the shoddy surroundings, the shoddy people—for all the people they had seen in the bar last night had that same aura of worn-down goods. There seemed to be no one there really successful and showing it, not even one flash of cash from a miner in from a good strike. There hadn't even been the grumbling hospitality of someone in from a run that had been a break-even business, simply okay. People had sat nursing their drinks like precious things, and had fought not out of anger, but boredom. It was distressing. In some ways it reminded Evan of pictures of Wales as it had been in the bad old days between the great coal-mining period and the inrush of high technology, when half the country was on the dole. People hadn't cared about work, or anything else, their spirit almost broken by years of never having enough. The comparison troubled him a great deal. "You told me," he said, "that this area was doing all right in terms of mining. Iron-nickel."

Joss nodded. "So the report said. But I think I'd like to go out and do a little assaying of my own, if time permits. We're not exactly set up for it in terms of hardware, but I can teach the chemical analysis software what I need, and we don't need to be dragging whole asteroids inside the hull. Cores will do."

Evan nodded.

They came to the police dome. It was primarily and officially a Solar Patrol office, but it also served as the HQ for the station's own tiny private security/police force. As they walked in the door—which opened properly for them, no screwdrivers here, thank heaven—Evan drew a breath and held it to keep from saying *"Diw!"* again, loudly, at the tininess and wretchedness of the place. *This* was the representation of the Solar Patrol in this part of the world? Another dome, the whole thing hardly the size of a decent office back on the Moon? A dome patched inside and out, cramped, piled up with filing modules and printout in great stacks, the situation desk almost lost in the midst of everything? And one young officer, in uniform, looking almost pitifully smart in the midst of it all?

He looked up as they came in, and an expression of shock came over his face. The young man was astonishingly red-haired, and very freckled, perhaps in his mid-twenties. As he leapt up to welcome them, Evan found himself wondering if he himself had looked like this before he got his growth—a bit on the gangly side, but of a frame and build that promised some heft to come.

"Gentlemen, come in, I wasn't expecting anybody, they didn't tell me—" the young officer said, hurrying over to them.

"I don't think they wanted to," Joss said, shaking the young officer's hand. "Joss O'Bannion. My partner, Evan Glyndower."

"Noel Hayden," the young officer said, and Evan was mildly pleased at his grip as they shook hands. If it was anything to go by, this lad would have no trouble in the bars, which was almost certainly why the SP had sent him here to hold down this job all alone.

"Come and sit down," Hayden said, leading them back toward a desk, and starting to unearth several chairs from beneath piles of paper. "I didn't think they were going to send anyone so soon. In fact, I wasn't sure they would send anyone at all.''

Evan sat down and turned his datapad on to take voice notes. He noted that the message area was flagged. The ship's computer must have picked up something for him from HQ during the night. It could wait, though. ''It was your report that set all this off, then,'' Joss was saying.

Hayden nodded. ''I hope so. The disappearances have been going on for a while now, and the place was starting to get nervous.''

''More than nervous, I think,'' Evan said.

Noel smiled gently, a remarkably knowing expression for someone so young. ''Yes, you passed your qualifyings last night, I heard. Hasn't been an officer here in twenty years that hasn't happened to. But you got a little more than the usual treatment.''

''I was wondering whether that was quite normal,'' Joss said.

''Nerves,'' Noel said, ''and there were two of you, and one of you was big.''

Evan raised his eyebrows in a resigned look.

''Can I give you something?'' Noel said. ''Coffee? Tea?''

''I'll pass,'' Joss said. Evan shook his head.

''Right. Anyway,'' Neil said, and spent a moment shuffling around on his desk looking for something. It promised to be an interesting search; there was enough paper on the desk alone to cover the whole inside of the dome. *Which might not be a bad idea,* Evan thought. *You wouldn't have to see the patches then.*

''This started about three months ago, as far as I can tell,'' Noel said. ''At least, that's the furthest back I can trace it. Though HQ doesn't find anything statistically suspect in it until about a month after that.'' Noel snorted. ''They don't take feelings into consideration, but if you've been out here for a few years, you start getting a feeling for real accidents as opposed to contrived ones.''

Joss looked slightly surprised. "How long have you been out here?"

"About eight years now." Noel smiled. "Oh. Don't let my looks fool you. I'm thirty-eight."

Evan smiled. "You have a picture aging in a closet somewhere, then."

"So people say. One of my nicknames here is apparently 'Snookums.' " Noel grinned, an expression that had a hint of satisfaction about it. "Everybody who comes here makes the predictable mistake in a bar—once."

Joss chuckled. Noel kept looking for his piece of paperwork. "Anyway, about four months ago, people started simply disappearing. Now, it's not as if they don't do that anyway. Mining is hardly a safe occupation, no matter how you look at it. Just the basic mechanics of it can get you killed. A cheap pressure suit goes south, your ship has a power failure and your transponder goes out—or doesn't work," he added, "possibly because someone's been fiddling with it. There's a lot of that around here, people killing their own transponders so as not to show where their claims are."

"I think we might want to look at the actual method for filing claims," Joss said.

"Surely." Noel kept digging about among the papers on his desk. "The worst of it all, anyway, is that there's no pattern I can find. My first suspicion was claim-jumping, of course. But that tends to be pretty easy to trace. Gossip is everything in this community, and it doesn't take much listening to find out who seems to have hit it big lately and whom they've told about it, if anybody. Or who's jealous, who's had a bad run of luck, and so forth. The result tends to be straightforward death by violence—shooting, or something of the kind. Sabotage happens occasionally, but it's rare. I think the perception is that it's too much trouble, and too easy to get caught. Also, the mechanics here are very careful about their work, since any ship that goes out and doesn't come back immediately brings them into disrepute even if plain old backshooting isn't apparent.''

Joss nodded. ''What's the population breakdown like here?''

''Mixed, of course, but mostly Russians and Japanese. We have a strong Baltic and Central European component, for some reason. I recommend Satra's over in the main dome—they have some pretty good *rostyas* there.''

Joss's eyebrows went up. ''There's a restaurant here?''

''Hey, this may be the asteroid belt,'' Noel said, ''but we're not quite the end of the world. Ah!'' He came up with a piece of printout, handed it over to Joss. ''Here.''

Joss scanned down it. ''That was the first one I found suspicious,'' Noel said. ''Yuri Brunoy's ship *Vastap*. Yuri wasn't the kind to have people trying to claim-jump him in the first place. Nice calm man, only shot people who needed it—''

''How do we determine who needed it?'' Evan said softly.

Noel leaned back in his chair and sighed. ''You've worked out this way before. No murders, though, I guess.''

Evan shook his head. ''Not from claim-jumping. Drug enforcement, mostly.''

''It's kind of a problem,'' Noel said. ''Someone jumps someone else's claim and gets shot for his trouble. The jumpee comes back with the body, claims self-defense. Short of a body that's been backshot, and sometimes even with one, without witnesses—and there are rarely witnesses out there since the family ships have fallen pretty much out of style—how do you prove that it *wasn't* self-defense? If there's even a body left. In zero gee, from the surface of small asteroids, bodies do get lost. And it's understandable when the person who's just been attacked doesn't particularly feel like chasing a tenth of a light-hour after the corpse of the person who just tried to backshoot *him*. Or if they do, they would have to throw ore out to make mass room for it. It doesn't seem like a good deal to a lot of people." Noel sighed. "So *habeas corpus* is a bit of a problem. And judges frequently refuse to hear these cases simply because they've seen so many of them end in the same way, with hung juries or dismissals. No," Noel added, "you have to manage these by feel, when it comes down to it. There's a certain amount of justice done here by the people themselves. You learn not to interfere too much. But if someone's taking the law into his own hands, he tends to die of that, too. Word travels fast."

Evan nodded. "Anyway," Noel said, *"Vastap* was a fifty-ton vessel, a small ore processor. We have a few people based here who prefer to crush and slag down their own ore. There's an advantage to it: you don't have to spend the money for reaction mass to haul around what's essentially going to be ninety percent waste rock after someone else processes it. It costs more in energy than just hauling ore back, of course, but if you're steadily turning over enough raw material, you can do a lot better than break even in a few years. Well, Yuri was well past that point. He had actually gotten married a few years back—they had a 'summer house' on Dacha Station around Jupiter—and he would work half the year, then take half the year off with his wives. Anyway, Yuri had just started his work year, when he went out and didn't come back. He was a careful pilot—"

"Yes," Joss said dryly. "I would think careful pilots would do well here."

Noel grunted. "I heard about your problem last night. Your assailants have already been cited—I did that just after breakfast—but you'll forgive me if I didn't fine them too much. They're fighting with inadequate equipment, like all the rest of us here. And the last thing this place needs is a landing guidance facility that's unfriendly to sops."

"Heavens, no," Joss said, "having seen what benign neglect looks like."

Noel coughed. "Yes. Anyway—Yuri always filed a course plan and he always kept to it. He was no hotdogger.

He was headed toward an area he had been mining for a while, about thirty thousand kilometers antiorbital from us, and about five thousand plus-zee. Still in the neighborhood, but an area that had plenty for everybody and wasn't in any danger of being mined out—a lot of nickel-iron there, but mostly iron, rather higher grade ore than usual, and more worth his trouble.''

"And there was no distress call or anything like it?" Joss said.

"Well, no," Noel said, "but the problem around here, of couse, is that even if there *is* a distress call, communications lag times being what they are, you're frequently too far away from the source of the distress to do any good by the time you get there. Our average response time here is about six hours, sometimes more if they're really far out there. But a lot of people are careless and don't carry enough emergency air to last them. They consider it a waste of mass and fuel for something that might never happen." Noel shrugged. "In that regard, I suppose you could say that natural selection is still operating."

"It usually finds ways," said Evan.

"There's nothing we can do for those people," Noel said. "But people who haven't had an accident that's an immediate killer can usually be brought back without too much trouble in ten to fourteen hours. I'm on call to do that myself, and we have a couple of volunteers with light haulers, or big engines, who go out if I'm already out on a job."

"Are you happy with your volunteers?" Joss said.

"Oh yes. Dav Myennes and Joan Selvino are heads of two of the big old families here. Probably the only really big families we have left. Since better facilities are available back around Mars, or Jupiter, we have a lot of people moving their families out," Noel sighed. "The place is turning into a bit of a ghost town . . . mostly singletons. It's a little sad. I miss the children."

Evan began to understand why the place had a dispirited

feel about it. "Anyway," he said, "our friend just vanished? No transponder trace?"

"None. Normally, when we start looking for a transponder with the high-powered gear, we can find it even if it's right out of the Belts. But there was no sign of Yuri's, which meant that his ship had either been completely destroyed, or the transponder had been shut down. That I find hard to believe. Yuri was very safety conscious—we did a pickup on him long, long ago, an engine failure, not his fault or the mechanic's—and I don't think I ever met anyone who was more against fiddling with your black box."

"So someone blew him completely away."

"Or he went out of range, which I also find hard to believe," Noel said. "He didn't like to roam; he had a good thing going where he was. And also, the converter ships don't have that kind of range; they trade it off for the energy they need to run their smelters. So—"

"But you don't think anyone would have bothered jumping his claim?" said Joss.

"Out that way, there would have been no need. See, mostly it happens when someone thinks that someone else is onto a particularly hot claim—an extremely high metal/ore ratio, or something that's not ore. We don't get much of that kind of thing around here. The last time we had a gemstone hit was, hell, six years ago now. Funny, that was Yuri too. But it was a small find, something like five thousand creds' worth of industrial diamonds. The rest of his load, just pig iron, brought him three times as much."

Noel did a bit more digging in the spot where he had found the first précis, and came up with several others. "Then came these. Les Bianco's *Loner*, Giselle Bollenberg's *Half Moon*, Dail Fissau's *Copernicus*, Rall Bevocic's *Lucie*—all gone. Within fifty days of one another— and no coincidence of times, places, anything. To judge by their filed course plans, they were all heading in different directions. One by one they all missed their return or check-in dates."

"Meaning they weren't planning to be coming back just yet, but they would come in close enough to send a message? Or stop in at another station and send one from there?" Joss asked.

"That's right. We only eventually found one ship, *Copernicus,* and that was by accident; someone from over at Cambrai Station found it while en route here. Its transponder was running, but there was no sign of Dail, and there was a big hole in the hull—the ship's fuel cell was blown out. It happens." Noel shrugged. "It was one of the older atomic ones: they're capricious at best. I don't know why people still use them, except that they're cheap."

Evan purposely did not look at the ceiling, or at something else he had noticed earlier: the obvious, and obviously used, emergency patching kit off beside one filing module, sitting there in case the passive sealing function of the dome should fail to work. "What about the claims proceedings?" he said.

"Well, we have a registrar, as most places out this far do. No one wants to make a special trip to Mars or Jupiter just to register a claim; you want to be able to lay over and resupply at the same time. The office is up in Main Dome. Claims still have to be filed in person—we're not that automated out here, I'm afraid—and the various station offices exchange records once a month just to make sure there are no mistakes, since asteroids do drift. Or are jarred off course." Noel grinned slightly. "We give a claimant a tag core to sink into the surface of the body in question. Like one of these." He reached down, pulled open one of his desk drawers, rummaged for a moment, and came up with something that looked like a sealed length of steel pipe, about an inch and a half wide and two feet long. "It transmits the claim number and the claimant's name to anyone with the right receiver, which around here is most people. Once in, it's almost impossible to get out without a bomb or a laser drill, and such removal always leaves signs. They're as tamperproof as we can make them.''

''But there have been exceptions, I take it,'' Joss said dryly.

''Oh yes. What technology can invent, technology can defeat. We've seen some very clever tamperings, even forgeries. But forgeries are easy to trace, since they don't match our records here. And tamperings leave traces. But most people consider it too much trouble to go to for one more hunk of iron, when there's likely to be a much better one fifty thousand meters further on.''

''Let's put the disappearances aside for a moment,'' Joss said. ''Have you had any claim jumps recently?''

''A couple, yes.'' Noel started rummaging again, and this time didn't have to dig too deep. ''Sorry about this,'' he said, paging through a few pieces of paper, ''but my data base went down months ago, and we're still waiting for the parts to fix it. I have to keep everything this way, if I want it accessible at all.''

''They keep promising us the paper-free office,'' Evan said. ''I begin to wonder when we'll see it.''

''Here,'' said Noel, and handed Evan the sheets. He glanced down them, and passed them to Joss. ''That asteroid was pretty promising,'' Noel said. ''Good iron content. Hek Vaweda there staked it out about two months ago. She missed a check-in, and I went looking for her. Found the claim—but no ship, no Hek. No traces of where she had gone, or what had happened.'' Noel shook his head. ''It was a pity. She was a nice lady.''

''I'd like to have a look at the spot,'' Joss said, ruffling through the sheets, ''and at the rest of these.''

''I'll take you out,'' Noel said, getting up.

''No rush,'' Evan said. ''You probably have things to do first—''

''Unfortunately, yes,'' Noel said, ''but any escape from *this* is a pleasure. I have considered setting fire to it,'' he added, getting up, ''but I'm the fire chief as well, and it seems a little pointless. Half a second while I get my suit.''

They made their way back to the hangar dome, and Noel stopped in the middle of it and simply stared at their ship. "I saw one of those once," he said, "in a vid. I didn't think they actually existed."

"Oh, they exist," Joss said, "and the trouble people give you for overrunning your fuel expenditure, you wouldn't want to hear." His voice was unusually dry. Evan glanced over at him questioningly. Joss shrugged at him, the "later" shrug.

"Open up," he said, and obediently the craft cracked its seals and let them into the airlock. Noel looked around admiringly as they stepped in. "It still smells new," he said.

"Not for long," Evan said, and made his way up front to unlock and rig the third seat in the front cabin. "Wait till my friend here makes his chicken with forty cloves of garlic."

"Forty cloves of—"

"It's very innocent, really," Joss said. "It's most people's first chance to find out that garlic is a vegetable—"

"Indeed yes," said Evan drily. "A vegetable that makes parts of you speak that were better silent."

Noel blinked, and declined to comment. "Look at these cabins," he said, pausing in the door of Evan's. "Why the hell are you staying at Morrie's?"

After cleaning out the 'fresher head, this was a question that had also occurred to Evan. "Public relations, I guess," he said. "It seems to work better than becoming known as the stuck-up sop who stays in his own ship and won't patronize local business. Even if local business does charge five times the normal rate."

They got strapped in, and Joss put the engines into short-start mode and turned on the transmitter. "Willans control," he said, "this is SP vessel CDZ 8064. You remember, the one with the ruined paint job." His voice was good-humored as he said it, but Evan, looking at Joss's face, saw a shadow of what Joss must have been like that morning with the radar techs, and smiled slightly to himself.

"Uh, SP CDZ, that's a roger," said a rather sheepish sounding, middle-aged female voice. "What color was your paint?"

"New," Joss said, but this time he smiled a little.

"Sorry about that, SP CDZ. I have some nail polish here that might do the trick."

Joss laughed. "You're on, ma'am. See me after work if you like, in the Astoria." That was the bar of the night before. Evan kept his smile to himself. Joss never missed a chance to butter up the ladies, whether he could see what they looked like or not. He was an equal opportunity flirt, and the fact had caused Evan considerable amusement on more than one occasion.

There was a chuckle at the other end of the connection. "You're on, CDZ. You going somewhere right now?"

"Out for a stroll. Noel, you have coordinates for this nice lady?"

Noel leaned in toward the pickup. "Cecile, we're headed out past Osasco Point beacon, anti-orbital from the beacon six hundred klicks, and about minus-zee six hundred."

"Got it, Noel. You have a nice time now. Nobody out that way but old Vlad Marischal and his friends, transponder one point four four three from a.o. fourteen, sixteen klicks, plus-zee one fifty."

"Confirmed, Cecile," Joss said. "And listen, about this morning—"

"The limbs will probably grow back, we think. You were in the right. No hard feelings."

Joss chuckled. "Thanks much."

"You're welcome, Mister Sop O'Bannion Honey, and good hunting. Bay doors opening. Willans control out."

Joss closed down the connection for the moment and said to Noel, "Mister Sop O'Bannion Honey'?"

Noel looked innocent. "I guess word travels fast," he said. "Seems like a lot of people approve of your performance last night. What I heard was that your friend here had to carry you out to keep you from really hurting someone.''

Evan smiled again, harder this time.

The bay doors opened for them, and Joss stood the ship up on its underjets and eased it into the lock, then out after the rear doors had shut and the lock had been evacuated. As the outer doors opened in front of them, Noel sighed and said, ''There goes another hundred credits.''

Evan was astonished. ''There can't have been more than twenty credits' worth of air in that lock. Twenty-five, tops.''

Noel smiled sourly as Joss took them away from the lock. ''Not when it has to be shipped out this far. And Willans isn't a water-bearing asteroid: we can't crack out our own oxygen from it. We buy our oxygen as a co-op with a few other stations in this part of the Belts, but the suppliers on Jupiter say they're just passing on the cost of shipping out *their* processing equipment from Earth . . .''

They headed out into the long night. Evan watched Joss lock in the course he wanted with a smile on his face. *He does love this ship,* he thought, as Noel showed Joss which frequency to set on the comms board for the claim marker, and then sat back to wait.

There was no way to describe space travel in this part of the universe as particularly exciting. Joss went off and made coffee, and made Noel have some, and the tea he brought Evan was actually drinkable. Beyond drinking their tea and coffee, there was nothing to do but wait.

Whump! went the iondrivers, and Noel looked up in startlement. ''What was that?''

''Engines,'' Joss said, sitting down in the right-hand seat again, with a look on his face like a cat that's been given cream to put on its canary. ''ETA is about seven minutes.''

Noel's eyes were wide. ''What kind of engines have you *got* on this thing?''

Joss leaned back and went off into a spate of jargon that

threatened to make Evan's eyes cross. It was nothing he hadn't heard before. The day they picked the ship up, Joss had carried on like this with the SP engineer at Andronicus, going on for almost half an hour about boost ratios and ion spill and "dirty" generation and heaven only knew what else. Evan had had to go off and get a drink. Here, he couldn't even do that.

"What's this blinking?" he said finally, when he couldn't stand it any more.

"Where?" Joss said, turning hurriedly back to the console. "Oh, this. That's the comms alert. There's your claim, Noel."

"So soon? You'd better slow down."

"No problem."

Evan peered out the plex, squinting. When he had first come out here, he had thought of the Belts as looking (from the inside) like the enhanced telescopic pictures Earth people usually saw of asteroids, or of the moons of the outer planets, with everything lit in the same stark black-shadows-blinding-white-light as the Moon. Well, the shadows were stark enough, but the light was nowhere near so bright. The level of lighting was about the same as on a dim winter's afternoon in Wales, during the part of the winter when the Sun ran lowest; even on a clear day, its light was attenuated, cool, spare. Here it was the same, when the light had anything to fall on—chill and clear, a very pure white, but somehow thin and stretched. No surprise, considering how far it had come. Nor were the asteroids crowded all around them, easy to bump into, or even hard to avoid. Evan could not think of any part of the other side of the Belts—the denser side, at that—where he could stand on one asteroid, and see another one with the naked eye.

They were drifting close to a little asteroid, about half a kilometer from one end to the other, shaped rather like a shoe that had been stepped on. There were gaping holes cut in it, blasted with energy weapons, rather than with explosive, judging by the smooth sides. Evan nodded to himself as Joss slowed the ship down and maneuvered it in close. "Are you going to put us down on there?" he said.

"It's safer," Joss said. "If this thing has been slagged out, its motion may be eccentric. I'd sooner not do any more damage to my paint job, thanks."

"Your paint job?" Evan said mildly, and went off to get into his suit.

It was the first time in some days, and he was glad of the chance. Quickly he stripped down to shorts and singlet and began, piece by piece, to get into the suit; stepping into the boots first, strapping on greaves and thigh-pieces, backing into the backplate and then holding it up from behind to let it seal onto the breastplate. The soft hiss of closing seals was music to his ears. The suit was newly overhauled: fresh neural and feedback sponge padding had been put in, the helm's optics and electronics had been retuned, and the negative-feedback circuitry itself had been reset and restrung, making the suit react with a bit more bounce. This restringing was something that needed to be done a couple of times a year, as a man "worked into" a specific suit and found its mass easier to carry; otherwise the suit would begin to overreact to his movements, and move too easily, too sloppily.

As Evan slipped into the upper arm and forearm pieces, and sealed them shut, he was glad of the restringing, but he was even happier about the replacement of the feedback foam. It was what translated the movements of your muscles into the much larger, stronger movements of the suit, but it wasn't exactly something you could just send out to the cleaners. And after you had sweated into it for a couple of months, you could scare away perpetrators in interior environments just by the sheer awful stink of you in the neighborhood. There was this to be said for vacuum work: in space, no one could smell you coming.

He checked the insides and far outsides of the forearms, where the gun ports were faired in, and found everything satisfactory, slipped on the gauntlets and sealed them shut, and then reached for the helm. For a moment he looked at his reflection in the cool grey-silver surface. Some people, he knew, saw nothing but blind menace and the threat of violence in the blank reflection of the helm, that usually allowed no face to show, no eyes. Evan didn't mind. It was a weapon, and he used it as consciously as his guns, and with a freer conscience.

He put it on, touched the seals closed, and stepped out into the hallway. In the front cabin, Joss and Noel were in their own pressure suits, helms under arms, looking toward him. Joss's expression was calm and accustomed, but Noel's face showed shock and astonishment. It was a look Evan had gotten used to over time. "Ready?" he said.

"All set," Joss said, and put his helmet on. Noel followed suit. Together they all stepped into the airlock, and Joss touched the controls to seal the inner door, evacuate the air, and open the outer.

There was almost no gravity to deal with here, so they all moved on personal attitude jets, with care, and slowly. Joss bounced ahead a bit, looking at the ground intently. Noel went behind him and pointed off to one side. "That's the biggest hole, I guess," he said. "Want to go down inside?"

"Absolutely," said Joss.

Evan paused for a moment at the edge of the huge hole, looking up. He had not seen this particular skyscape for some time, not from the surface of one of these tiny bodies. The light was less bright out here than in Earth orbit, certainly, and cooler, but you could still make out the Belts, and the further bits were more easily seen than the nearer. The biggest asteroids, and the most reflective, made a bright vague chain that you could trace with the eye, far off to one side and to the other, where the reflective sides of them were turned more or less toward you. Here and there a particularly reflective or large asteroid shone like a star, a pale spark embedded in the milky glow of millions of others. Nearer the sun, as the asteroids seemed closer together, the band grew brighter, though no more distinct, until finally it was completely washed out in the light of the Sun, which was still much too bright to look at directly with the naked eye. Evan did the jaw clench that brought his visible-light filters down, and looked at the Sun for a moment, long enough to count a few sunspots and make out the tiny points of some spicules around the edges. *Quiet Sun weather; no bad solar wind or flares to worry about, at least. That's something.*

He turned his attention downward to the hole itself. Energy weapons, certainly. That by itself was a little strange; explosives were cheaper, when it came to merely slagging out an asteroid. But if someone was claim-jumping, no question that a beam would be faster. Evan bent down to feel the edge of the hole. No crumbling: a fast cut, then, with a high-energy beam. Someone well-equipped had been here, someone who didn't want to wait around, and could afford the energy not to.

He stepped off the edge of the hole, giving himself a brief hit of jets to push him downward; there was no other way to fall, in such very light gravity. Joss and Noel had their lights on—understandable, since it was dark as the inside of a cat down there—and were already well down into the empty space of the asteroid. Joss was over by one wall, running a gauntlet-covered hand over the surface.

"Beamer, definitely," he said to Evan. "And fairly high-powered. There's nothing much here in the way of melt marks: it's mostly straightforward downward vaporization."

Evan nodded, and said, "Noel, who around here has that kind of equipment?"

"A few of our people do, but they all have alibis that stand up. Quite a few people in the parts of the belt adjacent have beamers installed in their craft, and use them. Maybe ten or fifteen percent of the total registered mining force. I can get you stats when we get back, if you like."

"It would help." Evan watched Joss move hand over hand across the wall, pausing here and there to examine the stone. "Anything?" he said.

"I'm not sure." The answer came back in a tone of voice that said Joss *was* sure, but was being polite. "Noel," he said, "have you done an assay on this stuff?"

Noel sounded surprised. "No. There didn't seem to be much point."

"I'd like to, if you don't mind." From the pack on the back of his pressure suit, Joss came out with a small portable specific gravity and ore assay kit, a little squat tube about six inches wide and a foot long. "Now then," he said, "if I can just keep this thing from spinning me around. It's had some torque problems the past couple of weeks, but I put a new diamond ring in it, that should have it straightened out—"

There was no sound, of course, but Evan saw that Joss had to brace and rebrace himself against the attempt of the tube to turn while the internal drill was working. Apparently he was in one of his perfectionist moods; he could simply vaporized a sample and tested that, but it seemed he wanted a friability and texture assessment as well. Evan sighed. Joss's hobbyist tendencies came out at odd moments, but as long as they didn't slow things down too much, Evan had learned not to protest. Anything that kept that lively mind working at capacity was fine with him.

"Right," Joss said, and did something to the outside of the tube. Beside him, Noel peered at it curiously. "When does the answer come out?" he said after a few seconds.

"Takes a while," Joss said, pushing away from the wall and heading for another spot. "Hey, come on, Noel, my name isn't Spock."

"Who's Spock?" said Noel, mystified.

"Baby doctor," Evan said. "Something wrong with his ears, too, wasn't there?"

"Hah," Joss said, in that tone of voice that suggested Evan was going to be made to watch more ancient vids "for his own good and to make up for his terrible lack of cultural education." Evan sighed.

Joss applied the spee-gee tube to another part of the

asteroid's interior. Evan turned to look at the rest of the
inside of the asteroid. The surface was much the same all
around, brownish-grey rock with here and there a fleck of
remaining iron or nickel in metallic form. Where such
pieces of metal had been shorn off mostly flat by the vaporization, some were showing the faint scratches of crystalline formation that etching and polishing would have
turned into the characteristic Widmanstatten lines that betray true asteroidal metal. There were not many of these
bits of metal left, but that made sense; any claim jumper
would have scooped out as much of the asteroid as was
good, and left the rest. And, indeed, about nine-tenths of
the body had been removed as neatly as a melon scooped
out of its shell, though through several holes front and
back, rather than by splitting the melon and getting at the
insides that way.

Now why didn't the bugger do that, Evan thought, *rather
than doing it this way? What was to be gained?* It was
something he would have to ask Joss.

"There," Joss said, moving to a third spot. "One more
for luck." He took the sample by plain vaporization this
time, which suited Evan. There was something about this
site that was making him twitch, and he would have liked
to get out and go find someone to bring to book for it.
Someone had come here, probably killed the person who
was working this claim, and then stripped it bare and run
off, secure in the knowledge that it would be difficult, if
not impossible, to find him or her. Evan hated the idea of
that kind of callousness; even more, he hated actually having to hang about in the physical evidence of it.

"Done," said Joss. "Let's get out of here."

"What does it say?" said Noel.

"Still working. Come on, let's get up top. I want to
look at something."

They ascended to the surface and landed on it as best
they could, though it was difficult to stay landed in what
was effectively zero gee. "Now, here," Joss said, turning
the readout end of the tube up into the light, so Evan and

Noel could both see it. "See that little graph there? That's metal content plotted against stone/waste content. Here are the three readings."

Evan peered over Joss's shoulder. Three small bars plotted themselves against the graph. Well above the three of them, which varied only slightly from one another, was a red line. "What's that, then?" Evan said.

Joss looked up at Evan, and even in the indirect lighting, Evan could see his expression of fierce interest "Viability," he said. "That's the one percent metal-to-waste scenario. There wasn't anything in here worth slagging out."

Noel stared at him. "But that can't be," he said. "The assay brought to us when this claim was filed was much higher than that. At least five percent. No one would bother jumping an oh-one claim!"

"Yes, that's right, isn't it?" Joss said, sounding illogically pleased with himself. "Let's have a look at the claim core, shall we?"

There was no finding it visually, but Noel's suit had built into it a transmitter and homer sensitive to the claims frequencies, and he led them to the spot as directly as he could. There were crevasses to overleap on the stony surface. Once past the crevasses, they carefully kangarooed over to one bit of flat ground. Embedded in it, protruding from the surface, only about an inch, was one of the tubular steel claim cores.

"It hasn't been tampered with," Noel said. "And it's reading just as it did when I checked it out to Hek two months ago. Same frequ cy, same code."

Joss nodded, unslung his spee-gee apparatus again, and tested the ground in one place, then another. "Hmm," he said again. "Evan, would you make me a hole here? About half a meter deep or so?"

"How wide?" Evan said. "A third of a meter be enough?"

"Plenty."

Evan performed the brief pattern of finger touches that activated his own beamer, and pointed his right arm at the ground. "Eyes," he said, scaling down the amount of light his own faceplate would let in. Joss and Noel looked away. He fired a two-second burn.

When he stopped, there was a slight crystalline snow falling through the vacuum around them, rock vapor frozen back instantly into solid state and drifting very slowly down toward the asteroid's surface. "How's that?" he said.

"Showoff," said Joss, and bent over to slide the speegee reader down into the half-meter-wide, third-of-a-meter deep hole. He took one more sample, then pulled the device out again. "Now, then," he said.

They looked over his shoulder once more as he brought up the graph readout. Every one of the three sample bars went well over the red line.

"Oh, no," Noel said softly. "Bad assay. It's just the surface that's good, not the interior."

"I'm not so sure," Joss said, with a look at Evan.

Evan frowned. 'True. Why would someone jump the claim if the assay was bad?And if the jumpers did their own assay—and you'd think they would—why would they go to the trouble of hollowing out a whole asteroid, if the inside was worthless?"

They all three stood there for a moment, considering this. Then Joss said, "I need to look at something," and kangarooed off across the surface.

Noel looked at Evan in confusion. Evan shook his head. "You've got me," he said. Together they watched Joss bounce a little way across the surface, then back a little, back a little more, studying the ground closely, then off to one side, and further off, finally starting back toward them. He paused briefly and dropped to his knees, bouncing a bit, running his hands over the surface. "Evan," he said. "How much lifting is your suit rated for? The top range."

Evan raised his eyebrows. Bemused, "It's rated for nine tons, but I've just been restrung, and it might be a bit less."

"Hmm," Joss said, and stood up straight again. He began to bounce toward them in a roughly circular path around the core. "Hmm," he said again, pausing to go down on his knees once more and check another piece of ground.

"It's like being at the damned doctor's," Evan said in good-natured exasperation. "For pity's sake, what're you up to?"

Joss came back to them. "Think you could do thirty or forty tons in zero gee?"

Evan did a bit of mental math. "Very likely. 'Give me a place to stand.' "

"Good. How about—" Joss headed off again, leftward, about five meters from the core proper, toward a smallish crevasse, and pointed downwards. "Right about here?"

Evan bounced over to him, and looked at the spot. "And lift what?"

"That," Joss said, pointing at the other side of the crevasse, and indicating the piece of ground that included the claim transmitter.

"You're daft!" Evan said. "Go trying to pick up pieces of the asteroid? Now, why would I want—" But even as he spoke he was looking more closely at the little crevasse, no more than a foot wide here. He kicked his helmet light on and looked at it more closely still.

The patterns on the rock on one side of the crevasse did not match the patterns on the other.

"*Jesu Crist* on a handbike!" he said.

He reached down into the crevasse, set his legs wide, bent his knees, took hold of the stone on the transmitter side of the crevasse, and started exerting pull.

Under his gauntlets, rock crumbled. He felt for another more solid handhold further down, but found none. He chipped through into the rock with his gauntlets to make a better place to brace his fingers, sank a bit more deeply into his kneebend, and heaved again.

Nothing happened. He could hear the suit creaking and straining around him as the servos tried to cope with what he was trying to get it to do.

He kept pulling.

Nothing happened. He wondered if he was going to ruin his negative-feedback circuitry. That happened, sometimes, when you tried to move something too large, like a piece of a planet—

Override requests and alarms began to flash in front of his eyes, or rather, on the surfaces of his retinas. Evan ignored them and kept pulling. Though nothing was happening.

Wait a minute. Something was giving under his hands—

No, it wasn't. The horizon was changing subtly. The claim transmitter was tilting away from him. A piece of the asteroid fifty feet across was tilting up out of the surface, near edge up, far edge down. A big, roughly semicircular chunk, now about a foot higher than the ground he was standing on—a foot and a half—

"Enough already!" Joss said. Evan let go, but mass in motion doing what it does in zero gee, the plugged-in piece of stone kept tilting up and up for several seconds before inertia set in and stopped it. Then it began to settle again, and a brief cloud of dust puffed up as it did.

"Pity you didn't have the suit on in the bar last night," Joss said. Evan saw Noel's head swivel toward Joss; it was a pity about the bad light, for he would have loved to see the look on Noel's face. "But how about *that,* then," Joss said smugly.

Evan was feeling smug too, though he was not sure that his biceps and the muscles of his forearms weren't going to have something to say to him tomorrow. "Someone," he said, "cut the claim transmitter whole and entire out of another asteroid. And cut a matching hole in this one, and dropped one into the other."

They both looked at Noel. He was flabbergasted. "Then the asteroid Hek claimed on is somewhere else entirely. With a big hole cut in it."

"Let's go looking," Joss said, and headed back for the ship. "It can't be far. If I was pulling a stunt like this, I'd be betting on never getting caught. I wouldn't bother going more than a few minutes away to find the place where I would dig the hole to stick this plug. Which means that Hek's real asteroid is nearby. Come on.''

They went after him, fast.

IT TOOK THEM THREE HOURS TO FIND IT, FOR there were about eighteen asteroids in the immediate area, and looking over every one of them was a time-consuming business. Joss swore at the ship for not being maneuverable enough (which it was) and at his scanning software for not being smart enough (which it was) as they sifted through the area, one rock after another.

And there it was, the fifteenth one; a small asteroid, very elongated, almost cucumber-shaped. One end of it had a roughly spherical hole cut in it. Joss sat there working with his controls for a moment, then said, ''The scan wasn't really built for this kind of thing, but I can tell that this ore pretty closely matches the ore around the claim core.''

Noel looked out at it and bit his lip. ''I wish I had this kind of equipment,'' he said, ''and time to use it.''

''No shame to you,'' Evan said. ''You're not exactly underworked as it is.'' He looked over at Joss and said, ''We ought to look this over pretty carefully.''

Joss nodded and started them in a slow spiral around the surface of the asteroid. There was nothing much else to be seen, at least not by strictly visual means. What *was* plain from visual examination was that this asteroid had been slagged out as well, through several apertures, and with great skill. Joss shook his head ruefully as they came to the end of the spiraling, at the far end of the asteroid.

''So,'' he said. ''A claim jumper with a nasty turn of mind.''

''Or someone who wants us to think he's claim-jumping,'' Evan said.

Joss nodded. ''Yes,'' he said. ''I didn't want to mention

it. I hate to start being paranoid this early on. But we'll see whether there's any evidence to support it.''

He sat for a moment and thought, then began to work with his control panel again. "Let's see," he said. "what else we can dig up around here."

A moment later he was done. Evan leaned over to look at the data readout screen. Joss had done something to its output; there was nothing on it but a sort of fuzzy glob of light off to one side. "You break that thing again?"

"No," Joss said, sounding abstracted. "I've got it reading for diffuse proximity. You set the radar so it—oh, never mind. I'll tell you about it later. This may take a while—there's too damn much rock and ore around here to attenuate the signal." He leaned over the screen, peering at it while he made some delicate adjustment to the command console. "And what do you mean again? *You* broke it last time."

"I never," Evan said. "You left it set up for radar, it wasn't my fault if the computer—"

"Ssh!"

Evan sshed, smiling slightly. There was a slight hiss of jets as Joss moved the ship, edging it away from the asteroid from which the claim core had been cut, and toward another one about twenty thousand meters away. Another burst of jets, and another, one every few seconds for awhile. Then, silence.

Slowly they drifted close to it, the asteroid body swelling into visibility on the screen, a spark at first, then a bizarre shape like a batch of lumps welded together. "Mmf," Joss said, sounding annoyed. The fuzzy patch of light on the screen had become larger, and fuzzier around the edges: the light at its center was more concentrated.

"No good?" Evan said softly.

"Further along on this line," Joss said, more to himself than to Evan. "Another twenty kilometers or so. Let's see."

More small hisses of jets, more time drifting in silence. They passed the lumpy asteroid and headed on. "It can't be far," Joss muttered. "Even with drift, even with the usual traffic, I wouldn't have risked it being much farther than this. Hope that's not just some wreck."

"We don't have wrecks drifting around out here," Noel said. "It's not like Earth orbit, where there are a lot of better ways to make money. Out here, salvage prices are too good to ignore, and worked metal is worth a lot more than raw."

"Good," Joss said, and would say nothing else for some minutes.

They drifted on. Stars moved in the plex window, but nothing else came into view. Joss sat hunched over and wouldn't take his eyes off the screen. The concentration of light in the middle of the fuzzy glob got stronger and stronger.

"Has to be," Joss said to himself. "Has to be." He hit the control console, and there was a short, heavy burst of jets, a two-second burn.

They began to speed up a good deal. The white core of light on the readout got stronger and stronger. "Look at that!" Joss said, triumphant.

"What is it?" said Evan.

Joss sat back and breathed out. *That* is metal under stone. Metal under *disturbed* stone. Side-looking radar sees half of it. The spectroscopy scanner sees the other half. A significant contrast in density between the surface and the substrate material. It's no good for mining, because the density differences are never this major, ninety percent of the time—the odds are too much against it being useful as a tool. Sorry, Noel. But that—" and he pointed at the screen "—*that* is something made of pure steel or other alloy, underneath a stone surface. *That.*"

He pointed at the asteroid they were approaching. It was another lumpy one, a sort of two-potato asteroid, the potatoes welded to one another side by side, the long way. Joss touched the command console again, slowing the ship down, and started to swing it around the asteroid. "Let's see, now," he said.

Evan looked with interest at the surface of the asteroid. It was the usual mess—pocked with microasteroid impacts, dusty, rocky, cracked. But there was something else interesting about it. "Joss," he said, "a bit lively, isn't it?"

Joss nodded. "Yes," he said. "It's tumbling too much, much more than from a simple collision. Someone's been interfering with it. Someone added something to its mass, and not too long ago—and didn't bother to stabilize its orbit afterwards."

"Not that that would have helped them," Evan said, "with Sherlock Holmes on the job."

Joss smiled slightly. "People get clumsy out here," he said, making another adjustment to the console. "You'd think they'd never heard of physics." He looked out the plex. "There!"

"There what?"

Joss was tapping at the console again. "We passed it. Half a second while I slow us down."

It took more than half a second, but that was the way it was on chemical jets. Evan told himself to be patient, and waited. They came right around the asteroid again, and Joss had them down to the barest crawling drift by the time they passed the point again. "Right there," he said, pointing again. "What does that look like to you?"

Evan looked down and smiled, an angry smile. There was no mistaking it; he had seen it on the other side of the Belts, as a convenient way to hide drug caches. "I'd say that someone dug a hole, dumped something big over it, raked some rubble in on top, and fused it."

"Something made of metal," Joss said, looking at one of his instruments, "and massing, oh, about thirty tons—eh, Noel?"

Noel nodded. "That was Hek's weight of registry, yeah?" he said. "Close enough."

"Now, then," Joss said, and reached for another part of the console, the part with the capped controls on it. One by one he performed the touch patterns that made the panel swallow the caps, leaving the pads for the ship's weaponry free. "Let's see if we can manage this without damaging the evidence."

"You sure you don't want me to go down there and just dig it up?" Evan said. He was only half kidding. He was getting angry again, and ripping an asteroid apart would have been oddly satisfying.

Joss looked at him with an expression that said he was tempted to let Evan try. "Better let me," he said.

He selected several controls, depressed them, and said, "Medium dispersion. This should take the first three meters off. Three seconds."

Evan breathed in, breathed out. The next moment, the plex went white with the asteroid-reflected fire of the weapons going off. Dust and vapor blew by the plex shield, and there were rattles and tinkles against the hull as bits of rock and other debris hit the ship and bounced. When the light cut off and the noise died away, Joss looked out the plex and scowled a bit.

"That's annoying," he said. "They were supposed to be tuned higher than that. Hardly the top meter went off. One more time."

Once more the blinding light lip up the cabin, and bits or rock rattled and banged against them. Evan saw Noel wince. He understood the feeling: Evan had never liked the sound of *anything* colliding with a ship he was in; you could never tell if it was going to come through.

"There," Joss said.

Evan looked out through the dust. There was no gleam of metal, not after heat like that, but a scarred, blackened shape that was definitely not something that occurred naturally in an asteroid. A corner of a cargo module was visible, though the blast of the ship's weaponry had melted it somewhat.

"That look familiar?" said Joss to Noel.

Noel looked stricken. He nodded. "That's Hek's ship, all right."

"We'll want to get it dug out, then," Joss said. "Can

you have someone give us a hand with that? It's not smart to try to dig and examine evidence at the same time.''

''Certainly,'' Noel said. He smiled weakly and added, ''They're going to give me hell about my budget, of course.''

''So what else is new?'' Joss said. ''Budgets were made to be broken. We're also going to want your records about the other claim jumps and missing people. There may be more tampering of this kind; we'll want to see if there's a pattern.''

He turned the ship slowly and carefully away from the asteroid, and touched his console. ''Call me suspicious,'' Joss said, ''but I'm going to put one of our little hockey pucks down on the surface.''

''Hockey pucks?'' Noel said.

Evan smiled. ''Don't ask him,'' he said. ''It's a motion sensor, with a little camera on it—eh, Joss?''

There was a slight kick of reaction as something left the ship from near its rear end. ''There,'' Joss said, looking at his instruments. ''It dug in its spike nice and hard. Anybody comes here and meddles, we'll know about it. There's no telling who might have followed us out this far, after all. And if anyone has, and comes around here, he'll leave a record.'' He smiled.

Noel shook his head. ''I wish I could get my hands on technology like this. But they only send us what they think we need.''

Joss kicked in the ship's jets and finished turning it around. ''Well, they sent you us,'' he said. ''Maybe we can do you some good. Anyway, let's get back and start sorting things out.''

SEVERAL HOURS LATER, EVAN LEFT JOSS HAP-pily buried in the ship, feeding it data from Noel's files. ''You sure you don't want to come out and get something?'' Evan said. ''It's been hours since you ate.''

"No, no," Joss said, happily inputting at a keyboard in his stateroom. "Damn." He stopped to correct a misspelling, tossed one piece of paper to the floor, and picked up another.

"Why don't you just read that stuff in?" Evan said.

Joss shook his head. "This helps me think," he said. "Besides, Tee tried to improve my voice recognition algorithm, and it got messed up somehow—it keeps misspelling for me. Damned if I need a machine to do that. I can do it myself. Anyway, you go ahead. I want to get as much of this stuff into the machine as I can. Pity I didn't ask them to put in an optical scanner, but who would have thought we would have to be dealing with paper?"

"Too right," Evan said. "Well, listen, I'm going out to get a bite. I'll be back in a while."

"Oh, by the way—" Joss fumbled about in the pile of papers, came up with his pad, and tossed it to Evan. "You didn't read your mail this morning, did you?"

"I was busy with the plumbing," Evan said, catching the pad. "Damned if I want to stay in that place another night."

"Possibly we should take turns," Joss said, tapping away. "But look at that."

Evan keyed the pad on and brought up the mail menu. *Oh, hell*, he thought, seeing the message waiting from Lucretia. He scanned down past the transmittal strings and routing codes and found:

"ABOUT YOUR FUEL EXPENDITURE: Your computer tells me that yesterday you used almost your entire allocation for altitude jets in a matter of fifteen minutes. I have cautioned you about hotdogging in your craft. You have had two weeks to work out the inevitable high spirits."

"*What??*" Evan said. "Why, that small, mean-souled beast, she'd pull a pacifier out of a baby's mouth if she thought it was having too much fun!"

"Gently," Joss said, tossing another piece of paper to

the floor. "Who knows whether she managed to have this thing bugged before we left?"

"I hope she may have! Lucretia, you're a cheap little bottom-line buggerer!" Evan said pointedly to the ceiling, and tossed the pad back to Joss. "What does she think you were using the fuel for, for pity's sake? We'd only be freeze-dried beef jerky by now, the two of us—"

Joss laughed. "I merely point it out to you to give you a sense of how this mission is already shaping up," he said. "If you're going for drink, better make it small beer."

"Huh," Evan said. "Well. You're sure you won't come?"

"No, truly. Bring me back something, if you want. And stay out of trouble," Joss said, not looking up, but smiling.

Evan snorted good-humoredly and went on out. Joss was usually a bit that way, a worrier about things he didn't need to worry about. Evan didn't mind it much. And there was an odd inversion to this behavior, for when things got really bad, Joss tended to stop worrying entirely, except as a logistical exercise. He was not incautious; he just stopped wasting time being concerned about what concern couldn't affect.

He headed out through the hangar dome and began to make his way through the corridors of the station. Joss was really right: the place was much dirtier than it needed to be. *Going moribund,* he thought. But Noel had promised him that there were parts of it that were better off than others, one of them being the bar he had recommended Evan and Joss should try. Evan was quite sure he had the directions correct, though they had been fairly complicated.

The people he met as he strode along looked at him as if he were from Mars, but most of them nodded in a friendly enough manner. Evan nodded back, and smiled. A lot of them were wearing skinsuits that were very much out of fashion—much patched, or combined with other garments in a way that suggested new clothes were either hard to come by in this part of the world, or prohibitively expensive. It was hard to remember, sometimes, that the Asteroids, though not quite, as Noel had said, the end of the universe, were still far enough out that imports were surprisingly costly.

At least they don't have to import their booze, Evan thought, sniffing the air, *or not much of it.* There was definitely a still in the area. *Potatoes,* he thought as he came around the corner, and the smell of spuds in advanced ferment hit him like a hammer.

And where there's a still, there's a bar, he thought, seeing the open door of a small dome not too far away. There was a metal plate over the door, and painted on it the words LAST CHANCE SALOON. Someone had a sense of humor: the plate had been streaked with a base coat to look like old wood. There were only a few places where the paint had chipped to show the steel underneath, and these didn't really ruin the effect.

Evan walked in slowly, glancing around him to see where the bar was. This dome had lights hung from its small ceiling, and, whether accidentally or on purpose, looked like some antique bars Evan had been in on Earth: yellow metal railings (not real brass, of course) and leather-covered benches and chairs (plastic, of course). The bar itself was off to one side of the dome, done in some composite plastic, dyed brown, and carved into Georgian-looking swirls and acanthus leaves. If this was a saloon, it was more like the great old Victorian drinking salons of Belfast and Liverpool than anything else, and it was certainly an astonishing place to find halfway between Mars and Jupiter.

Evan stepped up to the carved bar and caught the eye of the barman, a tall, black-bearded man with cool eyes. "Beer?" he said.

"Quarter-liter? Half?"

"Half, please."

The barman began to pull the pint. Evan leaned against

the bar and looked around at the patrons. They reminded him too much of those at the bar last night: hunched postures, nursed drinks, no conversation much above a whisper. And as he glanced around, the eyes that looked up at him were definitely unfriendly.

Again, he thought. *No. I'm not going to leave, and I'm not going to have any trouble, either. A nice quiet drink, and then dinner—*

Someone came up to stand beside him. Evan turned with a slight smile on his face. And didn't quite swallow.

"Well, Mr. 'Smith,' " he said. "And how are you tonight?"

"Smith" didn't say anything for a few seconds, which hardly mattered, for Evan could see the answer to his question perfectly well. The man's face was swollen to about a third again the size it had been yesterday evening. He had been bruised by experts, and Evan knew who the experts were. It was very embarrassing.

"Well enough," "Smith" said. And something poked Evan in the ribs, hard. "Gonna be better in a moment, though."

There were other people rising from their seats in the bar. Evan cursed silently for letting himself be distracted by the work of the day and the pleasant look of the bar. It had been well-lighted and airy, not like a dive at all. He had let that fool him. That had been a mistake.

And there were more people in this bar than there had been last night, Joss was nowhere in sight, and there was no way to call him, not right this moment, not with the bad end of a blaster stuck into his side. Evan breathed deeply once, and the slight movement helped him feel the muzzle aperture. At least three-quarters of an inch. *Oh, my maiden aunts, feel the flare on that. I'll have a hole in me you could install an Underground tube in. Unless something happens. But at least it's not a knife—*

He was being surrounded by those unfriendly faces, three deep. As far as he could tell, none of these people had guns, thank heaven, but all of them looked like they wished they did. Evan found himself staring at an assortment of gapped teeth, radiation-burnt, chewed-up noses and lips, and scabby, patchy, half-balding scalps such as he hadn't seen since the other side of the Belts, where there were also a lot of people who tended to be careless about their exposure to cosmic radiation. A lot of these people would come down with cancer within the decade, but he doubted they cared about that at the moment. *His* demise seemed to be a much more popular topic.

"Smith" was grinning at him. "You sops," he said. "You think mighty well of yourselves, insulting good hard-working people, starting fights in bars. But you're not so tough when you're alone, are you?" He went off into breathy laughter that smelled of cheap vodka and various food byproducts. "No, indeed. And we're gonna put a few nice little holes in you so you don't come bothering us a—"

The second or third sentence of a gloat, Evan had noticed some years back, was always a good time to do something. He did it without taking his eyes from "Smith's": simply put his hand around Smith's gun hand, and turned it right around in one quick motion till the muzzle was dug deep into "Smith's" belly. "Smith's" eyes widened.

"Now you go right ahead and pull that trigger," Evan said softly. "Go on, Mr. 'Smith.' Or do you need some help?" He felt for "Smith's" trigger finger, felt it struggling to slip out of the loop, refused to let it do so. Evan started applying pressure. "You know," Evan said, "you're the kind of guy who could get thrown in jail for assaulting a Solar officer. Except you probably won't live to." He pressed harder. "You'll probably wind up with a great fat hole in your middle. And so will the people standing behind you." Evan added, thoughtfully.

The people behind Smith abruptly moved to either side. *This isn't going to last for long.* Evan thought. *I can't resort to silly business like taking this man hostage. This has to be won straight out if these people are ever going*

*to tell us anything we need to hear. Dammit, why didn't I
leave my suit on—?*

"Then again," Evan said, "it'd be a waste of the tax-
payer's money to have to make out the paperwork after
killing you. Not to mention that the cleaning people here
would probably be annoyed with me." And with that he
stomped down hard on "Smith's" instep, holding onto the
gun.

"Smith" let go of it, screaming, and lurched away. Immediately three other people came at Evan, two from the
sides. He didn't dare fire. He pulled the gun's charge pack
out, threw it one way, and the gun the other, and with feet
and fists piled into the people who were coming at him.

The next several moments became a series of images,
as always happened in situations like this. An elbow here
(snapped), a kneecap there (one kick, missed, the second
one landing), a third kick at someone's gut (misjudged,
too deep, the person falling out of view with that terrible
looseness that meant a long hospital stay, if not the
morgue). Then his arms being pinned, shaking off that
pin, having another one attached, too heavy to lose, someone punching him in the side of the head, a kick in the
kidneys, the flash of pain up his back—

—a sudden thump in the back; not him being hit, but
someone else, the force transmitting through. One of the
people pinning him let go. He reached around with that
arm, grabbed the person pinning on the other side, found
his balance point, tossed him more or less toward the bar.
A sudden WHAM! as a table hit him in the leg and went
caroming away across the floor.

Someone went flying across his field of vision, a largeish
bald man. *Joss has arrived* Evan thought, and turned, delighted that the cavalry had come over the hill.

Another man was being held more or less horizontally.
The person holding him threw him out the door, almost
effortlessly, and then waded into one of the three or four
people left in the middle of the room. The woman was
sinuously slender: she could hardly have weighed more

than 125 pounds, and she was two meters tall if she was an inch. She had black hair half as long as she was, and she was wearing a smudged grey skinsuit with a quilted rusty black jacket over it, and heavy boots of the kind that locked into the bottom of a pressure suit. She was presently inserting one of them, hard, in some guy's midriff.

She glanced at him, barely more than a flicker of eyes, as the man she had kicked went down. Another of the crowd went for Evan, a big bear of a man hardly smaller than he was. Evan wasted no further time, but stabbed the man stiff-fingered in the larynx, and stepped forward to punch a tall, skinny man who was standing behind him, desperately trying to fit together the separated gun and power pack. Pack and gun went flying again, and the man went down. Immediately thereafter came a short, tough-looking man who had a metal chair in his hands; together man and chair described a short, graceful arc and fell on the tall, skinny man. Evan turned to see the woman dusting her hands off thoughtfully.

"Anybody else?" Evan said to the room at large, turning and glowering at everyone, one at a time. The patrons who had remained sitting either shook their heads, or dropped their eyes and got very interested in their drinks.

"Good," Evan said. He looked over at the barman and said, "Call Noel Hayden and tell him to come get this turkey and shove him out an airlock in his underwear. And then," Evan said, turning, "find out what this lady will have to drink."

She nodded, smiled at him, went to the bar, picked up one overturned bar stool, and then another, sat on one of them, and tilted her head at the other one, looking at Evan.

That was how he met Mell Fontenay.

THREE

★

JOSS STRETCHED, AND TOSSED THE LAST PIECE of paper to the floor, then sat back and flexed his fingers. *The best thing that ever happened to me,* he thought, *was my touch typing course.*

He drummed his fingers on the arms of his chair for a moment. There were a lot of data to sort through here, and it was going to take a good while for him to figure out what it all meant. One thing was clear, though: the disappearances had been going on for even longer than Noel had thought. It was at least four months since people had started disappearing in the same way. They would set out and they would not report in, usually within a period of no more than three days and no less than one. There might be more statistical factors involved, but Joss would let the computer play with its data and work out the details on those. He would follow the case that immediately attracted him.

He leaned back a bit farther and smiled to himself. Usually Evan was the one who had hunches. Joss had started out by laughing at them; then he had found that they weren't so laughable. Slowly he had started experimenting with following his own hunches. Sometimes, surprisingly often, they worked. They made him uncomfortable, though. His way of handling things had always been slow reasoning, logic, working things out step by step.

A man's got to learn new things, though, Joss thought, getting up and heading for the communications console.

He touched it and said, "Willans control, this is SP vessel CDZ 8064. Anybody home?"

"Sure are, Mister Sop O'Bannion Honey," said a cheerful voice. "What about that drink we were supposed to have?"

"Oh, hell!"

"That's what I like to hear," the voice came back: "enthusiasm."

"Sorry, Cecile! I got snowed under with paperwork." He looked around the control cabin with some regret, the white mass all over the floor did indeed suggest Crans-Montana around Christmas time. "How late are you on, anyway? I would have thought you'd be off by now. Don't you sleep?"

"Life's too short, Mister Sop O'Bannion Honey." She chuckled at him. "I've got a few hours to go yet. One of my night people is down with the Titanian two-step."

"Not catching, I hope!"

"Oh no," Cecile said, "it was something she ate. Some Hungarian thing at Satra's."

"Oh dear," Joss said, "so much for the one good restaurant here. . . ."

"Are you kidding?" asked Cecile. "There are about five good restaurants on this miserable rock, and my kids run two of them."

Joss shook his head in wonder. "Cecile, I promise you, I'll take you out to dinner at all of them."

There was another chuckle. "Mister Sop O'Bannion Honey, I bet you say that to all the girls."

"What the hell?" Joss said. "Sometimes it even works. About that drink, Cecile. I have to take a quick run over to the salvage heap. Take me about an hour, an hour and a half, to do what I need to do. Think you'll still be in the mood for that drink?"

"Sounds about right. Just give me a call when you come back. You know how to do the remote procedure on the hangar doors now?"

"First thing I checked," Joss said, "I tell you, Cecile,

this business ain't what it's cracked up to be. Glory and good pay, they promised me. I'd make more if I hired myself out as a secretary. And I wouldn't have to carry all these guns.''

Laughter at the other end. ''Always thought you guys liked the guns and all.''

''They're a nuisance to keep clean,'' Joss said, ''and if you walk into anything while you're wearing them, they bruise your legs up something awful. Never mind that just now. I've got to get out there and do sop things.''

''Right you are. Willans control out.''

Joss sighed and started picked up the paper from the floor, tossing it all in a pile on his bed, and shutting his stateroom door on it. There would be time to tidy everything back into order later; right now he was having suspicions, and those suspicions were distracting him from cleaning at the moment. He was glad of the distraction, too. He normally didn't like cleaning much, but Evan was awfully fussy, especially about their new ship and all.

He made his way back to the control console, tapped at it for a moment, and started the procedure that would open the inner doors of the hangar dome airlock. Then he started the heating process for the vectored jets and the iondriver engine.

There was an odd noise. He paused to listen to it: a sort of whine, it was, very peculiar indeed. He thought he knew every noise that this machine could make, but then again, they'd only had it for a few weeks. ''Hmm,'' Joss said, and shut the vectored thrusters down.

The whine went away.

''Hmm,'' he said again, and killed the warmup of the iondrivers as well. For a few moments he just sat there, staring at the control console, and thought. He thought first of the weird patches on the domes, and the bizarrely patched-together ships in the hangar dome. Then he thought of the work he needed to be doing, and how little of it he would get done if he had to spend the next two days crawling around in the engines of his ship.

He hit another control. "Willans control," he said finally, "this is CDZ 8064—"

"Done already, Mister Sop O'Bannion Honey?" Cecile asked.

"No such luck. Cecile, have you got a good mechanic on call? I mean, a really good one?"

"Only kind we have around here," Cecile said mildly. "We tend to lose all the others."

"Good," Joss said. "I think I need one."

"I have somebody I can get over to you in a little bit," Cecile said. "May take awhile. It's off-shift time."

"No problem with that. I still have to go over to the salvage heap. I'll just walk instead."

"Exercise'll do you good," Cecile said. "Especially if we're going to all those restaurants."

Joss smiled. "Cecile," he said, "what do you look like?"

"I'm tall, with no neck, bad breath, and six grandchildren."

"Ah," Joss said, "an *experienced* woman."

Cecile burst out laughing. "Never mind that, you. Have a nice walk. Mind the holes; there are some pretty big ones out there."

"Will do, Gramma."

"That's *Ms*. Grandma to you, Mister Sop O'Bannion Honey. Willans control out."

Joss chuckled and cut the connection, then headed back into his stateroom to pull his pressure suit down out of its clamps.

IT WAS A PLEASANT WALK, IF A LONGISH ONE. The salvage dump was well away from the settled part of the station, and was little more than a crater, somewhat slagged out to make it less easy for ships to be jarred out of position when others were dropped on top of them.

There were always four or five ships in there, according to Noel. The salvage assessors came through about once every month or month and a half, to determine amounts to be paid to salvaging miners, and to take away wrecks that had already been assessed and were ready to be scrapped. Joss was very interested indeed in looking at these ships to see whether any of them were by chance pieces of ships that had been reported missing, and to talk to the people who had brought them in. Noel hadn't immediately recognized any of them, true, but Joss had the feeling that Noel had so much to do, he might easily have missed something.

There really ought to be about four sops stationed here, Joss thought irritably, as he bounced gently along the rocky surface. The Sun was on the other side of the asteroid at the moment, and it was as dark as it might be on the back side of the Moon. There was nothing to go by but the bobbing light from outside his suit's helmet and the inertial tracker inside it, which he had programmed with the dump's coordinates before leaving.

He watched the dust puff up from where his boots scuffed the surface—not real dust, of course, but the remnants of micrometeorite impacts over days and years. *Not nearly enough people to handle an area of this size,* he thought. *What kind of police force are we supposed to be running out here, anyway? Poor Noel must have something like sixteen million cubic kilometers that he's responsible for. And a shoestring to run it on, poor kid.*

Joss paused for a moment, checking his tracker to make sure he was headed the right way. Even on a body this small, it was too easy to get lost. But Joss was Moon-raised, and had the habits and reflexes of someone who had seen friends of twelve and thirteen go out, get careless, and not come back. In one case not even the kid's body had been found. *At the bottom of some crater,* Joss thought, *or buried under some fall of moondust, I guess.* But it had tended to make the survivors careful.

He checked his tracker again. *A little to the left,* he

thought; *sunward*—He bounced off that way, and came over the short apparent horizon to see the dump.

What a mess, he thought. There, in a hole in the ground, was a tumbled pile of twisted-up metal: boxy bits, round bits, struts and pads sticking up in the air like the feet of dead bugs, all extremely untidy, looking like the toy box of an extremely destructive child giant. *Going to be the devil's own business looking at the stuff that's buried farthest down,* Joss thought. *Oh well.*

He bounced on over to the hole. It was nearly an eighth of a mile wide, and no more than about a hundred feet deep. He paused a moment to wake up the small reference pad mounted on the forearm of his pressure suit. It had stored in it all the makes and registration numbers of the ships whose disappearances had been suspicious, and its link to his main datapad, back in the ship, was wide awake and working.

Now, then, Joss thought, and hopped cheerfully down into the hole to start doing more clerical work.

For about three-quarters of an hour he strolled around the edges of the pile, pausing every now and then to peer more closely at something. There were about thirty ships here at the moment. According to Noel, it had been about two months since there had been a collection—something about a very large salvage find further along in the Belts, which had kept the assessors from arriving as scheduled. There was an astonishing assortment of junk here: VW's that had to be forty years old, Ladas that had to be fifty. *Heaven only knows how they lasted that long,* Joss thought, since Lada was really not the best of the brands; there were more jokes about Ladas than about any of the others. *Then again,* Joss thought, *maybe this one did break down fifty years ago. . . .* It looked likely enough. The thing didn't have a mark on it except for the usual slight collisions and bumps. Joss noted its number down on his pad and moved on to the next dead ship, wondering how a brand could go on so long when its craft had a rep for being so poor. *I guess there are always people who're willing to buy something cheap that works, and take their chances on when it might stop working. . . .*

Slowly he worked his way around the pile, pausing about halfway through as the Sun suddenly came up, throwing long black shadows over everything and momentarily confusing his directional sense. The asteroid had a slow longitudinal tumble; this ''day'' wouldn't last for long. *May as well make the most of it,* he thought.

Joss paused near the wreckage of an old Skoda medium-range cargo hauler and looked it over. Its engines had been cannibalized—no surprise, that: engine systems were the most adaptable parts of most of these craft, and could be fitted to almost anything if you had the know-how. The big squarish cargo shell was all that was left; its landing struts were broken off halfway by another craft, a Chevy, which had been dropped on top of it. The engine module was broken open like an eggshell, and cables and connectors dangled out of it, frayed and dusty. Joss leaned in to look at it, brushed some dust aside, and saw on the hull metal the scrapes and pinchmarks of a large waldo that had torn the module open.

He nodded to himself, referring to his notes. There was a Skoda of about this age missing. He climbed in among the wreckage, out of the light, and looked for the forward bulkheads of the thing, where the registration numbers should be engraved.

Hmm, he thought then, for the bulkhead had been shorn off. Well, that wasn't unheard of either. Many people who did salvage work were afraid that they might accidentally try to move a vessel that had been wrecked by foul play rather than misadventure, and rather than take the chance of prosecution, they burned off or otherwise lost the reg numbers. But still . . . He looked again at his notes about the Skoda. Like this one, it was a '38, and with the same cargo module. But he had no absolute proof that this was the one that had been lost. And besides, if it were, it would have come here from halfway across the Belts. *Who would haul a piece of salvage so far?* he wondered. *Doesn't make sense. . . .*

He stood there a moment, then looked deeper into the pile. It was hard to see anything much; his helmet lamp wasn't nearly bright enough to give him much detail, and its dull shine fell on twisted metal and showed very little about how it had been twisted.

Joss sighed. *Going to have to come back here and tear this pile apart with a lifter,* he thought, stepping back and starting to work his way around the pile again. He kicked his way through the dust, noting more VW's, a Rolls—that was a bit of a surprise. *Must have been pretty completely destroyed,* he thought, peering at it. *Usually their warranty covers anything short of the power plant blowing.* And that seemed to be what had happened to this one. He clambered in over a few broken struts and touched the hull of the Rolls. It had been sleek once. Rolls was one of the manufacturers who had not gone modular, and had built its own craft, with long, surprisingly graceful lines, and all in one piece. Even its cargo craft had been good to look at. This one, though, had holes blown in its hull in three places. The metal was bent inward in strips and ribbons, like a cartoon firecracker. *Bombs,* Joss thought. *Or rather, projectile weapons. Big ones, too. Who out there would be carrying such things? And why would they use them on a mining vessel?*

His curiosity was getting the better of him. He pushed into the pile again, past the Rolls, where there was a sort of alleyway between ruined pieces of metal. Carefully Joss squeezed between them and leaned up against the next craft, a very beat-up-looking VW Box. He was near the front end of it, and within reach of the front bulkhead with the reg numbers. Bending, he checked them, and found them on his list. This vessel had been reported lost half-way across the Belts, as had the Skoda he was suspicious of. And this time he had proof.

Joss worked his way further down the Box's body, being very careful of his suit—it was quite tough, but a rip would be hard to patch quickly in this tight place, and could kill him. He came to the engine pod. At first sight, much to his surprise, the engine appeared to be still in it. But then he looked into the hole in the side of the engine pod, and saw the truth of the situation. About half the engine seemed to have been simply scooped out. Not literally, of course; someone had used some kind of energy weapon on the side of this ship. The engine had vaporized; parts of it on the fringes of the effect had slagged. Nearest the edges of the hole, the slagging of parts of the hull had preserved bits of engine behind them, and the occasional piece of cable or chunk of bus bar had survived.

Joss leaned there against the beamed ship and sucked in a slow, contemplative breath. *That's no weapon that miners have access to,* he thought. *That's military level, that is.*

Better than we have. Possibly better than the Space Forces have.

Who has weapons like that?

Very carefully, he turned around and began to work his way out of the darkness.

The light started to change. There was no sound with it, of course, but the change in the light alone was quite enough to send a flush of pure shock right through Joss. It was not the Sun going down, though that would happen soon. It was the shape of the pile of wrecked ships changing.

Stupid, he thought instantly, holding quite still to see, just for that second, what was happening. *Stupid, to come out alone, to broadcast where you were headed, on an open channel. After this, I swear to God, I send them notes on little pieces of paper. In code—*

He looked ahead of him, back out toward the light, and saw the shape of the pile of ships visibly change. Someone was out there, in a good spot, pushing. Someone intended to see him extremely buried. At the moment, Joss was feeling more anger than anything else, and that was a good thing. Fear would come later. Right now it would be a nuisance.

They can't have a very good idea of where I am, he thought. *There's that comfort, at least. Let's just see if I can get out in time to surprise them.* He paused, leaning on the hull of the Rolls for a moment.

This time he did hear something—not with his ears, but with the way the vibration through the hull of the Rolls felt through his hand—a long, low, groaning rumble. Something nearby was shifting, a lot. This time the panic hit him, and he scrambled for the light.

It went out. The Sun had gone down, at exactly the wrong moment. *Oh, come on, now!* Joss said in great annoyance to whatever deities were listening. In the same moment, though, he tossed his head to turn his helmet light off. He might be blind, but at least whoever was out there trying to kill him would be no better off. Without hearing, or seeing him, they were helpless. So was he, but at least it meant the odds were even.

Meanwhile, the important thing was to get the hell out of the salvage pile, before the whole thing shifted in some new and exciting way and trapped him. Even as he started pushing and twisting his way toward the thin hole in the darkness that contained stars, there was a movement, and the Skoda and the Rolls started to squeeze closer together. He quickly turned sideways, pulling his arms in tight to him. This was a good thing; from the other side, with a sudden wrenching bump, a VW pushed over into the Rolls. He could feel the rustle and crunch of it right through his pressure suit. He winced, as if something with a lot of legs had run over his flesh, at the awfulness of what would have happened had that VW managed to pin his arm against the Rolls. The arm would have come right off, and it would have been a good question whether he would have died more quickly of blood loss or lack of air.

He panted for a second, and then started to squeeze past the Skoda. It had gotten a lot tighter. He could feel the rough edges of metal poking into the back of his suit, pressing in hard, scraping at him in a very pointed way. *Oh, please, hold together,* he prayed briefly to the suit and to B. F. Goodrich, and moved slowly and steadily, on the principle that he would be less likely to pick up a tear that way than by moving quickly. *All the same—how recently was my patch kit replaced? And how fast can I put it on my back when I can't see what I'm doing?—*

As far as he could tell by his last judgment of the distance, there were about three feet to go between him and the open space before the lights went out. He twisted and turned carefully, and edged his way forward. There was another movement, one that he again felt rather than saw. The mass of metal settled. He was being poked from both back and front, now, and one of the pokes was right in front, under his breastplate, where there was a lot of sensitive electronic equipment and piping under the plas-sealed fabric. All his life support hardware and software was there, and the insulated feed from the lox pads on his back. He was well and truly pinned, like a bug. Through the pieces of metal pinning him he could feel more motion, the remote groan of mass moving against mass—

Ever so carefully, despite the sharp pressures fore and aft, he kept edging forward. The pressure in front speared right into his solar plexus as he tried to slide past. He resisted the urge to throw up, since any sudden movement could tear the suit quite as thoroughly as a slow one. There was another movement around him, of something settling—then, abruptly, the pressure on his back lessened. Something was still pressing down on his helmet from on top, though, and there was an ominous growling resonating through it. Joss leaned back away from the pressure on his abdomen, and slowly, carefully, but as quickly as he dared, edged and squeezed and twisted forward. Another foot or so would do it. Just a little further—

—and then he took the plunge, throwing himself forward into the open space, twisting as he did so to make sure he didn't land on his faceplate.

Instead, he came down hard on his side, bounced, rolled

away from the pile. He managed to stop himself after just a couple of rolls, and saw the pile settling on that side, squashing down with a puff of dust that turned silvery as it rose high enough to catch sunlight over the horizon of the asteroid.

Right, Joss thought fiercely, and scrambled to his feet. Crouched over, he began bouncing around the pile, choosing his steps carefully in the dark. He reached into his holster as he went, drew the Remington, and thumbed the safety off. Normally Joss did not like shooting people. But at the moment, he was willing to like it a little. It might improve his aim.

He paused at one point, leaning up behind the bulk of one of the trashed ships that had splayed somewhat out of the pit proper, and peered around it. Nothing. *Come on,* he thought. *Come on, aren't you going to come and see what you killed?*

No movement. Then again—was that a puff of dust around the corner of the pile? Just more settlement, or a trick of the darkness? Or something else? He edged around the ship behind which he had been hiding and paused a moment, for even though his eyes were more or less used to the dark now, it was still almost as black as the inside of a cat.

Light: a flicker of light.

Oh, God, thank you for stupid perpetrators, Joss thought, at least as thankful as he had been to B. F. Goodrich a little while before. He edged forward a bit more. The light vanished, came back again, then vanished once more. A hand torch, and a fairly powerful one. *Idiot!* Joss thought with delight, as the torch bobbed away around the pile. *Now what? Go around the other way and take them head-on? Or slip up from behind?*

Joss occasionally had romantic tendencies and loved the old courtesies and traditions of the past, especially those about fair play. But he wasn't stupid. *From behind,* he thought, and started after the light, moving as quietly as he could, even though in this environment it wasn't strictly necessary. It was just that old habits were hard to break.

The light appeared again, and flickered over the pile.

Yes indeed, Joss thought. *Looking for something.* And the reflected light from the pile showed him what he was looking for: one figure in a well-patched suit, with blacked-out helm. Joss would remember the arrangement of those patches when he saw them again, even though the colors were iffy in lighting this faint. *Come on, sun,* he thought, as he edged around, hiding behind pieces of torn metal. *Come on, I want a clear look at what I'm shooting!* For Joss knew that his aim wasn't always of the best, and he didn't want to kill this person, not at all. An arm or leg shot, something quickly patched, would do him just fine.

The torch flickered away from the pile, leaving the figure that held it dark again, scarcely there except for some slight reflection of light from the ground. Joss bit his lip and edged closer while the figure stood there, pondering who knew what, then moved on around the pile again.

Joss sighed. *We're not getting any younger here,* he thought, and made his move, bouncing forward.

The dark shape came into view, its helmet turned away from him. It was about a hundred yards away. Joss lifted the Remington, not daring to use the radar sighting for fear that the other's suit had a passive warning system working. *Leg,* he thought, *legs are better than arms—arms are too close to the important parts—* He squeezed the trigger gently, and a white line lanced out—

—and went right by the suited figure's kneecap.

It was pure chance that the person in the suit was looking down: otherwise Joss would have had a chance for another shot before he—or she, perhaps, for the suit was on the small side—moved. But the target started at the sight of the Remington's beam, turned hastily and swept the torch in all directions. Joss dodged behind a twisted half-WV and ducked as the beam flashed by over his head, then away. He popped up and took another shot.

But the target was moving. *There's panic, if you like,*

Joss thought, with a mixture of relief and annoyance, as he saw the suited figure go bouncing away from the salvage pile at high speed. Dammit! He raised the Remington again, bracing it against the wrecked VW, increased the power to compensate for distance and narrow the spread, and fired again.

The figure hopped straight up, came down hard and bounced several times. *What the hell,* Joss thought, and then realized he'd scored a hit; the pressure of air escaping from the suit had knocked his assailant straight up in that first moment. Bingo! Fumbling for his patch kit, Joss went after his victim.

But the the victim had other plans. One leg held out stiffly, he—or she—went off at high speed, kangarooing with considerable skill across the bumpy terrain, and vanished over the horizon—which, on a body this small, was only about two hundred yards away. *Damn it to everything!* Joss thought, and followed. But when he had made it over the horizon himself, there was nothing to be seen. His quarry was probably two horizons over by now, and had likely gone to ground, possibly in one of the tunnels that led to the station. Joss knew that they were there, but hadn't had time as yet to investigate them.

He stood there with his gun in his hand, feeling very annoyed, but also somehow elated. There was at least one pressure suit in the station that he would recognize on sight. It would be easy enough to pick it out of all the suits in the place—but that could wait for later.

Right now, the situation had changed radically. He and Evan were obviously investigating something that made at least one person anxious to try to kill Joss, just on the off chance that he might find out something sensitive. He had information that some people would obviously much prefer that he didn't have. He was bruised in a few places, but no matter, at least, there were no holes—and what he needed to do right away was get back and send a note to HQ on the Moon.

Maybe now Lucretia would stop worrying about their fuel allowance. . . .

EVAN LEANED BACK IN HIS CHAIR AND SAID, "Do you come here often?"

She laughed at him. "I bet you say that to all the girls. Next cliché?"

Evan blushed slightly. That in itself was so unusual an occurrence that it made him blush harder.

She leaned back in her seat and took a long drink; then made a face. "A little too young, this batch," she said to the bartender. "What are you doing? Making the stuff out of the chips that don't get sold at lunchtime?"

The bartender glowered at her in a friendly sort of way and didn't deign to answer, just went back to polishing glasses. Mell looked over at Evan and said, "I really shouldn't complain. They tried making vodka out of soybeans last month, and it's taken this long for the smell to go away."

Evan shook his head. "Sounds foul."

"You have no idea," she said.

Evan was trying hard not to seem too interested, and failing. Mell Fontenay was, if possible, even better-looking sitting still than she was when fighting. For one thing, when she was sitting still, you could watch the thoughts go round and round behind that astonishing pair of ice-green eyes. Expressions variously calculating, humorous, scornful, amused, and thoughtful followed one another, only occasionally seeming to have anything to do with the conversation going on. It was the kind of thing that tempted you to say outrageous things in an attempt to produce the correct expression—or rather, to interest her enough so that the correct expression overrode the one that she was choosing to wear for her own reasons.

"You were going to tell me," he said, "why you mixed in when you did."

"Was I?" she said, looking abstractedly into her glass for the moment. She put it down, empty, and pushed it at the bartender. "Same again, please. You know," she said to Evan, "this is rather a closed community. Any stranger attracts a bit more attention than he might find usual."

"So it seems," Evan said rather ruefully.

"Well, it's worse for you," she said. "You're the Government, after all."

"I am not!"

"Of course you are," she said, "to us. Or rather, to these people."

Evan raised his eyebrows. "You're not 'us'?"

"Oh no," she said. "I'm an independent contractor. Thanks, Mike." She took a long drink, put the glass down.

Evan laughed. "I thought everybody here was an independent contractor. Except maybe poor Noel."

"Poor Noel," she said, and smiled a little. "Yes, well. We're used to him by now."

"Eight years," Evan said, "I should bloody well think so."

"Oh, but this is no different from any other small community," Mell said. "Some people will never become part of it, no matter how hard they try. Some people wouldn't be part of it even if they were born here. Noel is accepted because he was ordered here, and because he cares. But as for you and your friend," she said, taking another drink, "as far as you're concerned, we're just another job."

"It's not exactly like that," Evan said.

"And some people here," Mell said, "aren't any too sure just what your job is."

"I should have thought that would be all over the place by now," Evan said. "The disappearances."

"Yes, well," Mell said. "There are people who aren't sure that the investigation might not turn to something more general after a while. There are a lot of people out here involved in things that are, shall we say . . . marginal."

"Marginally legal, you mean."

She nodded, and stroked her long hair back out of her eyes. It was a habitual gesture, one which Evan had noticed she made even when the hair wasn't actually in her way at the moment.

"Quite so," she said, and for a second Evan thought she was mocking his accent. The glint in her eyes said that this was more than likely. "The illegality might be marginal, too. But most of the people who've come here to live have little rackets running of one kind or another, or else they have something in their lives that they wouldn't want looked into too closely. People like you coming here—" and the glint turned very definitely mocking for a moment "—make the man in the corridors here nervous. Nobody likes seeing the status quo disturbed."

Evan sighed a little and took a good long drink himself. He said, "I'm not particularly interested in disturbing *that* status quo. Unfortunately, the people who send us here and there take a dim view of us running off after problems that aren't the one we were sent to solve. Also," he said a little grumpily, "we don't have the budget for it."

"That's not what I hear from your rooming house," Mell said, a little wickedly.

"That thief," Evan growled. "Man should be ashamed to rent out rooms in such a state."

"And what were you expecting? Conrad Hilton and silver trays?"

That annoyed him. "Lady," Evan said, "I've spent five months living out in a little dome at Highlight, where the patches on the ceilings were even worse than they are here, and if you saw washing water twice a month, it was an event. But at least when it came it was clean, and you didn't have to spend half your morning scraping the bleeding grunge out of the plumbing!" He took another slug of the horrible vodka to calm himself. It merely shifted his annoyance to the vodka: he began to think he could taste a certain bouquet of rancid deep-frying oil. "The man," he said, with what he hoped was more dignity, "is a thief for all that. But you won't see me arresting him. I have other fish to fry.''

Mell looked thoughtful for the moment. ''So you say. Well, I guess you ought to be given a chance to prove yourselves.''

''I take that very kindly,'' Evan said.

''Ouch!'' she said, and rocked back in the seat, laughing at his mockery. ''We're even, I suppose.''

''Oh, indeed,'' Evan said, and chuckled a bit. ''Well, never mind that for the moment. Listen, Madam Chop-and-Change, Ms. Inconsistent, you still haven't told me why you decided to become the belle of the brawl.''

''Pity?'' she suggested. ''A momentary weakness in the head? Curiosity?''

''Curiosity I might buy.''

She shrugged. ''Your technique was interesting,'' she said. ''And maybe the odds were a little too high for my tastes.''

''Hah,'' Evan said. ''An adherent of the Marquis of Queensberry, out here? You're misplaced a bit, I'd say. But you know the rule, anyway. One riot, one sop.''

''They sent two of you.''

''So? We had two riots. Maybe now we can get down to work.''

''Third time usually pays for all, around here,'' Mell said, her eyes glinting again. And what was it this time? Anticipation? Evan breathed out in a moment's annoyance; the woman's moods came and went faster than a laser can tune itself.

''Are you implying that I'm going to have to take on Mr. 'Smith' again?''

''Who?''

''The lad who started the fight just now.''

''Oh, you mean Leif the Turk?''

''What?''

''Leif the Turk.'' She started laughing.

''Not a very Turkish name,'' Evan said.

''No,'' Mell said. ''But that's what everyone calls him.

I think his folks were Russian and Finnish, or some such thing. But he was born on the Moon.''

"So where does the Turkish part come in?''

"I think he killed one," Mell said. "Claim jump, apparently.''

Evan finished his drink, pushed it in the direction of the bartender for another one. "There seems," he said, "to be a lot more of that going on around here than in other parts of the Belts.''

Mell sighed and stared at her glass. "It would be nice if high-content asteroids were evenly distributed through the Belts," she said, "but they aren't. The explosion that created them is still geologically much too close to us in time. It's supposed to be thousands of years before the distribution evens out, and by that time will there be anything left to mine?" She looked thoughtful. "But in the meantime, what people find here, they take pretty seriously. And a lot of people find the competition too fierce over in the higher-yield parts of the Belts. The big companies are out there with their bulk sweepers, and the independent operators over there can afford better equipment than most of the people over here can." She turned her glass around a few times, staring at it. "So tempers run a little high. It happens a lot less than it might, I think. But people tend to get pretty secretive." She glanced up at him. "So when a couple of sops with a shiny new ship come barging in here and announce that they're intending to investigate claim-jumping, a lot of people get twitchy. Even the innocent ones. And the guilty ones start wondering whether some inner-system sop with his shiny SP badge is going to have the same ideas about justice as they do.''

Evan looked at her thoughtfully.

"Besides," Mell added, pushing her hair out of her eyes again, "some of the people based out of this station have their claims hidden in all kinds of interesting ways. They're not too willing to have information about how they're doing it made too public. For some of them, the secrecy of their claims' location is the only thing between them and bankruptcy.''

"I'm not interested in making anybody bankrupt," Evan said, "or anything else of the kind. I want to find out why in the past few months, more people are being lost than should be. And I want to find out why someone is willing to go to quite so much trouble to make plain murder look like claim jumping. I think that's legitimate. Don't you?''

She looked at him from under the sweep of hair that fell across her eyes. "Don't you find that hair a problem when you're in a suit?'' Evan said suddenly.

Mell smiled. "I tie it back. What do you mean, 'One riot, one sop?' ''

Evan drew breath in protest at being dragged off the subject again, then laughed resignedly. "It's an old story,'' he said. "There was once a group of lawmen called the Texas Rangers, back on Earth. The area they were policing was pretty wild—a lot of backshooting, robbery, rustling—''

Mell looked bemused. "People making crackly noises?''

"Not that kind of rustling. Stealing cattle. Anyway, these Rangers had a reputation for being extremely determined, and tough. One example: there was a saddlemaker who had a whole batch of his saddles stolen, and he asked the Rangers to do something about it. They did. Wherever they went, if they saw someone riding by on one of those saddles, they shot him off it. They got all the stolen saddles back,'' Evan said, playing to her shocked expression with some pleasure. "The saddlemaker went out of business a year later, though.''

"Very effective," she said, "I think.''

"Well. There was a town in Texas somewhere which was having trouble with rioting and looting, and they sent a message to the Rangers' HQ, saying, 'Having riot, send company of Rangers.' The message came back, "One riot, one Ranger.' '' Evan smiled wryly. The story was one of Joss's favorites, and got told with depressing regularity.

"And so you two are like those Rangers?"

"There are similarities," Evan said, "but we do try not to shoot people quite so much. Now about Leif the Turk; what's his grudge?"

"Grudge? Don't be silly. Leif's a mental case. There's nobody in this place he hasn't attacked at one point or another. But you sure bring out the worst in him. I don't know where he got a gun from. Usually nobody around here will let him have one."

Evan put that piece of information away for future reference. "Never mind him, then. My partner and I are going to need to start talking to people around here pretty soon, when we've finished our preliminary work. Have you heard anything about what we've found so far?"

"Hek's ship," she said, "yes. Digging starts in the morning, doesn't it?"

"As soon as we get our independents lined up, yes." He cocked his head. "Are you interested, then?"

"Not in my line of work," she said. "I'm maintenance. I can recommend some names, though."

Evan nodded at that, while thinking. *Maintenance? This is one of the people who repairs this place? Or rather, doesn't repair it? Dear sweet Lord, help us.*

"I need people who are good operators with mining tools," he said, trying not to change expression too much, "and who can be careful about what they find. I'll want to vet your suggestions with Noel, of course."

"If you like," she said, "I'll meet you in his office tomorrow and you can check them out with him right there and then. Most of the heavy-tool operators who work here I know pretty well."

"All right," Evan sighed and had another drink. "If Leif the Turk is so mental," he said, "why haven't you people sent him off where he can get some help?"

"Because he'd go twenty times as nuts," Mell said sadly. "The doctor here monitors his medication and keeps him pretty calm. Leif had a hard life: he worked hard, then lost his wife and children all of a sudden, in a transport accident, while he was out mining. What good would shipping him off to a padded cell somewhere be? Let him live out his life here where he knows where he is, and people can take care of him."

There was really no arguing with that. Evan nodded. "And what about you?" he said. "What brings you out this way?"

"Ah," Mell said, "now we get personal. Mike, you remember what happened to the last person who got personal with me?"

"You married him," said the bartender, and went back to polishing glasses again.

"I consider myself warned," Evan said mildly. "Never mind, then. I was just making conversation."

Mell stroked her hair back, looking slightly bemused. "Do you ever, really?" she said. "I mean, doesn't everything go into the investigative pot, so to speak?"

Evan had to smile a little at that. "A lot of things do, I suppose. But sometimes I do just talk. And what about you? Do you ever say anything that isn't misleading, provocative, or vaguely insulting?"

Mell laughed. "Ahh . . . we're even again, I guess."

For a moment they both just sat turning their drinks around.

"I was born on Mars," Mell said after a while. "The usual thing: one of the little terraformed settlements, down in a deep rille. O2 farming, water mining, and so forth. Some archaeology, but no one took the brick diggers very seriously. My mother and father had a garage." Mell smiled a bit. "They taught me my trade. Got started with skimmers, overcharging the archaeologists, then moved on to a lot of iondriver work when the Belts started to really open up. Even had an Opel dealership for a while." She made a face at that. "It went under after awhile, and just as well; we all hated it. It was one of those mistakes you make sometimes. After my dad died, and I got old enough to start making decisions about what to do with myself, I came out this way. It seemed the best thing, and emigration runs in our family: Dad left the Moon when he was about the age I left for the Belts. This was the first place I came, and I've been here ever since.''

Evan nodded. ''And you?'' she said. ''Surely you didn't spring fully formed from the Commissioner's forehead.''

Evan laughed and gestured to the bartender to get them more drinks, privately considering that the only thing to leap from the Commissioner's head recently was an extremely stupid budget. He sat back and told her about Wales for awhile: how it was to grow up there, with the place a great hotbed of industry and business, and pressure from all directions to hurry and make something of yourself—the memory of the bad old days of poverty and unemployment had not gone away, by any means. Then the army, and training to be a suited soldier, and the occasional police actions. But always there had been a feeling that there was something missing, something else he was meant to do. Odd, but when they had let him go at last, the anger had lasted only a very short time. The death of his first Solar Police partner. The detective work that led to the smashing of the drug ring that had caused that death. Finally his new partnering with Joss. It made a surprisingly short, dry tale, for all the thought and blood and tears and booze that had passed through it and him at one time or another.

When he finally wound down, Evan wasn't even sure Mell had been listening. She was about halfway through her drink, and looking slightly weary. ''I've bored you,'' he said, resigned.

''Lord, no,'' she said, though he couldn't have told it from her voice. But she pushed the drink away.

''I guess,'' she said, ''the tendency is to think of a sop like you as just a lump of dumb meat, isn't it?''

Evan smiled slightly. ''It's an impression I don't always try to correct,'' he said. ''Sometimes it works to one's advantage.''

She glanced at him with an expression of mild exasperation. Evan just shrugged.

"Well," she said.

He looked at her. *I am having unprofessional ideas,* he thought, without the usual shock. She was definitely an interesting woman.

Well, more than just interesting. She can fight, too.

"Where *did* you learn to fight like that?" he asked. "Seriously."

She laughed softly. "Childhood on Mars can be pretty educational," she said. "You grow up fast. And on some parts of the planet, the man-to-woman ratio is still pretty high. A lot of the men there are used to trying to take what they want." She smiled. "No point in letting them have it without a fight. And every now and then you get a chance to practice here."

"More than every now and then," Evan said, putting his unprofessional thoughts aside for good. The woman would probably bite his head off if she even suspected what he was thinking.

But at the same time he enjoyed the thought. *Dammit, they can't shoot you for thinking. Not yet.*

"Penny for them," Mell said.

Evan laughed out loud. "You know," he said, "no one's said that to me since before I left Wales."

She raised both eyebrows. "Has the price gone up or something?"

Evan shook his head.

"So let's hear it, then," she said.

What harm? said one part of his mind loudly, followed by another part commenting, *She'll only probably kick your nuggets in, that's all. But it'll be one of the more interesting ways it's happened lately.*

"You might become violent," he said at last. "It's dangerously personal. And I'm not available for being married at the moment."

Her eyes glittered a bit, even in the low light. "Funny," Mell said, "but neither am I."

"Then I was thinking," Evan said, "that in another

time, and another place, it would be fun to take you out to dinner.''

''Another time,'' she said, ''being when you're finished with this job. And another place being somewhere that has better restaurants.''

Evan thought that it might be interesting to find out whether their rooms down here had been bugged. But for the moment he merely nodded and said, ''That's a close approximation.''

Mell looked at him. *Astonishing,* Evan thought, *how the greenness of the eyes shows up even in this poor lighting. Like a cat's.*

''I must say,'' she said, ''that we have some pretty fair restaurants even here. No matter what the Michelin Guide says. Stuck-up snobs,'' she added, with a slight smile.

''Ah,'' Evan said. ''Then when we're finished . . .''

''I'm partial to Moussaka,'' she said, ''and we do some pretty fair Tandoori Pork.''

''Pork? That's not very usual,'' Evan said.

She shrugged. ''The cook is great Chinese. Likes his chilies, too. His tandoori mix is pretty lethal.''

Evan opened his mouth to say something he desperately hoped would be clever and witty, but he never got to find out whether it was—an insistent beeping began.

''Oh, hell,'' Mell said, ''so much for an evening off. I'm needed.'' She slid off the bar stool and smiled at Evan. Sweat broke out abruptly behind his ears.

''Good night, Evan,'' she said, and hurried out the door.

Evan looked at his drink for a good few moments, then picked it up and kicked back the last of it. He glanced up to see the bartender looking at him reflectively.

''Very nice lady,'' Evan said, unable to think of anything else whatever.

''Mmf,'' said the bartender, and turned away.

Evan slid off the bar stool and headed back to the ship, whistling ''We'll Keep a Welcome in the Valleys.''

★

JOSS SPENT A GOOD TWENTY MINUTES IN THE ship's 'fresher before feeling ready to sally forth again. Being shot at always made him sweat a particularly nasty, acrid kind of sweat that got into his clothes and his hair and his psyche, and needed a lot of hot water and soap to get rid of. He had just had the tanks charged from the station stores, and he paid the highish water price without a second thought. Let Lucretia think what she liked. No one was shooting at *her*.

When he came out, he made his way back to the bar of the night before, the Astoria, and went straight in without so much as a moment's hesitation. He was in uniform, with the holster of his Remington unclipped, and with a look on his face that he hoped would come across less like a fixed grin of terror than the expression of a man who might get nasty if pushed. People looked up at his entry, and stared at him. He stared back at them with that grin in place. Eyes dropped and heads turned away as fast as they had started turning toward him.

He stepped up to the bar, where there was only one other person seated at the moment, and said loudly, "I am going to have a drink with Cecile, the most beautiful woman in nine planets, and anyone who interrupts me is going to be shot." He paused, and added, "And then thrown in jail for breach of the peace and behavior likely to cause public disorder. So if you're going to do something, for God's sake do it now so honest people don't have to sit around all night waiting for it to happen."

There was a silence that was not quite dead; there was smothered laughter in it, and it was a much healthier silence than the last time. The other person at the bar turned around and said, "Why, Mister Sop O'Bannion Honey, I thought you'd gone and stood me up."

"Madame," Joss said, taking her hand and bowing over it, "I would have been desolate to have missed you. Unfortunately—" he dropped his voice so that only she could hear him—"I had to go out and let some idiot try to kill me, but now that that's been taken care of for the evening,

I can relax a while. What are you drinking?'' he added in a more normal tone.

''Gin and tonic, if you would,'' said Cecile, and pulled out a bar stool for him. Joss smiled at her. Cecile was about five feet tall, cheerfully round, with the kind of figure that used to be called ''pleasantly plump.'' She had hair that could only be described as pink, since it had been red originally, and was now turning beautifully silver. Her face was a map of friendly wrinkles, mostly smile lines, but it was still impossible to tell how old she was. And truly, Joss didn't care: her eyes were quite young, almost wicked.

''Your mechanic should be along presently,'' Cecile said, when her drink came, and Joss had one to match it. ''Sorry for the delay, but it was hard to find anybody who both felt like taking the call and had the expertise you need.''

''Ah,'' Joss said. ''Well, never mind.'' He had a long drink, and paused a moment. ''Something a little funny about this gin,'' he said.

''It's the juniper extract,'' Cecile said. ''It's synthesized. We can't spare the hydroponics room to grow juniper berries here.''

Joss shrugged. ''As long as you grow pigs here,'' he said, ''I don't care.'' And he reached across the bar for the bowl of pig tails.

Cecile looked at him with surprise and mild admiration. ''However did you know we raise pigs?'' she said.

Joss wiggled his fingers in the air. ''Basic research, madame. It would be too expensive to import such a relatively low-protein food—and a delicacy, at that—as pig tails and ears. But if you have your own, it's a shame to waste. And they taste too good.'' Joss pulled one out of the bowl and bit into it with a crunch of crackling. ''Besides, while I was out, I passed by the part of the aggie-dome complex where they're kept. Snuck a look in through the airlock. I see they're fed the skim milk and whey left over from your milk processing. Very sensible.''

Cecile chuckled. "One of my grandchildren is a cheese-maker," she said. "Another one is in hydroponics—grain, mostly, the stuff we feed the cows on. We only wind up using about ten percent of our output for food, according to Randie."

"That's what the records say," Joss said. "I've been at the station computers, you see."

Cecile raised her eyebrows. "So that's what all those protocol transfers were earlier. I was wondering."

"You noticed?" Joss smiled a little. This was what he had been wanting to find out.

"About three hours ago, yes? Right. You're welcome, I'm sure," Cecile said, "as long as your transfer software doesn't have anything in it that'll confuse ours."

"I don't think it does," Joss said. "But I was kind of surprised to get such easy access to your data banks. Exactly how much of the station's business goes through your part of data processing?"

Cecile laughed at him. "Why, Mister Sop Honey, *all* of it does. You think we're big enough to have separate computers for everything? No, indeed. The approach radars and so forth are in our offices because that way they'll be closest to the computers that drive them. No use putting them elsewhere! And if something goes wrong with them, it's easier to do something about it quickly."

Joss was a little taken aback. "But your backups—"

Cecile shook her head at him sadly. "You've been too close to the Sun too long," she said. "We can't afford total redundancy, not by a long shot. We have to mend and make do if something breaks. What do you think was happening when you almost got smashed flat coming in here?" She dropped her voice a bit and said, "You should have let us know you were coming a little sooner."

"The surprise is the best part," Joss said, "usually. But never mind that for the moment."

They drank in silence for a few moments. "What I want to know," Joss said at last, very quietly, "is who here can hear ship-to-shore traffic, like me to you in the hangar earlier.''

Cecile looked at him with slight bemusement. ''Just about anyone who feels like tuning in to the frequency,'' she said. ''We can't afford fancy scrambling and whatnot. Too many people's transmitters are the cheap and dirty kind, and we need to be able to hear them.''

Joss nodded. ''I can see the point,'' he said, and considered a moment. ''Cecile, do you keep tapes of the day's transmissions?''

''For three months,'' she said. ''It's the law. But there's never been much call for it. In fact, I can't remember the tapes being audited for as long as I've been working here. Fifteen years now.''

''And you just monitor ship-to-shore and close-in ship-to-ship.''

''On the main station frequency, that's right.''

''No suit traffic, then?''

''You know how much memory that would take? No way, Sop Honey. There are eighteen or twenty different suit channels, well away from the dedicated ship frequencies. We'd go crazy trying to keep track; there are few enough of us paid to work here as it is. And people are always fiddling with the frequencies anyway, trying to keep their communications private. We've got suits spread all over VHF, talking to each other all hours of the day.''

He sighed. It was what he had suspected. The thought had crossed his mind to try to rig some kind of surveillance, but his ship's computer core couldn't spare that kind of storage either; it had other business. ''Is there any other kind of record of when people go out in suits?'' Joss said.

Cecile shook her head sadly. ''Joss,'' she said, ''you're looking for a level of organization we just don't have here. If you think of us in terms of a town in the Yukon around the old gold rush, or in Outer Mongolia somewhere, you'll probably have it about right. The real world ships us people, some money, a lot of finished goods. We ship back raw materials, but the balance of our economy is tipped 'way toward the export side. We can't afford the kind of supervision—of snooping, really—that the inner planets take for granted these days. And I don't think we want to.''

Cecile sat back and held her drink in both hands, swirling the ice around in it. ''When I came here,'' she said, ''quite a while back, after my murder rap—'' Her eyes twinkled as she caught him trying to stifle his reaction. ''Oh, yes,'' she said. ''My first husband. I told him the first time he hit me that he wouldn't get to do it again. After I got out, it was a nightmare. I couldn't get a job— criminal record; it didn't matter that I'd done my time— couldn't get a loan, couldn't hold down a place to live that was any good. Everybody who wanted to could know everything about my life—right down to how much was in my piggy bank, I think—just by hitting the right buttons. The Moon was no better; neither was Mars. The chance came up to emigrate, and I did. Here, if I buy something on credit, I sign for it and my signature's good enough. If I contract for services with somebody, my word is considered my bond. And since people who break their word get thrown out where there ain't no air,'' she added, smiling slightly, ''most people's word is good. Life isn't like it is in the inner circle, but it has its own rewards. And nobody finds out anything about me that I didn't tell them. Hardly anybody has a fancy data acquisition rig like you have. You, I don't mind having it. You have an honest face—''

''Oh, don't say that,'' Joss said. ''After everything I go through to make myself look tough.''

''You do, you poor thing. And it's useful, isn't it?'' Cecile added, sipping at her drink. ''That bland, innocent look—no one can see all those little wheels turning in there. Now, now,'' she said to Joss's shocked look. ''I have grandchildren. You think this riff is anything new to me?''

''Of course not,'' Joss said. ''Heaven forbid I should ever have thought so.''

''You lie cute, too,'' Cecile said. ''Anyway. ' She lowered her voice. "You were asking about suits. No, there's no way to keep record of the in-and-out traffic. There are something like eighty airlocks scattered around this place. Possibly more. People put in new ones on occasion. You're telling me, I think, that someone heard our little chat, then followed you out and tried to do you dirt."

"Close enough for jazz," Joss said. "Cecile, who would want me dead? After I've been here all of two days and done nothing but get in a fight in a bar?"

The look she turned on him was thoughtful. "Sometimes that's enough," she said. "But I wouldn't think it was in your case. You just ran afoul of Leif the Turk. That happens all the time."

"Leif the Turk?"

"And you're sops," she said, "and sops always get beat up a little when they first get here, to remind them that this isn't a desk job."

"I would have mistaken it for one in a second," Joss said, "believe me, I would." His stateroom chair had not turned out to be much good for extended keyboard work, and his back was letting him know about it.

"Hmm," said Cecile. "Well, at any rate, it's doesn't seem like enough to get you killed. Word has certainly been going around about why you're here—at least, what you said in the bar. People are secretive enough here, some of them, but not enough to go out there and try to mess you over. What happened?"

Joss told her, in brief. Cecile sat quiet for a bit, then said to him, "I think that was a dumb thing to do, Mister Sop Honey. Even without somebody annoyed at you. Or just trying to do you a mischief. This asteroid's movements aren't completely stable. Every now and then one of the little internal faults shifts, and things move."

"The point is that someone was willing to help it move," Joss said. "But I managed to knock a chip off them, if nothing else. Maybe it'll make them a bit more cautious in future."

"Or a bit more determined to do something sudden and

permanent to you, the next time," Cecile said. "Tell me: would you know that suit again if you saw it?"

"In a minute. Observer training has its advantages."

"Good," Cecile said. "Listen. Most people don't bother taking their suits back to their domes with them; there's too little room at home, as a rule, to waste on the suit. Most people dump their suits near the airlock they tend to use to go in and out. I bet if you made the rounds, you might find the suit in question. It would give you a hint, at least, of what part of the station the one you're looking for lives in."

Joss considered that a moment. "It would mean a lot of legwork, which I don't mind myself," he said. "But Cecile, what proof would there be that the place where I found it had anything to do with the person's whereabouts? If *I* had just been trying to kill someone, I would try to leave that suit as far as I could from where I came in with it. If in fact I didn't scrap it on the spot. The person has to know that if I could see well enough to shoot, I got a look at the suit itself."

Cecile pursed her lips and nodded. "That's true enough, I guess. But I don't think anybody here is flush enough to just throw away a suit. It might turn up in different form, recycled, after a while."

Joss nodded. "All right. Meanwhile, I won't go out for walks alone. I just wish I had a motive for that little attack, that's all. Motiveless attempted murder bothers me."

Cecile looked at him. "You know," she said, "just by yourself, you represent everything that a lot of people here have come to get away from. Organization, taxes—well, they haven't got away from that, much—governmental snooping, trouble of all kinds. It's not your fault, I know. You do good work. But some of the people we have out here won't see it that way. It might just have been mischief. It's just as well that you shot whoever it was. Word will get around, among other people who would want to make mischief. It may make them a little more reluctant."

Joss took a breath, thought about what he was going to

say next, and let the breath out again. "You might hear," he said, "about anybody who needed medical treatment all of a sudden. An accident with a laser or something."

Cecile looked at him. "I might," she said. "And if I can find a way to let you know about it without jeopardizing my own position, Mister Sop Honey, I'll see what I can do. But I have to live with these people. And sneaks and snoops have a tendency to come to grief out here."

"So I notice," Joss said softly. "All right. And thank you. Meanwhile, what's your next one?"

"The same again," Cecile said, "a double."

"ANOTHER OUTBREAK OF WILD NATIONALISM, I see," Joss said when Evan came in through the airlock.

"What?" Evan said.

"You're singing that Toasted Cheese song again. At least you haven't started in on "Men of Harlech" yet."

"I never," Evan said, mildly scandalized.

"You do too. Constantly, and especially in the 'fresher. And usually in the key of M."

"W, surely," Evan said.

"Hush up, Supertaff," Joss said from the computer console. "Come look at this."

Evan leaned over Joss's shoulder to look at the computer's readout pad. "I see lots of registration numbers," he said, "the significance of which is presently difficult for me to understand. So suppose you explain, which you're visibly itching to do."

"I'm more interested in finding out who was trying to kill me just now," Joss said.

"Been in the bar again, have you?" said Evan.

"*You* should talk," Joss said, and Evan blushed. Joss noticed this with mild interest, but left it alone for the moment.

Joss told Evan about his excursion to the salvage pile.

"You bleeding idiot," Evan said at the end of it, "why didn't you wait for me?"

"Who knew when you were getting back from your little pub crawl?" Joss said. Evan blushed again. *Goodness,* Joss thought, *what's going on with our lad tonight?* "And besides, who knew someone was going to go to all that trouble to try to off me? It can't have been easy, pushing all that metal around." He sat very still for a moment, considering what he had just said. "And besides," he went on, looking up at Evan, "how would one person alone have done it? Without any lifting equipment? Without any heavy equipment at all? When I came out of that pile, there was nothing left but footprints."

Evan looked at him thoughtfully. "Someone," he said, "has been out there ahead of time, cutting through vital bits of metalwork. Making it dangerous for anyone to investigate too closely. Hmm?"

"You'd think that would be noticed," Joss said.

"Now why would it be, then? On this place's night shift—and there is one, apparently, though people tend to keep late hours—who would notice one lone person out there with a cutting torch?"

Joss nodded. "And there's evidence," he said, "that if people did notice it, they'd most likely keep it to themselves. You may have a point there, partner."

"Let's take a moment, some time in the next few days," Evan said, "and tear that pile apart."

"I was going to recommend it anyway. I want to see how many other ships we're looking for might be hidden in there. Probably not many more; it wouldn't be smart." Joss paged through the display of his data pad, brought up a graphic. "But look at this."

Evan bent in close to look at the vidsnap of the hole in the engine pod of the VW Box. "What the hell?" he said.

"Right," Joss said. "What made it?"

"Nothing civil," said Evan. "That's military."

"Nothing standard military, either," Joss said. "That's brand new weaponry that can do that, my friend. One of your new charged-particle scoops, or one of those damn muon-augmented braided noble gas lasers you were lusting after in *Jane's* last month.''

"I never lust after weapons," Evan said, and blushed again.

"Hah," Joss said, and his curiosity was really getting the better of him now. "Never mind that. Somebody out this way has been playing with state-of-the-art weapons that not even the Space Forces will buy yet because they're not yet fully tested—that is to say, the price hasn't yet dropped low enough for the boys in Acquisitions to justify buying them to the cheapskates in Accounting. This is not good news for us, Unka Evan, not at all. It means there are people running around out here who are *lots* better armed than we are; hell, lots better armed than the goddam Space Forces are—not that that would be hard. And these too-goddam-well-armed people have been getting terminally cranky with people who have been catching them at something they're doing. Maybe not even that. Maybe just being in the wrong places at the wrong times. But five'll get you ten that the people who have these weapons are somehow involved with the disappearances we're here to investigate. And ten'll get you twenty that someone has already attempted to get rid of one of the people investigating this situation, while *you* were in the bar shining up to the ladies. Hmm?''

Evan blushed furiously.

"I would have thought you were out starting a fight or something," Joss said, "to maintain parity, or the pride of the force, or some damn thing. Who is she?''

"Mell Fontenay," Evan said. "She's Maintenance.''

Joss sat back at his console and listened to the tale Evan told him. It was an interesting one, but there were aspects of it that bothered Joss. "You know," he said, "I'm not entirely sure you weren't set up.''

"What?''

"What's to say that she and this Turk character aren't in cahoots somehow? She seems awful full of the milk of human kindness for someone who was about to kill you. Not to mention that it was pretty providential that she walked in exactly when she did.''

''It was a good thing she did, my boyo!''

''Look,'' Joss said, ''I won't argue that it was a help to you. I'm just not so sure how accidental it all was. Any more than my little contretemps out at the salvage pile was accidental. Though someone was trying hard to make it look that way.''

''Now, wait a minute—''

''And it's pretty handy that this lady knows all these miners she can recommend to help us dig,'' Joss said. ''Well, we'll see what Noel says about her in the morning. But as for the rest of it. Evan, come on!'' Joss said. ''Cecile is nice, too, but I'm not sure I trust her as far as I can throw her. I'm not sure I trust anyone here, except maybe Noel, and Noel seems so busy that he's missing a lot of things that are going on around him.''

Evan looked at Joss as if he were out of his mind.

Oh heaven, Joss thought. *Why does this have to happen to us now?* ''Never mind,'' he said aloud. ''We'll handle it in six hours or so. Both of us have had long days, and we need time to assimilate what we've found. Not to mention getting some sleep.''

There came some subdued clanking sounds from outside the hull. Joss moved to one of the console screens, flicked it on, looked at it, and flicked it off again. ''Just the station techs,'' he said, ''come to look at that engine problem. I left the external access to the engine pod open for them. You want to sleep here tonight, or shall I?''

Evan looked suddenly stricken. Joss knew that expression: it was the one Evan had worn when first looking at the horrible rooming-house.

''Both of us, I think,'' Joss said, ''and to hell with community relations. We've got a long day of digging tomorrow.''

"Right," Evan said. He headed off to his stateroom, and the door shut behind him.

Joss sat down at his command console and looked at the closed door, in thoughtful mood.

FOUR

⭐

IT WAS A LATE MORNING FOR BOTH OF THEM.
Joss was up first, partly because the data he had been
amassing were on his mind, and partly because he was
the "lark" of the team. Evan was an "owl" and never got
up before ten hundred if he could avoid it—though he also
tended to be up till oh-three hundred the next morning, a
habit which Joss found hard to understand except when
one was out drinking. It generally meant that Joss got to
make breakfast, and Evan got to complain about how his
mother made it better.

This Joss was well used to by now. He was sitting by
the computer with a mug of coffee when Evan came hulk-
ing out of his stateroom, dressed and groomed, but otherwise looking as horrible as he usually did until he had
gotten some protein into him. "Morning," Joss said.

"Nnngh," said Evan, and headed down for the tiny
galley.

"Your eggs are in the nuke box," Joss said, "and your
tea is in the pot."

"Nnngh," came the reply. Joss smiled slightly and went
back to paging through his missing-ship data.

Muffled clanking noises were still coming from outside
the hull, and had been for some time. Joss had fallen asleep
to them, and had woken to them an hour and a half ago.
Evan put his head out of the galley and said, "They're still
at it out there?"

"Sounds that way."

"Incompetents," Evan muttered. "How long can it take them?"

"Drink your tea first!" Joss said; but there was no point in it. Evan was already on his way through the airlock to give someone a piece of his only half-formed mind. Joss sighed and got up to go watch.

Outside the ship, Evan was staring at a pair of legs that were sticking out from under the engine pod. "Excuse me," he said, "but how long does it take you to do a simple engine repair? It was just a noise in the—"

His voice simply stopped in his throat with a sort of "gluck" sound as Joss came out the airlock. The mechanic had scooted out a bit from under the ship on his— *oops*, Joss thought, *her*—back dolly, and was looking at Evan with understandable annoyance. But the expression was quirky and amused as well.

"That's a hell of a question to ask someone who's been up all night trying to find out what the hell is wrong with your goddam ship," said the mechanic. Joss looked at Evan and watched him blush right up into his crewcut.

Aha! he thought.

"Evan," he said, "you might perhaps introduce us."

Evan looked at him with an expression somewhere between incredible embarrassment and complete shock. "Uh. Joss O'Bannion—Mell Fontenay."

"Pleased, ma'am," Joss said, "and thank you for coming so late in your shift. I saw you starting up last night, but I didn't want to bother you. Have you found anything interesting?"

The lady looked up at Joss with cool green eyes and said, "I found the reason for at least one of your vectored thrusters giving you trouble. Under the circumstances, I didn't want to leave without checking the other systems as well."

"Oh?" Joss said. And then added, "Evan, your tea's going to get cold."

Evan made a suggestion as to what could be done with

his tea. Joss chuckled; Evan was waking up nicely. "Let's see," he said.

Mell got up off her dolly, walked over to one of her toolboxes, and picked up something from it. She handed it to Joss. It was a little package of something solid, wrapped in paper on the inside and plastic outside, with wires stuck in it, and a chip of some kind taped onto the front.

"Good God," Joss said softly, handing it to Evan to examine.

"I cut the wires as soon as I saw it," she said. "It was slipped inside one of your thruster gas vents. The explosive I recognize; it's one of the plastiques used for mining around here. The chip I haven't seen before. I would suppose it was pressure sensitive, or something like that."

Joss looked at Evan with interest. "So now," he said. "This is all very interesting. Ms. Fontenay," he said, "did you find anything else that worried you?"

"Not so far," she said, "but considering that thing, there are a few other checks I want to make before I'm done. Besides," and she smiled at Joss, "there aren't many ships like this one out here. I can't say I'm not having a good time rummaging around inside."

"Enjoy yourself, then," Joss said, and patted Evan on the shoulder. "Partner, can we talk for a moment?"

Evan nodded and headed back into the ship, still looking stunned. Joss nodded politely to Mell and followed him.

Evan headed straight to the galley and got his tea. Joss followed more slowly, making sure first that the airlock was shut.

"I'm impressed," he said. "She's quite a looker."

Evan glanced at him over the teacup. "She's got a mean right cross, too. I'd stay on her good side, if I were you."

"I'll leave that to you, thanks," Joss said. Evan blushed again. *This is too easy,* Joss thought: *I really have to stop doing it to him.* "I'm just not sure I'm entirely happy she's crawling around in the innards of my ship, considering the circumstances.''

''*Our* ship,'' Evan said, but his heart wasn't in it.

Joss smiled slightly. ''I mean, it would have been just as easy for her to have put the thing in there herself—''

''The timing,'' Evan said, with some irritation, ''is all wrong.''

''No it's not. She's a mechanic, she has access to this part of the station.''

''So does everybody else who lives here, as far as I know!'' Evan glared at him. ''Your paranoia is showing.''

''When someone is shoving little package bombs into my ship,'' Joss said, ''damn right it is.'' He took the little plastic-wrapped packet away from Evan and pulled off the chip.

''Let's see about this,'' he said, and took it over to the data reading console. He put the chip on the pad, contact side first, and brought up the pad's electronics-reading program. ''Here, now,'' he said, and let it rip.

The pad paused for a moment, then started drawing a graphic of the chip's circuitry, layer by layer. Joss looked at it with interest. ''Not just a timer,'' he said. ''The thing 'listens' for iondrive emissions, as far as I can tell. The next time we went out—like this morning, to start the digging—boom!'' He chuckled. ''Engine failure, it would probably look like. New ship, not run in properly . . . very sad. And no one would ever find out differently, because the pieces of the hull that would prove an explosive device had been in use would be all over the Belts within a day, and the ship itself would be salvaged within minutes, so the SP couldn't get its hands on it. Bets?''

Evan just looked at him.

''It could have been anybody,'' he said.

Joss sighed. ''You're right, of course. But now I'm going to have to arrange some gimmickry for the ship to make sure no one will tamper with it. It's going to take time that we can't really spare at the moment. And no one is going to tamper with the ship now, anyway, because they know we'll be expecting it.'' He shook his head in resignation. ''I guess I'd better get on with it. It's just annoying. Somebody out there is very quick on the trigger. And this technology,'' he said, pointing at the chip lying on the pad, ''is a little too shiny and new for my taste. There's money involved in this. Too much of it, much too much for this part of space.''

Evan nodded, but he was looking at the airlock door. Joss grinned at him a bit. ''From the looks of her,'' he said, ''I think you'd better eat your eggs. You want to keep up your strength, after all.''

Evan threw the teacup at him. Joss caught it in midair, looked into it with satisfaction. ''I must be getting better at making the tea,'' he said. ''Go get your eggs and I'll give you another cup.''

ABOUT AN HOUR LATER, THEY WENT ALONG TO Noel's office. He had actually managed to clear the paperwork away a little, and produce a couple of extra chairs. When they got there, Mell Fontenay was in one of them. Evan nodded to her, and casually sat down in the chair farthest from her.

Another chair contained a big man in his mid-thirties, another two-meter job, brown-eyed, brown-skinned, with a mop of brown hair; a man with a face like a friendly puppy's, and a likeable air. ''Officer Glyndower, Officer O'Bannion,'' Noel said, ''this is my deputy, George Klosters. George helps me out when there are physical surveys and claim investigations to be done. He'll give you a hand with your digging today, and act as liaison between you and the freelancers who'll be helping with the dig.''

''Pleased,'' Evan said, and shook the man's hand after Joss did. It was a considerable grip George had, the kind of grip a man uses when he's not nervous about needing to prove anything. But the look he gave Evan was cool and a touch cautious. *It's the uniform, I guess,* Evan thought. It was a reaction he had grown used to over time.

"Noel has been telling me something about your find," George said. "It sounds as if you're going to need a lot of delicate work with laser drills and so forth, rather than blasting."

"Definitely no blasting," Joss said. "We want the craft as intact as possible. It's going to be difficult, because of all the fused material around the ship. Its surface is likely to contain evidence of exactly what happened, but only if we can keep it from being scarred or burnt too badly."

"It sounds to me," Mell said to Noel, "as if this is going to be the kind of work that needs slow, careful people. Joe Siegler could do it, I think, and Vanya Rostropovich."

Noel nodded. "Sounds about right, George?"

George nodded. "Besides them," he said, "I'd suggest Lara Vidcic. She's got some pretty good laser equipment. She and her dad were doing some gemstone work a few years back, and they kept the fine-tuned stuff around in case they needed it again."

"All right," Noel said. "How soon do you think we can get everybody together?"

"Shouldn't take much longer than two or three hours," George said in his big, gruff voice. "I'll go make the calls shortly."

"Fine," Noel looked at Joss. "I hear you found a little present in your ship this morning," he said.

"That we did," Joss said, and described the bomb, for George's benefit. "Noel, the level of technology of the thing is surprising. It's very memory-dense, very smart— the palladium-arsenide detector in it is more miniaturized than I've ever heard of—but most of all, the thing is *expensive*. I'm pretty surprised to see it out in this part of the world at all. I'd love to find out where it came from. The station keeps some import and export records, doesn't it?"

Noel nodded. "They should be in central data processing. Feel free."

"Thanks," Joss said, "I will. I doubt I'll find anything straightforward, though. I think this thing was most likely smuggled in, and I want to see if I can figure out how. That'll be my morning, at least till the digging is ready to start. But somebody has been very quick about seeing how many different ways our work here can be stopped." He looked over at Mell and said, "In your opinion, is my ship clean now?"

"I can't vouch for the crew compartments," Mell said. "I don't do windows. But the engine is as your ship's computer claims it should be. The iondriver's pulse generator was slightly out of true, but I corrected that." She smiled. "It's a nice craft; some of the factory seals hadn't even been broken yet. I'm not used to engines that don't have chewing gum and sticky tape all over them. It was a pleasant change."

"Glad you liked it," Joss said. "Do you suppose I could get you to come have a look at it in the morning? Just for good luck, and to make sure no one's tampering?"

"No problem at all," Mell said. "My schedule won't be too bad for a while; my busy time starts with the next wave of arrivals, about two weeks from now. Routine scheduled repairs for people coming in from long runs."

"Fine," Joss said. "Thank you. Evan, what's your schedule?"

"I'd like to talk to anyone who saw Hek just before she left on her last run," Evan said. The thought that she might have given someone some sort of hint about what was going on had been preying on his mind for a day or so. "Friends, or any family."

"I can give you some names and addresses," Noel said, "but a lot of those people are out themselves right now. In fact, the Drury crowd, they're some kind of cousins of hers, headed out as you were coming in. I think you saw them."

"Yes," Evan said, thinking of the young man who had

so expressively spat at him on the way out. "They're not due back any time soon, I take it?"

"I don't believe they filed a flight plan and schedule, if that's what you mean," Noel said. "Most people here don't bother."

Evan sighed. This was something he was used to from his time on Highlight. "Right," he said. "I'll see what the people here can tell me."

"Good enough," Noel said. "If there's nothing else, let's get on it."

All of them got up and started to go about their business. Evan noticed George patting Mell's shoulder in a friendly goodbye as he headed out. "Friend of yours?" he said to her, after George had gone out.

Mell turned and looked at him, those green eyes glinting. "I should think so," she said. "That's my ex."

"Your ex-husband?"

"Right. See you later?" Mell said, and headed out the door.

Evan stood quite still for a moment, suddenly understanding that cool look from George. Oh dear, he thought, and blushed again.

Joss was standing behind him, saying nothing, and saying it with a slight smile. Evan didn't bother responding to this, but went over to Noel to get the list of names he was scribbling. "Most of these people are over in our old town," Noel said, "the more antiquated part of the station. It's the only part that's tunnelled very much. You'll get lost; everybody does. Don't let it bother you: anybody you meet will give you directions." He handed Evan the list. There were only four or five names on it. "This lady," Noel said, pointing to the first name, "and this gent," pointing to the second, "are probably your best bet: they were Hek's drinking buddies. You should be able to find them—this is their waking shift, the last I heard."

"Right," Evan said. "Thanks much, Noel. Joss—" He waved at his partner and headed out, before he started blushing again. This situation was acquiring aspects he hadn't been expecting, and didn't really care for. But there was nothing to do but get on with things as if everything was normal.

But he kept seeing sea-green eyes looking at him.

"CECILE," JOSS SAID, "HOW'S THAT?"

"I can hear you fine," she said. "This is interesting: we've never had a scrambled circuit before. Never needed one."

"First time for everything," Joss said. The first thing he had done on getting back to the ship was to start writing some new communications software for the station's data processing department to use. He had been shocked to see what they were using, a barely functional sort of block-by-block cyclic redundancy checker, with one computer shouting instructions at another between gaps in data. But the proprietary software was expensive, too expensive for a little place like this. No one would know, though, if Joss cloned off his ship's own programs—the simpler ones—and adapted them to the station's needs. Now he could be sure that material he borrowed from Willans' data banks came to him uncorrupted, and as a by-product, his ship-to-shore communications would be secure. He desperately hoped that someone out there would be very frustrated by the whole thing. "While I'm thinking of it," he said, "no news of any discarded suits lying around, huh?"

"No," she said, "no such luck. None of the medics saw anybody with a leg burn, either."

"Oh, well, can't win 'em all. At least not today," Joss said. "Cecile, I'm going to pull that list of trading manifests. Is this the one?" He used his data pad to bring up a menu of files in the Willans computers, and had the pad point at a particular one.

"That's it," Cecile said.

"Right," Joss said, and told the machine to fetch it

down into his ship's computers. It did, and while it was doing so, Joss said to Cecile, "Tell me something, Gramma: if you were going to try to mislead somebody about where you were going, how would you do it?"

"I'd tell them I was going somewhere else," she said mildly. "You must run into that kind of thing every now and then."

Joss chuckled. "I mean, if you were a miner."

"Heaven forbid. Horrible lifestyle it is." There was a brief pause. "You're asking about how people hide their claims, I think."

"It was just a thought."

Cecile laughed. "Mister Sop Honey," she said, "there's probably more ways to do that than there are to skin a cat. Not that anyone I know would skin one; we have too many rats as it is, nasty things. Well, certainly the claim transmitter lets you know whose the claim is, if you can get close enough. But nobody wants anyone to get too close, right? Because that way they can avoid trouble. You'll have noticed that people tend not to file flight plans."

"Yes," Joss said, "and only the fact that we have five hundred million cubic kilometers of space in this part of the Belts keeps them all from ramming into each other."

Cecile laughed at him. "Sop Honey, flight plans are an inner-planet invention. No one here needs to know where somebody else is going."

"They do if that somebody doesn't come back! And besides," Joss said, "the kind of electronics some of these ships are carrying, they couldn't tell if anyone else was coming if the other ship was exploding nukes to announce its presence. A lot of the ships in that hangar dome seem to think navigational hardware is an unnecessary luxury."

"For a lot of them, it is," Cecile said. "They can't afford it. They need drills and waldoes and explosives much more than they need fancy machines to talk to other ships. They don't *want* to see other ships, anyway."

"So they don't have the fancy equipment," Joss said.

''But even the least sociable of the miners has a check-in routine.''

''Most of them do,'' Cecile said. ''They arrange to send us a signal, oh, every week or so. Since most of them tend to work a circular course around the station, and then spiral in toward the end of it, that works pretty well.''

''I can see where it would,'' Joss said, seeing that the data transfer had ended. He cleared the pad, and brought up a scribble surface, reaching for his stylus. ''So the station might be here—'' he drew a dot ''—and the miner would be out here somewhere,'' he said drawing a circle around it. ''And at different points along that circle—or along a set of circles, since he might do more than one— he has his ship send a signal.''

''That's right.''

''And the signal is directional, of course.''

''Along one line, yes. We can get a pretty crude triangulation, if we have reason to try: we have receiver masts at both ends of the asteroid. But it's not much of a baseline, and the parallax measurement is very, very tight. Mostly we don't bother.''

''Well, you'd have no real reason most of the time. But a snooper who was keeping track of the direction their signals were coming from, and who knew the timing, could get a pretty good triangulation if he or she were out in a ship on his own, say fifty or a hundred kilometers out, and caught the new signal as it was coming in. He would use Willans as the other end of the baseline, and nail the location of the signal in three dimensions.''

''Sure he could,'' Cecile said thoughtfully. ''And then if he did that several times, whoever was out in the other ship would be able to establish the location of the circle, in three dimensions, as you say, and probably find the other guy's claim as well.''

''It would take time, but it's doable,'' Joss said, doodling on the screen. ''I'm trying to think of ways to subvert this process. I mean, if you know people are going to be doing it—''

There was a pause. "You know," Cecile said, "I would find a way to send a signal from somewhere I wasn't."

"You have a sneaky mind, Gramma," Joss said. "So would I. I would rig a relay of some kind, and shoot it off on that circular orbit. And then I'd be somewhere else."

"But where?" Cecile asked.

"The other direction? If I were being mulish and individualistic and all?"

"Enough people here would do that," Cecile said. "I think the word you're looking for is 'ornery.' "

"Exactly," Joss said, considering that it was time he had another look at *Death Valley Days*. "Unfortunately, that only leaves about four hundred million cubic klicks of space in which to look for you."

"Seems like an advantage to me," Cecile said.

"You've got a point there." Joss stared at his pad. He didn't say what he was thinking—that the present proposition was a problem only if you had a single trace, or set of traces, to work from. If you had quite a few of them, and plotted those traces all at once, you might well have a better idea of where to look for that relay—or relays. It seemed likely there might be more than one.

"Heavens," Joss said, "this is frustrating. What would you do next, Cecile?" Joss, cleared the pad, asking it covertly to pull the entire Willans communications records for the last three months, without telling Cecile. The pad got busy with this.

"Go out for dinner. I know a nice little Italian place—"

"Run by one of your grandchildren?"

"I can see why you're in the police. Indeed I can, Mister Sop Honey. Do you like *calamari?*"

Joss was amused. "You raise *calamari* here too?"

"No," Cecile said, "but the grandchild does a pretty fair fake out of soy protein."

The pad quietly told Joss that it was finished. "You interest me strangely, madam," Joss said. "Tonight, maybe?"

"Depends on work," Cecile said. "I'll give you a call, if I may."

"You're on," Joss said. "Later, Cecile."

"Right, Mister Sop Honey."

Joss stroked the pad's control surface for a moment, getting it to connect up to the holographic display over the command console. When the connection was made, he started plotting, in three dimensions, every location fix from every ship that had reported in for the last three months. It was going to take him a couple of hours, he knew, but after that he might have something worth working with. And with some luck, Evan might have something to add to it that would be of use. From initial indications, there were an awful lot of people using this kind of technique; the first few plots were showing various exaggerated curves and parabolas. What they would need now was anecdotal evidence.

No one like Evan for getting that, Joss thought cheerfully, and got on with the business of the plotting. *People hear that silly accent of his and spill their guts on the spot. . . .*

EVAN'S PINT FELL OVER IN FRONT OF HIM, spilling all over the counter of the bar where he stood.

Evan sighed, and cocked his fist back, and hit the man who had knocked his pint over.

It was not nearly as big or noisy a fight as the last two, but this mob had knives. Evan hated knives. They were much harder to take away from people than guns, and if you stepped on them, they tended not to break as easily. *Why don't I have my suit on?* he thought, and punched the next person who dove at him over a table.

"Ah, hell," said a voice behind him. There was a grunt, and a rustling sound, and from behind him someone was picked up and thrown across the room. Another face got punched next to him, and Evan recognized the slim wrist attached to the fist that did the punching.

"Your social skills just aren't up to small communities, you know that?" Mell said, and kicked a large man in the goolies, making her way toward Evan. "What have you been *saying* to these people?"

"Hello, mostly," Evan said, and backhanded a small man who was raising a knife at him. There was a crowd of about ten more people to deal with, and he was thinking seriously about his gun, community relations or no community relations. "At least Leif the Turk isn't here," he added, tripping someone who was running at him from the side.

"Hey, you all—cut it out!" Mell shrieked. In a small space, the sound was most extraordinarily piercing, and a lot of people dropped things—glasses and bottles and knives—just out of shock. "Evan won't hurt you, you assholes, he wants to find who cacked Hek, that's all. Now, shut up and sit down, or your ships are going to start having problems real soon now!"

Evan propped himself up against a table and watched the crowd warily. All of them stared at him: some of them put down what bottles or knives they were still holding, and their expressions were slightly more forgiving than anything he had seen yet. *Possibly,* he thought, *because the idea of an annoyed mechanic works better than anything I might say.*

"You just let these people be," Mell shouted, "they're here on our side for a change. What about your buddy, Luke, forty years out on the rounds and all of a sudden he didn't check in? You think that was accidental? What about Mary LaBianca and her two kids, the best-maintained ship anybody ever saw? You think that was engine failure? What about Dele Marigny! What about Leo Ballinger!"

Faces were beginning to look somber all around. "Now you people come talk to Evan here," Mell said, "and you tell him what he needs to know about when you last saw the folks who disappeared. He doesn't give a shit about where your claims are. He wants to find out who's murdering our people, and all you're giving him is crap and more crap! You cut it out before I start sending you people bills for what you owe me!"

A visible shudder went through the whole crowd. The last time Evan had seen anything similar was in a crowd outside a besieged apartment building, when the residents had been told there was a nuke inside with the terrorists who were holding it. He couldn't say the effect made him entirely unhappy.

"Here," Mell said, and gestured Evan over to a table that had avoided having glass broken over it. It was wet, but Evan didn't care about that. He sat down at it, trying not to look either too smug or too relieved.

"What do you want to drink?" Mell asked Evan, as people around him started picking up chairs and setting them upright again.

"What do you suggest?" he said.

She looked at the crowd. "Ask for a Swill."

Evan looked up into those sea-green eyes with some bemusement, then said to the bartender, who had come out with a drying cloth, "May I have a Swill, please?"

The man nodded and went off. All around Evan, people were beginning to sit down in the chairs they drew up, and look at him. He wasn't sure he found this situation preferable to being punched. The people's looks were variously curious, suspicious and mistrustful, with degrees of fear, distaste and interest mixed in. Evan felt more threatened than he had in many places where guns were being pointed at him, but there was nothing he could do, and certainly no suit to hide behind. *Cope,* he said to himself, as he had that day he found himself outside the building with the nuke. He took a deep breath and went about coping.

"Baba, you come over here," Mell was saying to a small silver-haired lady who had been coming at Evan with a knife when he last saw her. Evan was glad things had broken up before he had to throw a chair at her; she reminded him uncomfortably of his mother. Also, "Baba" was one of the names Noel had given him to see, one of Hek's drinking buddies. Mell sat her down at the table with Evan and said, "You tell him about when you last saw Hek. And what she said."

There was a pause while the bartender returned with a tall glass with ice in it. Evan looked at this with trepidation. Too many times in the army he had been given glasses that looked innocent on the outside, and on the inside were a great deal of trouble to him, either immediately or eventually. But he accepted this one, thanked the bartender, and looked at the people all around him.

"Thank you," he said to them.

They watched him, as if something was wanting.

He looked at the bartender. "Won't they have something?" he said.

All around the table, heads shook.

"Oh, come on," Evan said suddenly, "do." The memory of his mother brought back another one, of being coaxed over a plate of cakes at his auntie's house, and coerced into having another one, whether he particularly wanted to or not.

More heads shook.

Evan took the bit between his teeth. "Oh, now, you have to," he said to all the people around the table: smiling at them as he would have at his aunt, in cheerful revenge for all those afternoons when he was stuffed until he could hardly walk. "Won't you have something to drink? On me, for pity's sake," he added, "is there any question?"

There was an abrupt babble of voices, as about six people at once grabbed the bartender by the sleeve and began issuing orders, some of them very complex. Evan smiled slightly and waited until everyone's hand was filled. This took some time, while aromas floated up to him from the glass of Swill that hinted that this was one of those drinks for a brave man to fear. At least he wasn't in college any more, where some real wit might be tempted to make the traditional Broken Kneecap with any hard liquor and dry ice, or a Bubble and Squeak with metallic sodium.

He didn't quite dare glance at Mell. She was sitting quietly to one side, with a drink identical to Evan's, for the moment doing nothing and saying nothing. When everyone had their drinks, Evan said to them, *"Slainte va,"* and knocked the drink back in one.

He was aware of their watching him as he raised the glass. He simply drank fast, without bothering to try to savor any specific flavors. It was just as well. He didn't breathe for the next few moments.

A sop doesn't need to breathe, Evan told himself, as he worked very hard indeed to keep from choking. His vocal cords felt as if they were paralyzed, and someone inside his head seemed to be hitting the backs of both his eyeballs with a very small, sharp-pointed hammer. His throat appeared to have had a grenade shoved down it, and someone seemed to have lit a fuse at the end of his spine. Evan wondered how long he had before he went off.

Some time later, he found that he could breathe, and there were people looking at him and applauding. He managed a weak smile and looked at the glass to see if he'd dropped it or tipped it over. Miraculously, it was intact, and mercifully empty.

Evan resisted the urge to shake his head, pant, or do any of the things that he felt like doing. He concentrated on making something like intelligent conversation with the people around him. He wasn't too sure how he was doing, but since he saw many of them drinking the same thing he was, Evan decided not to worry too much about it. He did turn to Mell, though, and when the people he had been talking to were distracted, he said, "What was in that?"

She smiled at him. "Industrial spirit. Some other things."

"Og diw," Evan said, and sighed. He looked up and said, "Bartender? May I have another Swill, please?"

All around him there were looks of great pleasure. *This*

*is probably going to be even worse than being beaten up,
later on,* he thought, *but hell, a sop must do his job. . . .*

He had no clear idea of how long he was there. He
talked for quite awhile with several of the people gathered
around him, specifically the little silver-haired lady, Baba.
She wasn't able to tell him much about where her friend
Hek had been headed, only that Hek had said she had her
claim very securely hidden indeed, though she didn't know
how. Baba, unfortunately, was not a miner herself, just
the mother of one, and was short on any knowledge of
technique. "But she said," Baba said, "that she didn't
expect it to stay hidden forever, the claim. She always said
someone would probably stumble on it by accident. 'It's
all just folly, that's all,' she would say to me." Baba shook
her head sadly. " 'Just folly.' I guess she was right."

The old lady sighed and drank. Evan looked from her
to Mell, and found Mell wearing an oddly intense expression. "Folly?" she said. "Baba, did she say just 'folly'?
Or maybe 'Langton's Folly'?"

Baba looked up, frowning slightly. "Maybe. Maybe she
did. It was a while ago. She would always say, 'Out by
the folly.' "

"That's an old station that failed," Mell said to Evan.
"It went bankrupt about fifteen years ago, and it was too
small for anyone to start it going again. It was salvaged,
nothing there but empty shells, and a beacon to warn people that it's closed."

Evan nodding, filing the information away, and turned
to the others. Quite a few other people had things to tell
about friends who had disappeared—but again, they were
short on hard details about coordinates and so forth. Evan
was somewhat disappointed about this, but against the
paucity of information he could weigh the fact that a lot
of these people were much more kindly disposed toward
him than they had been, and some help might be forth-
coming from them now. At least, he wouldn't get beaten
up every time he came into a bar. If nothing else, his
social life would improve.

He looked over at Mell, who was leaning back in her seat with a Swill of her own. The cool green eyes were resting on him in a reflective sort of way.

"You make a good native guide," Evan said, while the gossiping went on around him.

Mell put her head to one side. "I think perhaps you needed one."

At first Evan felt embarrassed to admit it, but abruptly the embarrassment fell off him. Maybe it was the booze. "I think perhaps you're right," Evan said. "Thank you. I owe you one, *cariad.*"

She raised her eyebrows. "Careful. I might collect."

Evan raised his eyebrows right back at her. "Think I'm scared, then?"

"You?" She chuckled softly. "You'd hardly show it if you were. Not your style, I should think."

Evan smiled slightly at that. "Well, then."

She reached out for his hand.

He took it.

They got up and went out, leaving the gossip running hot behind them.

JOSS SAID TO GEORGE, "I SUPPOSE HE'S BUSY. Best we get going."

"We're all set," George said, from inside his own ship at the other side of the hanger. "Let's go."

"Cecile?" Joss said. "We're out of here. Evan comes looking for me, tell him we'll be back in a few hours."

"Last I heard, he was over in Old Town, in the Hole in the Wall," Cecile said. "Some kind of fight."

"Oh, no! Is he all right?"

"Oh, yes. He was drinking again, last I heard."

Joss chuckled. "He's conducting business, then. No problem: we don't really need him for this. See you later, Cecile."

"Hasta la vista, Mister Sop Honey."

Joss had had the ship's engines heating up for a good while now, and had been listening to them with great care, besides running every diagnostic that he could think of through the systems. Everything came up negative. He wasn't sure whether to think of this as good or bad. If someone was going to try to sabotage his ship now, surely they'd try something too sophisticated for him to catch. *Small consolation it'll be,* he thought as he lifted the ship up on its underjets, *to die of something completely unexpected.*

He eased the ship out into the airlock, waited for it to seal behind him and to open before. The doors cracked open slowly, and he soared out. Joss was getting a better feel for the controls than he'd had for the first couple of weeks, and he was now getting more enjoyment than ever out of the way the ship moved and carried itself. Even on attitude jets, it maneuvered quickly and well, and it accelerated more and more nicely on iondrive. *Running in finally, I suppose,* Joss thought. *Or maybe Evan's lady friend tweaked it.*

Evan's lady friend. Joss had to chuckle a bit at that, as he angled the ship away from Willans and headed out to where the other three diggers' ships were waiting for him. Evan was usually such a conservative type; it wasn't like him even to look at a lady, though he could be gallant enough when it pleased him. Now, though—all this blushing! It was hilarious—except for Joss's uncomfortable suspicion that the lady in question was somehow involved with the trouble they were investigating.

Then again, he thought, *in a place this small, almost everybody is likely to be at least involved with it . . . in some small or marginal way. No help to us, either. It's going to mean a lot more information for us to sift through.*

Behind him, Joss saw George's ship slip out of the airlock. "All right, everybody," he said to the other three ships, "you've got the coordinates. Let's head along."

"Right," and "Gotcha," came the answers; and a third

voice, a heavily accented Eastern European one, said, " 'Ey, Sop Honey, what you call your ship?"

Joss snorted good-naturedly. He had a feeling he was already so stuck with the nickname that there was no point in even fighting it. "Doesn't have a name yet," he said.

"Not good," said another of the voices. "Bad business to fly a ship with no name, Honey. They have a way of turning on you."

"Then what do you do with it in the meantime?" Joss asked.

There was a chuckle from the Eastern European voice. "Nickname, at least. But you can't give it. Someone else must. When real name comes along, you give it proper, with wine. And the person who gave the nickname gives real name too."

"This is just another clever ruse for us all to go out and get drunk," Joss said, chuckling.

"And so if is? What better to drink for? Big strike, wedding, baby, name baby, name ship, funeral, wake, what else?"

"You've got a point there," Joss said. He kicked in the iondrivers; around him, with thoughtless skill, so did the others, and they all accelerated together. "So what's the nickname then?"

There was a brief silence. "You ask me to give nickname?"

Joss paused, and said, "Madam, I ask."

There was another pause, and then the voice said, "We call her *Nosey*. See, she has bump there."

Joss had to laugh. The one thing he was most sensitive about on this ship—"Good enough," he said. "We'll make it official when we get in."

There was laughter from the other two ships as well. "Mister Sop," one of their pilots said, "there's hope for you yet."

"I surely hope so," Joss said.

They accelerated for about twenty minutes, then flipped end-for-end and began to slow. Hek's asteroid swelled before them, with its lopped-off end and the slight crater where the skin of the ship was exposed. Joss waited until everyone was in position, then said, "There she is. That's what we have to dig out. Ladies and gentlemen, we need to be as careful as we can about the digging. I don't want to lose anything we might find lying around the excavation site that might belong to the ship. We may—or may not—have some extensive reconstruction to do on the site, or when we get home. But any bit of waste metal could be what gives us the clue we need to find out who killed this lady."

"We be careful," said the Eastern European voice.

The ships landed at the far end of the asteroid, and after a few moments, the pilots got out and began pulling out light mining tools and the generators to run them. Joss put *Nosey*—he chuckled again; the name was going to take getting used to—down last, next to George's ship, got suited up, and got out.

They were there for six hours. It was not a simple dig. The material thrown down around Hek's ship had fused unevenly. What was very solid melted rock and metal would give way quite suddenly to piled-up aggregates, and dust and molten stuff would suddenly be spraying all over the place as the laser drill found it had nothing in particular to work on. Flying rock became a problem. Joss's new faceplate got scratched. He found himself looking enviously at the miners' tougher composite faceplates, and wishing the SP would shell out for the same material.

But slowly the ship began to emerge from the piled-up, fused rubble. Joss had asked the workers to leave the door areas for last—they weren't a priority—and to concentrate on the engine end; he was interested to see just what had happened to this ship. At one point, George said to him, "What are you expecting?"

Joss touched helmets with the man, to keep it private. "Listen," he said, "do you ever hear stories of military vessels in these parts?"

George looked at Joss warily. "Sometimes. A ship will

come to grief, and we'll find out there was some kind of Space Forces thing going on out in the Belts. Some kind of 'organized maneuver,' they'll say. And we'll demand to know what happened to our ship, and we'll never find out. It hasn't happened in a long time—not for years now. But it used to happen quite a bit, before things got more settled out here.''

Joss thought of old stories of fishing boats getting their nets caught by cruising submarines. At best, they were dragged ten or a hundred miles; at worst, they were never seen again, and their fates were never revealed, since security forbade even admitting that the submarines had been there at all. *I wonder,* Joss thought, *how much of what we're investigating could be attributable to that? Has the SP sent us on some kind of wild goose chase for political purposes?*

But what was in front of them needed investigating, politics or not. Joss turned his attention back to the ship's pod, which was coming free. The boxy shape was partly hidden by dust from the drilling, but there was a long scooped-out sort of walkway down to where the side of the craft went into the ground. Joss went down and stood as close as he dared. Lara, the Eastern European, was standing there with a small drill, hunched over, alternately breaking the stone away in short bursts and scraping loose bits away with an old entrenching tool. Joss picked up the tool and nodded at her. Lara blasted and Joss picked and shoveled for a few minutes. Then he stopped her with an arm on her suit, and said, ''There. See that flange sticking up?''

It was a sharp, curved piece of metal, protruding at almost a forty-five-degree angle from the ship's hull. Joss could see no expression inside Lara's polarized faceplate, but she held quite still for a few seconds, and finally said, ''Blowout hole, huh?''

''Looks that way, yes, ma'am,'' Joss said. ''But let's get a closer look.'' Together they began to work around the edges of the hole, and, when it was defined, down the front of it. The hole in the ship's side turned out to be at least three feet wide; flanges of metal bent out from it all around. Lara looked in sadly at the twisted and burnt cables and burst batteries inside.

"Fuel cell," she said. "They blow often. I think they build them wrong. Not enough compartmentalization, not enough protection for these damn things."

Joss said nothing for the moment, just patted Lara on the arm and said, "Keep working, I'll be back."

He went around to the front, where George and Joe and Vanya were working. Vanya in particular was busy at the vessel's front hatch. "Let's see if we can get inside," Joss said, and started to help him.

It took them about half an hour to finish clearing the rubble and fused rock away from the door. When it was free, all work stopped for a few moments while Joss and Vanya worked, first with crowbars, then with a drill and a crowbar, to pry the door open.

Inside was dead dark, dusty, and in utter disorder. Hek's ship had been fairly roomy inside, for all that it was small; there was room enough for quite a few belongings. Now they lay all over the floors, stained and blackened by smoke; books, tools, a spare suit, plates, a blanket, a lacquered tray for tea. The teacups lay shattered. On top of them lay Hek's body, in its pressure suit.

No one moved for that first moment. Then Joss stepped forward, and slowly and carefully turned the body over. It was like a board—not surprising, considering how long it had been exposed to vacuum. The faceplate was webbed with cracks; there was one neat hole straight through it. The face was a mummified mask of freeze-dried blood. Joss ground his teeth, thinking, *She was a nice-looking old lady, once.* But he said nothing aloud.

He put her down gently, got up, and made his way toward the back of the ship. The entry into the engine pod was a cramped little access that Joss had to fight with to get unclamped and open. When he succeeded, and crawled in, he was only slightly surprised by what he saw.

There was a small neat hole in the wall of the fuel cell on this side. Joss touched it with his gauntlet, brushed at it. Almost no carbonization at the edges. Somebody with a very high-powered weapon had pushed its total power through here, and the fuel cell on the other side had quite understandably blown up. Joss stood there thinking. A change of plans, somewhere along the way? This destruction, followed by a decision that someone might see through the coverup, and it was safer to bury the ship, and move the claim core to confuse the issue?

If Joss had wanted reinforcement of the military connection, he had it now. The problem was, again, that he was sure not even the military had weapons like this just yet. Certainly they were being built, and certainly people were buying them. And using them. But not here.

He made his way back out to the group standing over Hek's body. "Let's finish getting the ship up out of the ground," he said, "so we can bring it home, and give this lady a decent burial."

"It was fuel cell?" Lara said.

"It was meant to look like fuel cell," Joss said, "but it was not. That explosion was caused from inside. Someone came in here, shot this woman, then went back and blew her engine out to make it look like an accident. And then someone else decided that the whole thing was better buried away. Tell your friends that; spread the word around. I want to know about anything military that has happened in this area that *anyone* knows about. Rumors, gossip, I don't care. This evening I'll be in the Astoria. I want to know why Hek was murdered. Ask your friends to help me."

There was silence, and nodding.

"Come on," Joss said, "let's finish getting this dug up. I want to go home."

It was a couple of hours more before they were ready to take the ship in tow. Joss longed for the tractor beams of the old space serials, but technology hadn't got along that far as yet. They had to make do with cables strung between two ships, an incredibly twitchy and finicky business that Lara and Joe nevertheless brought off with great finesse. *Better them than me,* Joss thought as he headed home.

They dropped the ship a short distance from the salvage pile. George grounded his ship nearby, to keep an eye on it until someone from Willans' private security could come and start standing watches there.

Joss put *Nosey* back in the hangar dome and went looking for Evan. He bumped into him in one of the corridors leading to the dome. "You have any luck?" Joss said.

Evan blushed.

"Not that way," Joss said, and cuffed Evan good-naturedly on the arm. "Come on, you look like you could use some coffee. You *smell* like you could use some coffee," he added. "What've you been drinking?"

"Swill," Evan said. He was blinking sightly, as if the light hurt his eyes.

"I believe you." Together they made their way back to the ship. Once they were inside with the airlock closed, Joss said, "We finished our digging just now."

"And?"

"Somebody with one of your braided tuned lasers did Hek's ship in," Joss said, and gave him the rest of the details.

Evan sat there with his brow furrowed. "Tea?" Joss said.

"Yes, please. What I'm trying to understand," Evan said, "is why, after faking it, and well—if that vessel had been brought in for salvage as usual, probably no one would ever have noticed—they then tried to cover everything up as they did."

"I've been running afoul of that one too. A sudden change in command of the operation?"

Evan sighed. "We'll have no way of knowing until we find out who did it, will we?"

"And we can't do that until we trace them," Joss said. "I'm going to send a note back to Lucretia and see if she can't find out something about any covert Space Forces business in this area."

"I don't think they'll tell her anything," Evan said.

Joss shrugged. "It's worth a try. I take it your meeting with the locals went well?"

"I got into a fight," Evan said. But there was an expression on his face like a smile trying hard to happen, and being restrained.

"And what else?" Joss said mildly.

Evan blushed again.

"Look," Joss said, chuckling, "if congratulations are in order, then congratulations. She seems like a nice lady. Just be careful what you say to her."

"Joss," Evan said, "she's been a great deal of help. Those people wouldn't have talked to me today without her." His tone was pained: it was one Joss couldn't remember hearing from Evan before.

"That's all very well. But I'm not sure of anybody's motives around here, not yet. Something fairly major is going on, and anyone who gets too close to it is getting killed. I'd sooner that didn't include us."

Joss sat down at his data pad and brought up the graphic that he had been working on while he was talking to Cecile. "Take a look at this," he said. "You may have been able to pick up something that'll be of use. I've got them labeled by ship names."

Evan sat down next to Joss and began puzzling over the graphic of nested circles and ellipses, the path of people's radio checks. "I don't know," he said finally. "I got a lot of rumor from those people, but very little in the way of hard coordinates where the missing ships were supposed to be heading."

Someone knocked on the outside airlock. Joss whistled the door open.

George came in. Joss nodded at him. "Everything set up out there?"

"All set," George said, looking over at Evan. "Station

security has the ship under guard. Though I don't think anything in particular will happen.''

"Neither do I," Joss said, looking with mild interest at the glances Evan and George were exchanging. Quite cool, those looks, and appraising. *Uh oh,* he thought, and resolved to have a little talk with Cecile later, if it seemed wise on second thought.

"George," Joss said, getting up, "I was talking to Cecile about the check-in patterns of some of the miners hereabouts. How familiar are you with the reg numbers and dates that ships have been disappearing?"

"Too goddam familiar," George said. "I did the original number crunching for Noel when he started to get suspicious."

"Good. Let me bring this chart up on the holographic display. See if you can help us fill in some details."

The pattern of circles and ellipses and long hyperbolae came up in midair over the map stand, looking very much like a messy ball of yarn tangled around a set of X-, Y-, and Z-axes. "There are the official radio checks, as far as I can pin them down," Joss said. "The ones in red are the ones that vanished. You can see they're all spinward of the station, but that's not a great deal for us to go on; that only leaves us about half the Belts to look at."

George stared at the display for a long moment. "We never thought to plot it like this. Even if we had, I don't think our machinery could have handled it. It's not numbers I can help you with here," he said. "I think I'm better equipped with gossip. This one—" He pointed at one narrow red ellipse. "That was *Cutty Sark,* wasn't it? Nick told me not too long before he disappeared that he was working five-fifty in, and nine-twenty up and over. That's a diagonal course, an average of Y and Z, about here." George stabbed at one spot in an empty part of the hologram; Joss quickly marked it with a dot. "But his checks are all over here. Nowhere near where he said."

Evan looked suddenly alert. "Where's Langton's

Folly?'' he said. "Baba told me that Hek said she was going to be working some rocks over by Langton's Folly.''

George looked at him with surprise. "Right about here,'' he said, and pointed at a spot about five hundred kilometers from the first spot Joss had marked.

Joss marked that one too. "This,'' he said softly, "is statistically significant. Do you see what those spots have in common?''

"No,'' Evan and George said together. And then looked at one another in what seemed like mild annoyance.

"If you draw a line between them,'' Joss said, "the line is just within maximum transmission distance of all of both those ships' official check-in points. Those two points are the foci of an ellipse, possibly. But there's still much too much space to cover in that shape. Come on, you two, I want all the gossip you've heard, whether you think it's particularly important or not.''

They spent another hour at it, tagging either specific points or fuzzy globes meant to indicate loci of probability: areas where people were reported to have been headed, to have been, or even just to have been interested in. By the time they were done, the original ball of yarn was almost hidden within an outer surface of dots and cotton-ball globes. But one little patch of globes and dots was well removed from the ball of yarn, and at its heart was the maximum-transmission line that Joss had pointed out.

"It's been drifting,'' Joss said, as they sat there drinking their tea or coffee, slumped in their chairs. "But there's a relay out there that all these ships were using to send fake check-in signals. The relay is somewhere here—'' he tapped the little blot of dots and globes. "Not too much space to check. A cube of space about three hundred miles to a side.''

"Child's play,'' George said, his voice dry and ironic.

"Exactly. George, what's out there?''

"Nothing at all. That spot's a lacuna—the distribution level there is very low. I'd be surprised if there were more than fifteen or twenty asteroids bigger than a klick on a side.''

''A good place to hide a relay, then. It's high up, almost out of the orbital plane; it gets good coverage of everybody's fake check-in points. No one is likely to stumble over it, since no one goes there much. No miners, anyway.''

They looked at one another.

''When do we leave?'' George said.

Joss looked at Evan. ''I wouldn't mind an evening to detox,'' Evan said, ''after the morning I've had.''

Joss nodded. ''Tomorrow morning, then?''

''Fine.''

''George? Can Noel spare you?''

''I should think so. I'll check and let you know.''

''All right, then.''

Joss noticed the two men looking at each other. ''I've got to run over to Noel's office to bring him copies of this,'' he said, working at his comms console for a moment, and touching the controls necessary to make a solid copy. A second later the little data block popped up out of the slot. ''I'll be back in a little while.''

He headed out of the airlock, whistling softly to himself. One thing he had learned fairly early on in the business of being a partnered sop as that there was no point in interfering in some things.

Even if your curiosity was killing you. . . .

''I JUST WANTED TO SAY,'' GEORGE SAID, ''THAT I want you to be real careful.''

Evan looked at him coolly, trying to give away nothing.

''There are several ways that could be interpreted,'' he said.

''She's very special,'' George said. ''Very.'' He was wearing a frown that was getting deeper by the second.

''I agree,'' Evan said.

It was maddening. He desperately wanted to dislike the man. He was too good-looking, too intelligent—*entirely too much of a threat,* some part of Evan's mind remarked, and was immediately shouted down by the rest. But it was true. Mell had loved him.

Mell had left him.

"She speaks very kindly of you," Evan said. It was the most neutral thing he could think of. *Dammit! What is it about this woman that leaves me with nothing to say but clichés?*

"It's a little late for that," George said. Was that a spark of regret there? Even desperately hoped so. Mell had not gone into details about what had broken up her marriage, except that the split had been acrimonious; and as far as Evan was concerned, it was none of his business. But at the same time, he was very angry at the thought of anyone's having hurt her, for whatever cause, no matter how good the reason. And this man had.

He wished he was wearing his suit.

He wished he was somewhere else. Anywhere else.

"You guys have a rep, that's all," George said, a little sullenly. "You come in, you go out, you—" He broke off. "I just don't want her hurt."

The urge to laugh in his face was considerable. But Evan squelched it. The man's face was screwed up like that of a perp making a confession, trying to hang onto his control. God only knew what his own face looked like.

"I don't wish to hurt her either," he said. It was all he could think of.

"See that you don't," George said, and his anger showed in his eyes very plainly for just that second. It was not a look that Evan was used to having turned on him. His hand was empty, and his suit was in its clamps, and this man was on his side.

Damn it all straight to Hell!

"Leave that to me," Evan said. He was going out of his way trying not to sound threatening. After all, who knew how he looked to this man? The glamorous career sop, with his shiny ship, practically the white knight on his steed. He had to understand that Evan wasn't really about to sweep anyone off her feet—

But those sea-green eyes. And the soft voice, and the— *How can I be so sure?*

"Look," Evan started to say, almost in desperation. *A truce for the moment—*

George got up, nodded stiffly to Evan, went out.

Evan slumped back in his chair, and a little sound, almost a moan, escaped him, much to his surprise.

Then he got up and headed for the 'fresher, to get ready for the evening.

And her.

JOSS GOT UP EARLY. EVAN WASN'T IN YET; NOR had he been expected to be, under the circumstances. His communications console, which he had quietly left running the afternoon before, had recorded Evan's conversation with George, which Joss had listened to and then destroyed, not entirely without mixed feelings. It was not exactly ethical to snoop like this. But these were not exactly usual circumstances.

There was a clanking noise outside the hull. *That'll be Mell, making her morning check,* Joss thought; *so Evan will be along shortly.* He had a word with the control console and got it ready to run its diagnostic checks as soon as she was gone. It wasn't that he didn't trust Mell; it was just—well, he didn't trust her.

He put his head out the airlock door. "Good morning, madam," he said, and stopped very abruptly when he realized that it was not Mell out there, but a tall skinny man in a rusty black skinsuit, doing something to one of his attitude jets.

"Hey!" Joss shouted. The man looked up at him with a face that was so radiation-scarred, you could hardly tell where the nose stuck out. Only the eyes were alive and lively, and, at the moment, shocked. The man threw down what he had been carrying, a metal rod with a rounded end, and ran for it.

And limped as he ran.

It's my boy from the salvage heap! Joss leapt down out of the airlock, voice-locked it behind him, took just a long enough glance at the attitude jet to see that a great gob of some kind of metal putty had been shoved down it, and then took off after the man, drawing his gun as he did.

"Stop!" he shouted, rather uselessly, but you had to do it, regs said: "Solar Police!" The man kept running, limping but still very fast, on out of the hangar dome, down the corridor, passing two rights, taking the third into a major intersection of corridors.

Oh, hell, Joss thought, for in that intersection was a parking place for the little electric carts that people in the station used for moving cargo, and—when it pleased them or they were feeling lazy—themselves. *Well, at least I won't have to run much further. I just pray I get one that's charged up. . . .*

He plunged into the corridor, came to its junction with the others. There were about fifteen of the pink carts parked there, and the man was already on one of them, zooming away, turning a corner. *Oh, hell and damnation!* Joss thought. In a few days he had come to learn some of the ways around here. He knew the man was heading for the Old Town. Down there, in the little mazy tunnels, Joss could chase him for a week and not catch him if he didn't want to be caught. All the same, he had to try. Joss leapt into one of the carts, turned the key, and headed off after the fugitive as fast as he could.

It was a bad situation. The man had a head start on him, and was on his home ground. Joss could do little but try to catch up with him, possibly shoot his tires out. And as for backup—there wasn't any. No way Noel could get to him. And as for Evan—

Joss snorted, swerved to miss a surprised woman coming out of a doorway. "Sorry, ma'am!" he shouted, driving with one hand, waving the gun with the other. Ahead of him he just barely had the man and his cart in view. The sound of more surprised screeching was coming from that direction, as other people in other carts or on foot got out of the way. *I need a siren,* Joss thought, turning a corner hard, another one, first left, then right. The man was ahead of him again. Sight was almost useless at this point, with so many corners and twists and turns; Joss was going by sound alone. He cornered hard, almost turned over, but not quite. The man was a hundred yards ahead of him, down a long straight corridor with no turns for a good while. *Aha,* Joss thought, and speeded up.

He began to close. Fate had been kind to him, this once, and had given his saboteur a cart with less charge. Joss crept up behind, closer and closer, pushing the cart to twenty klicks an hour, twenty-five— They were approaching a T-junction. The cart ahead of him swerved left; Joss turned the corner after it—

—and from out of corridors to the left and right, about fifty yards ahead of him, other carts leapt out, two from one side, three from the other. Joss hit the brakes, trying to see faces and to manage the cart at the same time. It was hopeless; he spun, the thing's braking system cut out, cut in again; he skidded, rammed sideways into the wall, and sat there stunned for half a second.

Before he could do anything about it, the other carts took off, losing themselves down turns out of the corridors from which they had come.

Joss sat there for a few moments, breathing hard, then put his gun away.

Hell, he thought. But he had to smile a little bit. He now had a piece of evidence that had been lacking. The sabotage that had been going on was *not* random mischief, but organized. He had been led down this corridor on purpose, and his saboteur, the man who tried to murder him, had been rescued by friends. Five of them. More, they had taken care that their sabotage should seem to be nothing but Mell doing her morning work. They would certainly have known she was doing it.

Or possibly even arranged to have her do it? Was Mell on their side?

He made his way back to *Nosey*. It took him about half an hour; he had gotten extremely lost down those corridors. Back at the ship, he checked the outside of it over most carefully. Nothing.

He looked at the clogged jet outlet. If this had been missed, when he tried to lift the ship up, it could well have blown the jet assembly straight backwards through the hull and into his stateroom on liftoff. *Tacky, tacky,* he thought, and picked up the discarded metal rod to dig out the putty before it hardened.

When that was done, he went into the ship and began running the diagnostics. About halfway through the process, they went red. There was something wrong with the iondriver.

Joss revised his estimate of the number of people involved in the sabotage. While he had been off on his wild cart chase, someone had been busy trying to ruin something else.

Now I wonder, he thought to himself as he went out to get the engine cover off, *would Mell have noticed it when she did her checks?*

He turned and went back inside to make himself a cup of coffee.

"LOOKS LIKE THE BEAM GENERATOR'S HAD ONE of its chips shorted out," Mell said, her voice slightly muffled, since she was under the ship on her dolly.

"Can you replace it?" Evan said.

"Not from anything in station stores," she said. "You insist in coming here in brand new equipment, you're going to have this kind of problem. If you were flying a VW, I could do something for you."

"Nosey is definitely not a VW," Joss said, coming down out of the airlock.

"Nosey?" asked Evan, looking at his partner with mild concern.

"Have to call a ship something," Joss said, "or it'll turn on you. Here, Mell, is this the right part number?" He held down a small plastic packet with an antistatic stripe around it.

Her hand came out from underneath, took it, pulled it under. "Oh, good," she said. "I was hoping you would have one."

"We carry triple spares," Joss said blandly, "for everything except our brains. Want some tea?"

"Yes, thanks. I didn't get any breakfast."

"You're mean to this lady," Joss said to Evan. "Come on."

Evan was unsure whether to take this statement as read, so he said nothing, merely followed Joss inside the ship. "Is there something wrong?"

"Just a few things I didn't want to mention in front of her," Joss said. Evan sat down as Joss closed the door, and listened to the tale of his morning's chase with ever-increasing bemusement.

"So they are organized after all," he said.

"That they are. And they're getting nervous."

"So are you, from the look of things."

"I think we have reason," Joss said. "We are going to have to start being very careful, Evan. I don't want one of those braided lasers up *my* backside, thank you."

"No," Evan said, "I would have to agree with you on that. Where is George this morning?"

"He's already waiting for us off the station beacon. When Mell's finished, we can head out." Joss looked at Evan with something that might have been pity. "Are you okay?" he asked.

Evan laughed out loud. Despite the various complications taking place around him, he had never been more okay in his life. But how was he going to explain that to Joss?

"I take it that means yes," Joss said.

How do I tell him? Evan wondered. *I've never been in love before—or not like this. I don't know what to do, and Diw, I don't care—* "It does," Evan said finally. "Truly, don't worry."

He will anyway, Evan thought. And, "I will anyway," Joss said immediately, so that they both laughed. But on Joss's part, the laughter was a little more restrained than usual.

"Yes," said Evan, "I thought you would. So worry. We have work to do."

Joss nodded. "Let's go see how she's doing, and then let's get out of here and go relay hunting."

FIVE
☆

THEY WENT COASTING OUT INTO THE COLD
dark.

It took them a weary while to get to the spot they had
in mind. Not that it was one particular spot; there was a
lot of space to cruise in it, listening for the tiny electronic
whisper of a relay that might or might not still be broad-
casting. Joss had the ship's communications "ears" listening carefully for any breath of radio communication that
seemed too close to be coming from where it said it was.
But so far there was nothing but silence.

And Evan was having a hard time keeping his mind on
his job.

"You must know a bit more about all this than you've
been letting on," he had said, in the darkness.

Laughter. "I've fallen into an old vid," she said. "Now
that the handsome cop has seduced me, I will tell him all
my secrets. Where the gold is hidden. How I've been spy-
ing on the Government." She laughed harder. "Isn't this
where the armed men come out of the closet and herd you
off? No, that won't work. I don't have a closet. Wait, I've
got it. Photographers come in, with those old cameras
with the flashbulbs. The blackmail pictures are sent to
your home with a note attached, saying, 'Lay off or the
local paper will get these.' "

Evan had laughed at that himself. He tickled her, then,
and she squealed and hit him with the pillow.

"But seriously. You seem to know everybody in this

place. I keep getting this feeling that you must know something else that could be of some help to us, if I could just figure out what it was.''

''Ah,'' she said. ''Subtlety.''

''Mell, come *on!*''

''Evan, you big dumb lug, listen! And stop looking so hurt. You try the dumb bunny act with me, I'm going to hit you right back with it. Of course I know illegal things that are going on here! People are always making mechanics the sort of peculiar offers they think the mechs can't ignore. Except. . . .''

''Except?''

''Except I don't usually have time for that kind of thing. I prefer a quiet life.''

''Don't usually?''

''What do I look like, the Virgin Mary?''

''To tell you the truth, I had not been under that impression . . . no.'' A chuckle.

She hit him again, harder. ''Listen,'' she said, after the giggling had died down. ''All kinds of people come through here. Some of them wave money around and try to get the people here to do things for them. Sometimes people do them, because, hell, money is scarce! A lot of the miners working this station have more than themselves and their ships to worry about. The rest of us here understand that. No one tries to scare away harmless trade. No one calls more attention to it than it needs. If something really bad's going on, of course people will have nothing to do with it. But if it's something that seems innocent—''

Her voice trailed off.

''So you've done the occasional 'innocent' thing.''

She just looked at him quietly.

''Do you really think I would be involved in something bad? Really?''

He gazed at her. The hair was a veil, the eyes were cool and a little sad.

''No,'' he said, ''No, of course not. But I had to ask.''

She nodded, still looking sad.

"Knowing," Evan said, "that you wouldn't tell me."

"But I would," she said. And after a moment's silence, added, "I *think* I would."

Evan sighed, drew her close, and kissed her again, sank into her, drowned in the depths of her—

"Wrong signal," Joss said down the commlink to George, shaking his head. "That's a live ship. Check your screen. I've got them tagged."

"My screen isn't getting your fancy tags," George said, sounding cheerful enough even though he was mocking. "Doesn't have the graphics capability."

"Oh, Lord," Joss said. "Well, never mind. Get your grease pencil or whatever and mark off that one at, uh, two six eight mark niner four, because it's a live ship and nothing we want. I think we're still too close in."

"Okay, got that," George said.

Joss sighed, sat back in the seat and stretched. "I can barely stand the excitement," he said to Evan. "You look similarly captivated."

Evan glanced over at Joss, and had to smile a little. For all his studious, careful, methodical act, Joss really did get worn down by prolonged chases, by those long periods during which they sat waiting for something significant to happen. "You ought to go watch a vid or something," Evan said.

Joss smiled a little. "You're *encouraging* me to go watch vids?" he said. "Possibly a historic occasion. What should I watch, then?"

Evan thought for a moment. "What's the one with the mouse in it?" he said.

"Your tastes," Joss said, "are in serious need of adjustment."

"What, all of them?"

Joss raised his eyebrows. "A few of them seem to be intact." His comms board cheeped at him; he turned, looked at it, then hit a control and said, "Ignore that, George. It's another live ship."

"Gotcha."

"No mice," Joss said. "We'll discuss it later. You look like you could use some distraction."

"Not really," Evan said, but he knew it was hopeless. Joss had been with him long enough to have learned something about reading his moods.

"George," Joss said, "must be something of a problem to you."

Evan looked up and said, "Partners though we are, I'm not sure we really need to be discussing this."

"I think maybe we'd better," Joss said, "since your performance is being affected. Visibly affected. You don't usually wool-gather in situations like this."

Evan sighed and said, "It won't make a difference once things start happening."

Joss looked skeptical. "You can't be sure of that," he said. "You said yourself that this has never happened to you before."

"I said it won't make a difference!"

"All right," Joss said, very gently, as his board cheeped at him again. "Let it be for the time being." He looked at the board, and at the screen next to it, and suddenly straightened up.

"George," he said, "what do you have at oh oh six mark one eight up?"

There was a pause. "Ship signal," George said. "Not very strong."

"No surprise, that," Joss said, "because if the tag on my screen is correct, that ship almost fell on me in the salvage pile the other day."

"Holy shit," said George, sounding completely delighted.

"Indeed, yes," Joss said, as Evan hurriedly came up behind him and peered over his shoulder at the screen. The signal tagged there was winking on and off with increasing and fading signal strength.

"Look at that," Joss said. "See that fade? That signal's being bounced off an asteroid about a hundred klicks from here. It looks as if it's coming from there to someone listening at Willans. I wonder, have they installed another relay on that little rock? Or maybe just a reflector?" He began fiddling with controls. "Never mind. George, are you getting the apparent direction of that signal?"

"Yup. It's weak, though, and I'm getting two of it."

"Secondary reflection," Joss said. "Perfect. You mark that. The stronger one of the two is the one we want. Here the relative strengths are obvious," he said to Evan, making adjustments to his board, "but they won't be obvious at Willans; they wouldn't be able to hear the primary signal from the relay at all. What a great system! What a twisty little mind somebody has!"

"We hope they still have it," said Evan.

"Hard to say," said Joss. "But we should find out a few things shortly. George, you heading for the primary signal?"

"Straight in."

"Mind our signal, then. This would be a bad place to rub elbows. Evan, you might want to think about getting your suit ready. If the thing's little, I'd like you to have a close look at it."

Evan nodded and headed for his stateroom. "I could bring it in, if you liked."

Joss looked after him, thoughtful. "Hmm. I don't know. You think that would be wise? If anybody were to notice that someone had been tampering with the relay—"

There was that, after all. "No," Evan said, starting to get into his suit, "I see your point. Let's leave well alone, then. How long till we're there?"

"Hard to tell you exactly, but I'd be surprised if it took us more than half an hour."

"Probably more like twenty minutes," George said. "I'm getting the signal a lot more strongly now."

They coasted closer. Steady soft beeping began to fill the control room. Joss was letting the relay's pulse output stay audible. After a little while Evan stalked back into the control room and looked over his shoulder.

"Do you know how heavily you walk in that thing?" Joss said, not looking up, but sounding quite amused. "Good thing there's nobody sleeping in here. You'd wake them up for sure."

Evan chuckled. "The suit wasn't exactly made for tiptoeing up behind people, that's true enough. How long now?"

"You really do want to get out, don't you?" Joss said. "About ten minutes. I think. George?"

"I make it about eight," he said. "Beginning to decelerate now."

"I'd better too, then," Joss said, and reached over for the command panel, swinging it close.

Evan braced himself a bit against one wall of the front cabin as the gee-stresses shifted. "Do we have any idea what this thing is going to look like?" he said.

Joss shook his head. "I would suspect that it's mostly batteries, since it has to be able to throw pretty concentrated beams of signal around. Solar panels wouldn't be any help to it this far out. Nuclear batteries, or chemical, I don't know which. But it'll be fairly massive."

"Right," Evan said, glad of the warning. Weightlessness was all very well, but heavy things retained their mass no matter what happened to their weight, and a careless move could get him crushed in very short order indeed.

"When we've had a look at that," Joss said, "we'll be better able to find out how signals are being sent to the thing from farther out. Possibly we'll even get some indication of where they were sent, if I can break into the relay's software."

"You think you can do that?" Evan asked, putting on his helmet.

Joss flexed his fingers expressively. "Just try me."

"You missed your calling," Evan said. "You should have been a safecracker. Or a spy."

Joss smiled and turned back to his console.

Evan finished closing the seals on his suit and went forward to look out the plex at the front.

"A little too soon," Joss said, touching controls here and there. "But look, here comes George."

Evan looked out and saw the glint of distant sunlight off George's ship—one of the station's typical designs, a box and a globe welded together, with struts to stand on. It was hard to miss George's ship. For reasons best known to himself, it was painted with gaudy black and yellow wasp stripes, and looked (to Evan's way of thinking) rather like the wrath of God.

"Hard to miss him," Evan remarked.

"Just as well," said Joss. "Three minutes, now. You see anything? I have a small mass in scan, straight ahead. We might be on top of it already, to judge by the signal."

Inside his helmet Evan tossed his head, and flipped down his specs, the binocular light augmentation filter. "Something out there," he said. "About a meter and a half long, if I'm judging correctly. Hard to tell without any other reference."

Joss nodded and started applying braking jets with a vengeance. "Here we go," he said. "On finals. George, you have a visual yet?"

"Of you, yes. Nothing else."

"Evan has it at our eighteen hundred low. Close now."

For a few moments more there was no sound. Then George said, "Got it."

"Meet you there," Joss said. He made more adjustments to his console. "Just one minute."

Evan gazed out the plex and watched the little thing draw slowly nearer as Joss decelerated and they coasted past it. It was a sort of double beer-can shape, with a third beer-can sitting on top of the first two. Joss gave a final blast of the attitude jets, stopped them, and set the ship to station-keeping. George's ship drew near, and hung there, poised.

"Your baby," Joss told Evan. "You know the cable that's coiled up in the clips in the airlock?"

"The one with all the weird heads on it? Sure."

"Take it with you and plug one end into the port at the nose end of the ship. If I can't get this relay to dump its guts by remote, I may have to do it the hard way."

"Physical connection?" George said drily, giving an opinion that nobody had asked for. "How primitive."

"No kidding," Joss said. He looked over at Evan, who was heading for the airlock.

"Be careful," he said.

Evan smiled at him, not minding, since Joss couldn't see it. "Shall do."

He went out to the airlock, snagged the cable, and shut the inner door behind him. "You want to pull the air in?" he said to Joss.

"At the prices we're paying on Willans, you better believe it." Sound hissed out of the airlock along with the air.

Evan picked the cable out of its clips, put the loop of it over his forearm, and reached for the first of the set of hull handles to his right, to pull himself along the skin of the ship. In front of him, Joss had put a spotlight on the relay.

"I think you were right about the batteries," George said. "Those two cans on the bottom."

"Yup," Joss said. In his earphones, while he plugged the comms cable into the hull, Evan could hear the sound of Joss's comms console being tickled. "Hmm."

"Stubborn?" Evan said.

"Mmf," said Joss. "Thing has a satchel code filter between it and its outputs. Nasty."

This was Greek to Evan. "Can't get in?"

"Might take me a few minutes," said Joss. "Patience."

Evan made his way to the thing, letting go of the ship and giving his personal jets a light kick. He stopped himself a little distance from it, using his chest torch to look it over. The black surface coating was somewhat scarred with micrometeorite impacts, as might have been expected.

"You think this might be booby-trapped?" he asked Joss.

"Seems unlikely, but it's best to check. Move your hand toward it, but don't touch it."

Evan did this. "Okay . . . take it away again." He did.

"No change in impedance," Joss said.

"Is that good?"

"It's not rigged to go off with mere proximity," Joss said. "Could be pressure-rigged, though."

"Oh, wonderful," Evan said. "Shall I just hit it and see what it does?"

"How good is your armor?" George said, sounding worried.

"Well, if there were a nuke in here I wouldn't do too well," Evan said, looking the relay over, "but I don't think this thing is big enough to hold critical mass, even with a squeeze field. I'll just take my chances."

He reached out and gave the relay a quick poke, a stab of the right index finger that would have put a hole through the proverbial brick wall.

Nothing.

"You are an idiot sometimes," Joss said, sounding slightly testy. "Why didn't you just back off and lob a rock at it?"

Evan chuckled. "Now where would be the drama in that?"

Joss told him what he could do with drama. "Never mind that now," Evan said. "How are you doing with that thing? Got it to spill its guts yet?"

"Whoever designed this thing," Joss said, apparently between clenched teeth, "didn't know anything about subtlety. The damn cryptography is all hard-wired."

"Cheaper that way," George said. He sounded like someone trying to be helpful, who knew perfectly well he was being no such thing, but had a good line he didn't want to waste.

"Hmmf," said Joss, and it was now quite apparent to Evan what the source of his testiness was. Joss liked to think that there wasn't a machine made that he couldn't outwit, blandish, or subvert.

"Shall I try the cable?" Evan said.

"Oh, go ahead, dammit," said Joss, sounding very cross indeed.

Evan moved carefully around the relay, looking for anything that might be a communication port. The upper body was quite smooth and unbroken. He gave himself a quick blast of downjets and started circling the lower part. "Hmm," he said. "Not much here. Let me try underneath."

"George," Joss said, "are you seeing that?"

"Seeing what?" George asked, as Evan looked over the bottoms of the two beer cans. There was nothing that looked like a port at all.

"Sort of a ghost at one oh one mark three five up and over."

There was a brief silence. "Joss," Evan remarked, "this thing is determined to remain as tight as Aunt Ellie's jam jar. Not a hole to be found."

Joss growled. Evan almost laughed out loud, but restrained himself. "Don't see a thing," George said.

"Hell. Never mind, I just lost it. Some reflection or something. Evan," Joss said, "make a hole."

"Where?" Evan said, looking the relay over.

A pause. "At the top, by preference. Then you see the little cable at the end where all the port connections are? The one with the little alligator clips on it?"

This time it was Evan's turn to pause, an uncomfortably long pause, before he said, "Yeah, got it."

"Just clip them to anything. A radio rig that well sealed is going to leak signal inside like a sieve. I may be able to upset its innards a little."

Evan chuckled and gave his jets a little push, so that after a moment he was floating above the top can. *Not too deep, now,* he thought, and did the wrist twist that set the beamer in his right arm to wider dispersion. He flipped down the polarizer inside his helm, and gave the top of the relay about three seconds.

Metal boiled away. When the vapor cleared, Evan peered inside and saw a few exposed wires and cables. *Perfect,* he thought, and tucked the alligator chips in, making sure they made good contact.

"All set," he said to Joss.

"Good. Here we go—"

"I think I've got your echo now," said George, sounding slightly surprised. "Not a reflection at all, I don't think."

"Aah, hell," Joss said, practically snarling now. "Keep an eye on it for me. Come on, you wretched tin can, spill it!!"

Evan hung there and listened to the swearing, while keypads were tapped and thumped and, to judge by the noise, kicked around the command cabin. "Nothing?" he said.

The answer that came back was florid and original, but didn't provide much information.

"Stronger," said George. "Whoever it is, they're coming in at a good rate. Should I identify us?"

"I'd rather you didn't," Joss said, and paused in his swearing a moment. Then he said, "Holy shit! Evan, get in here!"

Evan did not pause to question advice given in that tone of voice. He kicked his jets in and started cursing them himself, for they never seemed to move fast enough when he wanted them to. It was only a few seconds, but seemed like a lot longer before he had his hands on the nearest hull grip and was pulling himself hurriedly, hand over hand, along the hull toward the airlock. Joss had started turning the ship under him, and Evan waved like a flag in the wind.

"What the hell is the matter with you?" he said, groping for the last handhold before the airlock, and grabbing it at last.

He got his answer. A line of hot blue-white fire went right by them. It had to be three meters wide if it was an inch, and *bwn Diw,* there were separate lines of pale hot energy in it, curved around one another in a braid of long flat sine curves like the interwoven strands of pressurized flame that made up the shock-diamonds in the venturi of a conventional rocket's nozzle flare.

Evan slapped the airlock open, dove in, and slapped it shut behind him. It took a moment for the lock to reoxygenate itself; then the inner door sprung aside for him, and he stumbled in. The gravity was going in all directions at once again as Joss spun the ship.

"There's our little surprise for today," Joss said. "Damn! Damn it all to Hell! I almost had it!"

Another line of blue fire lanced across their bow, and it was wider this time. The braiding was horribly visible. "Why didn't they hit us?" Evan wondered.

"Can't tell. Don't wish it on us! George, run like hell!" Joss shouted down the link. "Don't wait around! Don't answer! Go!"

There was no telling from the screens what George was doing. Joss had them enlarged to show only one thing, the incoming vessel. Its blip was close enough to show some shape when enhanced. A box. A globe. Some struts.

"Look familiar?" Joss said.

"It's a scow," Evan said, not quite sure he was believing what he was seeing. "What miner has weapons like *that??*"

"No miner," Joss said, desperately kicking the ship over on its side with the attitudinal jets. Things fell over in the galley. "I do wish you'd put your teapot away when you're done with it," he added.

"Not a miner," Evan said. "But someone trying to look like one."

"Look at the weapons signature there," Joss said. "Then look at the engines. They can't put an engine on that ship that's worth anything. It would give them away instantly. All they can do is stick the best guns in the Solar

System in it, and sneak up on people, and potshot them. Like Hek. Oh, God, George, run like hell!''

"Is he away?'' Evan asked, suddenly nervous. It had just occurred to him that he might have some questions to answer Mell if George should fail to come home safely. And he would understand her reasoning.

"Can't tell. Oh, jeez, come on, you dumb bucket of bolts! Come on, *Nosey!*''

The ship veered abruptly in the other direction. Blue fire shot past her nose, missing it by about twenty meters. Joss kicked in the iondrivers, hard; the ship leapt forward. Evan hauled himself to his seat and pulled himself down into it, fumbling around for straps. The seat was not intended for him to be sitting in it when he was wearing the suit. All the straps had been adjusted for his shape when he was in nothing more bulky than a uniform.

"Never mind that,'' Joss said, "just hang on!'' He began doing things to the command console. "Unidentified vessel,'' he said to the comm link, "this is the Solar Patrol. Cease fire and prepare to be boarded, or prepare to receive fire.''

There was no answer. Joss shrugged. "Oh well,'' he said, "they had their chance.''

Evan nodded, and concentrated on hanging on and praying. It was surprising, the prayers that he remembered when he were being shaken in twelve directions at once, and someone was shooting at him, and he couldn't do anything about it at all. Joss was sweating bullets, and his face was fixed in an expression of concentration and rage that Evan had never seen before. Joss was paying no attention to the view out the plex, but was staring at his radar screen as if his life depended on it. It did.

He laughed shortly as another bolt went by and missed them again. "We're doing circles around each other,'' Joss said. "The damn thing's fixed.''

"What?''

"Fixed! It's stuck on the front of that ship in a fixed frame. Or installed fixed inside. Dumb thing can't move, otherwise we'd be all over this part of space at the moment," Joss said, and chuckled a bit. It was not Joss's usual chuckle. It made Evan look hard at his partner, and shudder a little. "They can only fire straight forward."

"Whereas we, of course—"

"You watch," Joss said, hands dancing over his console.

"The best part is, he can't run."

"Can't he?"

"Not as fast as we can. Come on, *Nosey* honey," Joss said, "come on. . . ."

The ship began to vibrate. "Good thing Mell found what she did," Joss said conversationally. "Just about now, we'd be pretty dead. Either here, or further back, before we got here. We must be getting close to what's going on, Evan, my lad, because somebody's getting pretty eager to kill us."

"There must be another way to find out you're right," Evan said, still fumbling for the straps as Joss tossed them in another strange and unexpected direction.

"Probably," Joss said, grinning, "but would it be this much fun?" He started to hum something Evan couldn't identify. "Na na na na na na na na naaaaa . . ."

The man's lost it, Evan thought. "Should I recognize that?" he asked, trying to sound conversational.

"Probably not," Joss said, very cheerfully. "It's what you sing when you're driving your go-cart down Dead Man's Hill, and the wheels are threatening to come off. Na na na na na na na na naaaaaa . . ."

Joss went off into a rather truncated version of the *William Tell Overture.* Evan breathed out. *If it works for him as well as praying does for me,* he thought, *I shouldn't complain. . . .*

The ship shuddered again as the iondrivers rattled more emphatically in their mounts. "All right," Joss said softly, "all right, you poor son of a bitch. Now, then." The ship shook again, but in a different way this time, as if something had kicked it in the side, hard.

"Missile away," Joss said. "Five seconds."

He flung the ship in yet another direction. More blue fire went by the front plex, again so close that the braiding of the tuned lasers was clearly visible. *It's actually very pretty,* Evan thought—and abruptly, the beam cut off.

Joss crowed with delight. "That's his power plant," he cried. "Perfect surgical strike. Now let's see what happens."

The whine of *Nosey*'s engines' began to back down a bit. "Unidentified vessel," Joss said again to the comm, as he turned the ship, "prepare to be boarded. Any further fire will result in punitive action."

Evan looked at Joss, a little concerned. "You wouldn't blow them up, would you?"

"Would you prefer spanking?" Joss asked, and then laughed. "Of course not, you asshole. I like a good fight, but these people are evidence, whoever they are—"

A blinding flash lit up the plex. It was autopolarizing, but even so, both of them had to turn their heads away. Only a moment later they found themselves looking at a blooming, burning cloud.

"Shit on a shingle," Joss said, glancing at his console. "Dirty. They were carrying atomics, too. But at least I didn't do it. They would have gone up right away."

"How's *our* shielding?" Evan asked.

"Oh, we can take it. But goddam it," Joss said as he looked at the comms board again, and his face fell, "that last shot of his got the relay. Damn, damn, damn!"

"Did you get anything from it at all?"

"Not a syllable. Oh, damn it to eff all!"

Evan sat there shaking his head for a moment. "Well," he said finally, "one thing we can be sure of, now. We have definitely been heading in the right direction."

"Yes," Joss said. "But dammit all, do you know how much that cable cost me?"

To this, Evan could think of no reply.

"Oh, well," Joss said after a few moments, "let's get

home. I want to file a report. And then I want to think. And then I want to ask some questions.''

"Such as?''

"Such as who knew we were coming out here,'' Joss said. "I didn't tell Cecile.''

"Well, obviously George knew.''

"Yes, and he bugged out right and proper, didn't he?'' Joss said, sitting back in his chair.

Evan was outraged. "You told him to!''

"He didn't fire a shot to help us, Evan. When we get back, I'd better find that that boy didn't even have a pea-shooter on board, or I'm going to start carrying on cranky. And who else knew?''

Evan looked at Joss uneasily. "Well, Mell, of course—''

"Of course.''

"Joss, are you out of your mind? What are you suggesting?''

"That somebody at the station,'' Joss said, "is feeding somebody out this-a-way information about where we're going to be. Evan, we weren't here five *minutes* before that ex-bozo showed up. Doesn't that evidence suggest something to you?''

Evan sat still and held onto his temper for a moment. "It does,'' he said finally, and very quietly, "but the evidence is circumstantial at best. And you know it.''

Joss knew that tone of voice by now, and held his own peace for a moment. "All right,'' he said. "But Evan, it needs to be looked at nonetheless. You had better ask your lady friend a question or three.''

Evan held still again, and then said, "I think that might be inappropriate, under the circumstances. Don't you? If you want to ask her something, do it yourself, Officer.''

Joss was quiet for a couple of breaths. "I will,'' he said. "But it can wait a little while. First of all, let's get back to Willans and make sure that this little shakedown hasn't done more than shake us up.''

IT WAS A LONG QUIET TRANSIT BACK TO THE station, and neither man seemed especially willing to say anything to the other. The tension on board ship was un-usual, and because of that, uncomfortable. It was Joss who finally broke the silence.

"You're coming with me," he said quietly, not giving orders, not even making a request. Just assuming that his buddy would do it without needing any more elaborate explanation. He was wrong.

"To where?" said Evan. There was something about the way he spoke, and the way he stared at Joss when he said the words so carefully, that had a challenge and a defiance in it. He knew where, and why, and to whom they were going, and he seemed to be waiting for Joss to come right out and say it.

"Mell's place." Joss tapped a few keys on the nearest console as if it were more something for him to do than anything relating to piloting the ship. He looked Evan straight in the eyes. "Because I want to be absolutely sure about your lady friend, and just right now, I'm not."

Evan felt himself expanding inwardly, the rush of blood or adrenaline or inhaled air that usually meant trouble for someone. The suit hid it, and he controlled the expression on his face, so that the only thing Joss might have noticed out of place was a slight hesitation in his partner's flow of speech. Then Evan, voice completely steady, said, "What's the point in that?"

"Come on, Officer Glyndower," and Joss said it right, *glinn-doo'wer,* instead of his usual mangled mispronun-ciations, "we've just been shot at by a ship whose crew can't answer questions, a ship that had no business being where we were, a ship that had double no business car-rying that sort of weaponry. I think that since we've few enough suspects who might know the who and the where and the why, we should start with the one who's been closest to us both."

"I resent that, O'Bannion," said Evan. He did, too, really and truly, rather than the slight, easily controlled outrage that would have been more usual in any of the several other circumstances. Maybe because, in those other circumstances, he could have been sure of his position as defendant. This time Evan wasn't sure at all. Maybe that was why he resented it so much, taking refuge in formal names and stiff-necked annoyance rather than letting Joss have his say.

And maybe both of them saw it in time.

Either way, Joss and Evan saw where the dialogue was headed, and both of them stopped talking in the same moment. The sudden quiet sounded even sillier than the slow, polite rising of voices, so that both men looked at one another, uncertain of how the next word or breath was likely to be received.

"Okay," said Evan. "The point to you, then. Did we take any damage that you can see, by the way?"

Joss shook his head. "No, but the diagnostics aren't equipped to assess the kind of damage I'm worried about. Do you have any idea how hot that damn braided beam is?"

"Hot enough to blister *my* ass, at least," he said.

Joss snorted. "I measured it at five hundred thousand C, or thereabouts. Trouble was, the hull sensors aren't built to handle that kind of thing. The estimate might have been low."

"Low," Evan breathed. *Diw. . . .* "That's hotter than the inside of most stars," he said.

"Just about all of them," said Joss. "The slightest contact would have boiled our hull off. Vacuum is a pretty effective insulator, but don't ever let one of those things touch you. It doesn't require anything like a direct hit, on man or vessel."

Evan shook his head. "How are they *doing* that?"

"Pocket fusion, probably," Joss said. "But that's technology for you. Wouldn't the Space Forces just love those?"

"Not sure the Government would let them have them," Evan said softly. "Might give them ideas, might it not?"

"Somebody has ideas already. Evan, who *are* these people?"

Evan shook his head.

"It's not drugs," Joss said. "No one out here has the kind of money to attract the drug trade. What other kind of people have enough money to buy weapons like that? And how many other ships equipped like that are running around out here?"

Evan looked at Joss and thought for a moment. "One might make inquiries," he said, "through the SP, to see which of the big companies have sold weapons of this sort to whom recently."

Joss sighed. "They'll fight it," he said. "Dammit, most of them are based on Earth, out of our jurisdiction, and SP subpoena powers won't work."

"They have offices," Evan said, his eyes glinting, "on the Moon. They might have copies in their computers of some of the records. Joss, we have to start somewhere—assuming that other methods of inquiry," and he frowned at Joss, "don't pan out."

Joss frowned back for a second. Then his expression lightened. "It'd given Lucretia something to do besides complain about our expense account, wouldn't it?"

Evan was stricken at the thought that he hadn't even looked at his data pad for a couple of days now. He sat there in shock. *Can he be right?* he thought. *And is she affecting my ability to function?*

And oh, good God, how can I function without her?

"There's this, too," Joss said. "Even if the weapons manufacturers on the Moon have the records we're after, you know perfectly well that the end-use certificates will have been tampered with. We won't be left with any clear idea of who the braided lasers were really sold to, or where they went. They'll certainly have covered their tracks that well."

"But it will be a start," Evan said. "All we know at the moment is that someone out this way is doing something clandestine—and expensive, to judge by the presence of the weapon, if nothing else. And what do they want with weapons like that? What are they planning?"

Joss tapped briefly at the command console as a light came on indicating the Willans approach beacon. "And we can't drag our feet about this, either," Joss said as he worked. "They've run across us, now, getting close to whatever they're doing out there. Someone will try to cover it up."

"Or cover *us* up," Evan said, "six feet deep or so."

Joss nodded. "The sooner the better," he said. "Willans approach control, this is SP vessel *Nosey*. Is the airlock clear?"

"All clear, Mister Sop Honey," Cecile said. "Come on in."

"Cecile, do you *ever* sleep?" Joss said.

"Depends on who asks me."

"Later, Cecile. We've got fish to fry. Is George back in?"

"Yup. Came in in a bit of a hurry."

"I just bet he did," Joss said, keeping his tone light; but Evan could see his face, and wasn't sure the tone would stay light when Joss found George. "Okay. Call Noel, will you, and tell him we need to see him in his office in ten minutes?"

"No sooner said than done. Willans out."

THEY FOUND HIM IN HIS OFFICE, ON TIME, AND looking agitated. This suited Evan well enough for the time being; he was feeling rather agitated himself.

"Are you two all right?" Noel demanded, leaving off sorting through yet another pile of paper, and hurrying over to them. "George was just in here in kind of a state."

"I don't doubt it," Joss said, "since somebody with a nuclear laser just tried to put salt on his tail. And ours."

"A what??"

Joss told him. Noel sank down to sit on one of the piles of paper on his desk, and never even noticed. "My God," he said, "Joss, you do know that his ship isn't armed?"

"I was hoping so. Never mind that, then. But Noel, someone on this station is feeding information to the people who have been causing your disappearances."

"What?"

"I have been collecting radar signatures of the ships that went missing," Joss said. "Your approach control has them on file in the computers as part of the docking management and recognition systems. The ship that attacked us exactly matches the radar signature of one of the ships that was reported missing a month and a half ago, and is *not* in your salvage pile. At least, to the best of my knowledge. I want that pile torn apart, Noel, so that I can go through my little list and cross off ships I know I don't have to worry about. Because apparently others of them are going to turn up to haunt us."

Noel nodded. "Right away."

"This evening at the latest. And there's the matter of finding out just who here is passing out information to the people who were shooting at us. And how they're doing it. And if possible, why. And there's someone I want to find." He described the skinny, scarred man who had been tampering with the ship that morning. "This is the lad who tried to do me in the other day in the salvage pile. He has about five friends who very conveniently helped him get away from me. They were organized. The sabotage was planned, and well planned. What they did to our ship, or would have done, would have killed us very dead. And doubtless solved all their problems for the moment. But I *like* being a problem." Joss grinned in a manner that suggested to Evan that he was getting ready to be more of one, somewhere else. "Anyway, I want that man found and arrested. Pass the word around that there's a five thou-

sand credit reward from the SP, payable immediately.''
Joss smiled slightly, as Evan inwardly cringed at the
thought of what Lucretia was likely to say.

Noel's eyes bugged a little. "Five thousand?"

"I should think that would provoke some action," Evan
said, "and action would seem to be something we need."

"Right," Joss said. "Oh, and a one thousand credit
bonus if the perp is brought in before eighteen hundred
tonight. We may not be here when he's brought in, but
we'll get to him as soon as we can. You work on him
and soften him up in the meantime. Let him know that
we're considering extended law in his case." Evan glanced
up in approval. "Extended law" meant that a sop was
ready to serve as judge, jury, and executioner to prevent
a loss of order in a jurisdictional area. It was not invoked
too often, but once an SP court had confirmed the cor-
rectness of the action, no other court had any power of
appeal against what had been done. "Let's see; what
else?" He thought for a moment. "That should do it for
a moment. One thing, though, Noel—"

"Anything."

"Why the hell are all the golf carts painted pink?"

Noel stared at him for a moment, then laughed. "Oh!
It's tradition. Willans is a Swiss name, it turns out. The
founding family came from Basel. In Basel City, they used
to have a stock of city bicycles. Anybody could use them.
If you needed to ride somewhere, you picked up a bike
from one of several depots, or just off the street, wherever
you liked. When you were done with it, you left it for
someone else to take. They were all painted pink. When
the Willanses came here, they did the same thing with the
carts, that's all."

Joss shook his head. "All right," he said. "Evan?"

"I think we need to go ask some people some questions," Evan said to Noel. "If you should chance to see
Mell Fontenay, I'd appreciate it if you'd tell her we're
looking for her."

"Will do," Noel said.

EVAN LED THE WAY. HE KNEW IT WELL ENOUGH by now, the twisty path through the corridors into the Old Town, where the ceilings grew lower, and the walls closer together, and the air got cool as the path sloped downward, letting them know they were tunneling into the rock. It was actually a very small area, relatively speaking, not more than half a mile across or so, but the tunnels twisted and curved, servicing the places where natural pockets in the stone had made it easy to cut cubic out of them.

"Down there," Evan said, "around the corner."

Joss nodded, his face expressionless. They came to Mell's door, an old-fashioned one, with a knob and a metal lock. Evan lifted his hand to knock.

Needlessly; the door was open.

"Mell?" Evan said, and looked in.

"Where is she?" someone screamed from inside, and a body hurtled out the door and hit Evan about chest-high. Normally he would have gone right over, but at the moment he was still wearing his suit—*community relations be damned,* he had thought on getting out of the ship— and with the bracing from the built-in servos, the effect was rather the same as if George had jumped straight at a brick wall. For it was George. He bounced, stood there staggered for a moment, and then jumped at Evan again.

This time Evan caught him, as gently as possible, and held him away. George struggled in his grip, but it was of course completely useless. "Damn it all," George shouted, "this is your fault! Where is she?"

Evan shook George, not hard, then put him down hurriedly; there was something embarrassing about holding so strong and angry a man helpless, like a child. "Hush now, George," he said. "We don't know where she is, either. We were just coming to look for her. What's happened here?"

George glared at Evan, gestured angrily at the room,

and turned his back on him. Evan stepped in and looked around.

"Oh, heaven," he said, and drew a long breath at the look of the place. Just yesterday it had been as cool and handsome a set of rooms as one could hope for: the furniture and decorations all very simple, elegant, plain, mostly white, with some pieces of real antique Danish Modern that must have cost a great deal of Mell's savings and went spectacularly well with the rough stone walls. But now half the furniture in the sitting room was overturned, some of it broken, drawers and cupboards thrown open and their contents scattered on the floor with books, dishes, clothing. In the next room, the bedroom, the place had been ransacked in the same way. How neat it had all been just yesterday, how calm and dim in the candlelight, with the big Amerindian tapestry over the bed glowing orange and cream and brown. But now the tapestry was pulled down and the bedcovers were flung away.

"No sign of forced entry," Joss said from behind him, and the clinical sound of his voice brought Evan down from the crescendo of fear that was beginning to build in him. "She must have known whoever it was who tore the place up, and let him in."

At that, Evan looked at George, and George looked at Evan. "You two stop it," Joss said sharply. "Neither of you would have had the opportunity, or the time. Evan has been with me, and as for you, George, you didn't do it, because I watched your radar trace all the way back in and you barely landed five minutes ahead of us. Now, who *would* do a thing like this?"

George shook his head. "No one would have," he cried, "if she hadn't been seeing *you!*"

Evan went ashen.

"Whether that's true or not," Joss said, "it's not helping us. And George, I hate to say it, but at the moment we're dealing with things that are a little more important than one disappearance—though they're almost certainly connected. I just hope that by solving one, we can solve the other. Now listen to me.'' Joss grabbed George and steadied him. ''You think about who around here might have lots of money to spend on guns like the one that almost burned your ass off. And when you have some answers, come back and talk to us. We'll be here for awhile. But for pity's sake, man, don't radio us anything on an open channel.''

Joss headed into the bedroom, had a quick look around and came back shaking his head. ''Trashed,'' he said, ''that's all. No shots fired that I can see, no blood.''

Evan had flipped down one of the analysis plates in his helm and was looking around for traces of chemicals and bright infrared traces, but there was nothing to be found. ''A struggle,'' he said, ''and then someone dragged her off. Several someones, it would have had to be, knowing Mell.''

Joss nodded. ''My friends from this morning, possibly. Damn! I want that man found.'' He stalked around the room one more time, looking at things. ''Someone she knew,'' he said softly. ''But she must have known everybody in this place.''

George nodded. ''Just about.''

''Wonderful,'' Evan said. ''That leaves us only everyone on the station to talk to.''

''Well, we have some hints, anyway,'' Joss said. George looked at him blankly, which was possibly what Joss had in mind. ''Evan, let's get back to *Nosey;* we have some nosing to do. George—don't leave town.''

Joss headed out. Evan went after him, giving George what was meant to be a sympathetic look as he went. He wasn't sure how sympathetic it looked to George, since the man scowled and turned away.

Evan's insides were one huge scowl of anger and fear themselves, but he kept the feeling out of his face and headed after Joss, to work.

☆

"TWO AND A HALF GODDAM HOURS," JOSS SAID softly, sitting at his command console again. "And God knows how long until they get the information out of the weapons firms. If they can get it at all. Maybe I am spoiled," he muttered. "Inner planet work and all."

"Just get the information, for pity's sake," Evan said, "and stop worrying about whether you're spoiled or not. Are we ready?"

"That we are," Joss said, and sighed. "You sure you have everything you want from here? This run's going to be a long one."

"Not everything," Evan said quietly.

"Yes," Joss said, "well. Willans control, this is *Nosey*."

"Listening, Mister Sop Honey."

"We're heading out. Prolonged absence, unknown flight plan. Sorry we can't be more specific. If anybody calls for us, tell them we'll catch them later."

"Will do. Good hunting, now."

"From your mouth to God's ear, Cecile," Joss said, and closed the channel down.

"She really must never sleep," he said, lifting *Nosey* up on her underjets and keying the release codes for the airlock doors. "Or maybe she has a clone."

Evan just sat in his seat beside Joss's, and looked out the plex.

"Anyway," Joss said, "no one here knows where we're going. Some people may guess, if they hear about it from George . . . or someone else. Which is why we'll come at that area in a nice wide circle, and take a day or so about it, while our data comes in. Then we'll see who shows up."

"If anyone," Evan said.

"Oh, someone will. There's too much at stake. We turned up once, and saw something that we shouldn't have. So someone else will be out there to make sure it doesn't happen again. And my guess is that word of what we've been doing at Willans today will spark some interest out in the great nowhere. There should be a little more going and coming than usual. In fact, I'm counting on it. So we head out there, nice and easy . . . and we wait.''

AND SO THEY DID.

About half way through the second day, Joss was quite aware that the waiting was driving Evan nuts. The problem was that the surveillance they were embarked on at the moment was essentially computer-driven. There was no use concentrating on what appeared on the radar screens or the scanners, because the computers could watch better and more completely than they could. They hung there, waiting, not too far from where the relay had been, with the plex polarized to keep visible light in, and maintaining radio silence except for the briefest squirt of signal to ac- knowledge the receipt of incoming material from friendly sources.

Joss had been watching the monitoring equipment— nothing much to that—and the times in between he spent cooking, watching old vids, doing crossword puzzles writ- ten by a program in his datapad, and having an occasional nap. Evan had been trying to catch up on his reading, and failing miserably; he kept going into his stateroom to pol- ish his suit, an act that Joss suspected as being profoundly symbolic of something else. What, he wasn't sure. The fourth or fifth time Evan had started doing this, Joss had shrugged, and busied himself with Noel's report on the radar signatures of the ships in the salvage pile, passed not directly to them (for fear of someone in the station dis- covering their whereabouts), but sent first to the Moon, and then to *Nosey*'s computer with the daily data dump. They were not revealing—there were no other ''killed'' ships in there—but Joss fed their radar signatures into his computer, on the off chance that whoever salvaged the wrecks might sell them to someone interested in scrap of good enough quality to fit with braided lasers.

Of course, other things had come in with the data dump as well, and they served to distract Evan, at least temporarily.

"REGARDING YOUR EXPENDITURES: I thought you two told me with your hands on your hearts that this was not going to be an expensive mission with vast bribes and benefactions flung around in all directions. You had better pray that the Commissioner is as impressed by your recording of what was shooting at you as I was. It's just as well that no one was able to claim the interesting little speed-of-capture bonus you were offering, since I think I would have more trouble explaining that to Upstairs than almost anything else. This is supposed to be good, steady police work, not a game of Interplanetary Beat The Clock. In the meantime, your bar bills are also of concern to me. I know that it is sometimes necessary to lubricate the natives somewhat, but the way you two are going about it, these people seem to have been subsisting on water vapors for years. Please try to keep some control over this, as the Commissioner is likely to get the idea that this is some clever ruse to hide the fact that both of you are closet alcoholics."

Joss snorted. "We don't have a closet," he said, and tossed his pad away. "What else does Miss Cheapskate have to say for herself?"

Evan looked oddly at him for a moment, then said, "Nothing much, except that the information from the weapons manufacturers will of course take time, et cetera, et cetera . . ."

Joss sighed. "Typical. What the hell is the use of being the police if you can't . . ." His voice trailed off. "Never mind. I still don't know what their problem is. Five thousand seemed like such a nice round number."

His console cheeped softly. This had happened before, twenty or thirty times a day, now, and it was always some remote radar pick-up that meant nothing of interest to them. But hope sprang eternal. Joss went over to look at the screen.

"Hmm," he said.

"Don't start!" Evan said. "What is it?"

"Hard to tell. A mark, certainly. And coming our way. Hmm."

"You need a hmm-ectomy," Evan said, coming over to look at the holographic display screen. He could make little of the radar tag that shone there, pale orange, hanging above the plane of the local Belt, and some few hundred kilometers further sunward, to judge by the X-, Y-, and Z-axes in the middle of the hologram.

"Nope," said Joss. "Heading the wrong way." He sighed and flopped down in his seat by the command console again, reaching for his pad.

Evan sat down beside him, staring at the blanked plex.

"I wonder where she is," he said.

Joss shook his head. "So do I, buddy," he said. "Not exactly like that lady to go off suddenly." He sighed, then, and put the pad down. "Unless, of course, this whole thing was a setup, and she's been working with them all along, and this was their way of lifting her and at the same time making her look above suspicion—"

Evan looked at him with that scowl again. Joss restrained a smile; he was getting used to it. "Why do you always have to suspect the worst of people?" Evan said.

"Because that way, when I discover the best about them, I'm pleasantly surprised," Joss said.

The console beeped again. "Damn thing," Joss said, tossing his pad down and getting up to go look at the chart. "I think I need to recalibrate it. It's too sensitive."

Evan picked up Joss's pad and stared at it. "Five-letter word for boredom?" he said thoughtfully.

"You should be able to tell me that, I would have thought," said Joss. "Hmm."

Evan pretended to throw the pad at him.

"No, no," Joss said, "really hmm. This is interesting."

"Oh?"

"Yes. You saw that last trace. We saw him earlier this morning, doing a big, easy circle. Well, now look at him."

Evan looked at the hologram as Joss told it to display the previous course, and the present projected one. "How about *that,*" he said.

"Yes. He's changed right around. Heading out this way." Joss pointed at the little red light that represented them. And the line between them, and the suddenly suspect vessel, pointed straight in the direction that the ship with the nuclear lasers had come from.

"Let's go!" Evan said.

"Oh, no. Here we sit. We let him pass us nice and easy. What about it, then?"

"All right."

"No, I didn't mean *that*. The five-letter word for boredom. Where's that classical education gone?"

"Da always said that crossword puzzles were entertainments for the vulgar mind."

"Didn't take the *Times,* did he? 'Ennui.' Put it in there. Then I should be able to get 54 Down."

They sat with the pad between them, and alternately watched the hologram. The trace they were watching arced closer and closer to them. At its closest it was no more than ten kilometers away. It slowed down, lingering, then curved off away from the line they were interested in, heading sunward again.

"Damn," Evan said, and went back to staring at 23 Across.

Joss sat there for several seconds trying both to slow his pulse and find an eight-letter word for an assault, in which the third and fourth letters were C and A.

The console beeped again.

"I knew it," he breathed.

"Escalade," said Evan.

"I knew it, I knew it," Joss said, jumping to look more closely and make sure of the holograph. "Look at him!"

The radar trace had changed course again. It was heading back along the line out into the emptiness, the line they were interested in.

"There he goes," Joss said, almost dancing with glee. "They think we're out here. They're acting like we might be, and they've been wasting time, waiting to see if we would jump them, And we didn't. So now they head on out—"

"To what?" Evan said.

Joss shook his head. "You got me, partner. To a place where you can keep all the guns you've been buying, without nosey neighbors seeing anything there? A place where you can take ships you've ripped off?"

Evan shook his head. "An asteroid off the beaten track?" he said.

"Probably. I would. It'd be cheaper than building a free-standing station. But who is it . . . *who?*"

"Let's go!"

"Not yet."

They waited for another three hours. Every now and then the trace they were following would execute an arc off its proper line of approach, then get back on the line again. Joss watched it, and rubbed his hands, and went back to working on 36 Across, which was "Italian casein-ate" with a Z in the middle. Evan polished his suit, and Joss didn't tease him about it.

And finally there was nothing to do but go after the trace, before they lost it entirely.

THEY FOLLOWED IT FOR A DAY AND A HALF, AT dead slow speed, inching along behind at what was the very edge of their detection range, and what Joss hoped very much was the very edge of their quarry's. They should look more like a shadow to him than he did to them. Only the signal-processing equipment that had been installed in *Nosey*, at Joss's insistence, before leaving the Moon, was making the ship they chased visible to them at all. At the time Evan had thought Joss was just showing off by impressing the techs with the obscure equipment he wanted attached to the computer. Now Evan wasn't so sure.

At the end of the day and a half, something happened to the trace: it began to be fuzzy, as if other physical objects in the area were confusing its signal. "There, then," Joss said to Evan, looking again at the holograph. "What do you make of that?"

Evan looked at the holograph. "We're well above the plane of the Belts now," he said. "But there would still be a few rogue bodies up this high, here and there."

"Of course," Joss said. "So. Radio silence, and slowly in."

Evan nodded. "I wish Lucretia would come up with the bloody information about the guns," he said.

"I do, too. But now we have other things to worry about. There's no settlement in that area on any of the ephemerides. We have definitely found a clandestine operation of some kind. I just think we should get a much closer look, and a better idea of what's going on, before we report in."

Joss looked at Evan, and waited.

He nodded. "I'm with you."

"We'll do it, then."

And they spent another day about it, creeping along through the dark. Evan polished his suit less, and discovered that 36 Across was "Gorgonzola." Joss minded his instruments and kept his curses to himself. He desperately wanted to kick in the iondrivers and blast out along that line, but that was a good way to get extremely dead. He let the computers handle their approach, a long, accidental-looking hyperbola—he knew better than to head straight after the ship they were following—and lay around trying to make sense of Evan's copy of *Pride and Prejudice*.

And at the end of the day, they found the asteroid.

They got a better trace on the ship they had been following first, of course. Joss had his little list of radar signatures ready, and as they started to curve past that distant ship, now slowing greatly, the computer saw a set of readings they recognized. Joss looked up sidelong from the console at Evan and said, "Know who that is?"

"Who?"

"That's another ship made out of pieces of missing craft. Atypical power curve, from what little signal I can get. Like his friend the other day. Not much engine, but too much gun."

"A patrol?" Evan said. "Sent out to find out what happened to the other ship?"

Joss nodded thoughtfully. "It seems likely. And sent out to kill whatever killed its buddy, if at all possible. As you say: a patrol. But he didn't find what he was looking for, meaning us, and he's just heading for home. And there's home."

He pointed at the larger, fuzzier trace in the holograph. Slowly, some other traces were becoming apparent in the area, some of them moving quite fast, their dots in the holograph shading up through blue or down through red as they Dopplered. "It's a base," Joss said.

"And for some pretty big stuff," Evan said, noticing the size-and-mass readings on some of the traces becoming visible around it.

"Yes. But much more small stuff. And some of it seriously overengined. Look at that one there. What the hell kind of driver have they got stuffed into that little shell? Or worse," Joss added, "what kind of weapon have they got attached to it? Makes you think, doesn't it?"

"No question," said Evan, sounding somber.

Joss nodded. "This is going to be interesting," he said. "Shall we go closer?"

"I think we'd best."

Joss nodded. For the first time in a good while he sat down at the command console and took control of the ship away from the computer. "Now," he said, "we tiptoe."

He spent another six hours, all told, edging the ship in closer and closer to the base they were stalking. When people had money of the kind it took to buy state-of-the-art weaponry, there was no telling what kind of imaging equipment they had. But the image system hadn't yet been invented that could cope with a trace that was hardly moving at all. Joss moved them in closer and closer at what was barely more than a walking pace, though it made him half mad with anticipation.

At seventy kilometers he let *Nosey* coast to a dead stop, with only one blast of the attitudinal jets to help, and said to Evan, "I think this is a good place to consider our options."

Evan sat down by him and nodded. They both considered the holograph.

At the middle of it was an asteroid: a fairly big one, about ten kilometers by five by five. Its own radar signature made it plain that there were large holes in it; it had been extensively slagged out. Various vessels were moored to its surface. Every now and then the asteroid's signature changed as a vessel came out of it. There never seemed to be less than five or six small vessels in space around it at any given time.

"Close patrol?" Joss said to Evan. "They're in and out of ten kilometers, usually."

"Possibly. Possibly just training maneuvers of some kind."

Joss nodded. "Not a lot of incoming traffic at the moment. But there seems to be some outgoing, heading sunward. Larger vessels. Cargo, perhaps?"

Evan tilted his head, thinking. "Probably."

"And our young friend," Joss said, "just popped inside there. Did you see that? For service, probably. Check the tires and water, then go out again and try to shoot up the sops who shot up the last ship out. Anybody who sees the vessel without looking for a specific radar signature will see just another mining ship. Until it blasts them to kingdom come."

Evan looked at him. "It would be a useful way to hide a little space navy," he said. "Further in toward the Sun, who looks twice at a beat-up trawler with a Belts registration? A poor cousin, in from the sticks to see the big city lights."

"And carrying one of his own," Joss said.

"I should very much like to go in and blow them all up," Evan said, "but I think we're a bit outgunned. What do you think, Officer O'Bannion?"

"Officer Glyndower," Joss said, "I think this is a good time to hold very still, and very quiet, and scream like hell for backup."

He went off to get his pad and write a note to Lucretia.

SIX

☆

AND TWO AND A HALF HOURS PASSED; AND
two and a half hours more; and they were very, very long.

"What's a six-letter word for diatribe?" Evan said.

Joss shook his head at him, staring at the hologram.
Evan sighed and leaned back. He had been that way for a
good while now, not very communicative at all. Evan's
grandmother would have said he looked "fey," which
meant grim and dangerous to most people, but with Evan's
grandmother the word had been meant to indicate any expression she didn't like the look of. As a rule, she would
hit anyone who was wearing such an expression, as hard
as she thought appropriate for their age, and ask, "What's
up your tail, then?"

Evan wouldn't have minded having his grandmother
around at the moment.

But there was someone else he would have preferred
having around even more.

"Penny for them," he said to Joss.

"Huh?"

"I said, a penny for your thoughts."

Joss stretched and sat back, faking an annoyed expression. "I would have thought they were worth more."

Evan's mouth set wryly. "Some might think so. But are
they people who know you?"

'You're no help," Joss said. "What the hell is keeping
Lucretia? *That's* what I'm thinking."

"The thought had crossed my mind as well," Evan said.

There was a deep, black silence for a few moments.
"You know," Joss said, "even if they send us the whole
damn Space Forces as backup, how long is it going to take
them to get here?"

"There *is* that problem. And how are they going to get
in here without being massively noticed? And possibly cut
into many tiny pieces?"

Joss nodded. It was a conclusion that was difficult to
avoid. The Space Forces were famous for the speed of
their craft—which most sops described as "nine speeds of
reverse"—and for the oversize and antiquity of their weapons, bought for them slowly and grudgingly by an acquisitions department that found anything more advanced than
rubber bands "needlessly complex and likely to malfunc-
tion in combat.' The truth of it was that the Space Force
had very little to do, since the planets had become feder-
ated. The nations on Earth were at peace with one another, by and large, and as far as the planets themselves
were concerned, it was economically unfeasible for them
to make war on each other. Each of the worlds had re-
sources that the others vitally needed, and any one of them
who tried to attack or invade another would pay for it
within months with the utter collapse of its own economy.
Space travel was not *that* cheap, not yet, and maybe
wouldn't be for centuries yet.

The Space Forces were still there because whenever
anyone suggested dismantling them, there was a ruckus
similar to that long ago when someone suggested that the
Swiss army might benefit from being abolished. The Space
Forces were widely seen as a far-flung peacekeeping force,
like the armed detachments of the old United Nations, and
people had become fond of it in the worst possible way.
That is, they had come to think peace depended upon it,
rather than upon them.

But the Space Forces were fairly useless when it came
to quick mobilization or any kind of military intervention
that didn't involve planetkiller bombs. "When they do
show up," Joss said gloomily, "these little ships will come

out and cut them in pieces. That's all. Those huge scows they have bobbing around out there have all the delicate maneuverability of an elephant seal in a double sink.''

Evan nodded. But then he looked up at Joss with an expression of growing horror.

''You don't suppose . . .''

''What?''

''You don't suppose they're dragging their heels about answering us so that we'll go in there and try to sort this mess out ourselves?''

Joss made an unhappy face at him. ''One Ranger,'' he said, ''one riot.''

''I hate you sometimes,'' Evan said.

''Possibly not as much as you should,'' Joss said, ''but fortunately, it always seems to be temporary.''

They looked at each other for a few minutes.

''No way,'' Joss said finally. ''I come down with limb paralysis at the damnedest times. This is a little above us, boyo. Us and about five heavy cruisers, yes. But alone??''

Evan shook his head.

''Let's wait,'' he said.

They both sat back and listened to the silence for a few seconds.

''And what if they don't say anything at all?'' Joss said. ''For, say, a few days?''

Evan raised his eyebrows. ''By then,'' he said, ''you'd think someone would have found us. We're not exactly a long way away from these people.''

''If we don't move, we're all right.''

''But the odds still favor their stumbling on us sooner or later, Joss. We might *have* to do something.''

''Horrible thought,'' Joss said, and made a great show of going back to *Pride and Prejudice*.

Evan bent back over Joss's crossword pad and started worrying away at the six-letter word for ''diatribe'' again.

''Evan,'' Joss said, ''tell me something.''

Evan looked up, raised his eyebrows again.

''Do you really think you love her?''

Evan's mouth fell open. Then he closed it and thought.

"I think it has to be love," he said, and put the pad down, folding his arms. "She seems to get in everywhere. I can't stop wanting to talk about her, even when it feels stupid to do it. I don't want to believe bad things about her, even when I know they might be true. I feel like part of me is missing." He shook his head. "I don't know what else to call it."

Joss looked at him, almost pityingly, Evan thought. Had it come from anyone else, Evan would not have been able to cope with that look. From Joss, it was acceptable, even slightly funny. "What are you going to do about it?" Joss asked him. "Your lifestyle, if that's the word for what we have, isn't going to make for much of a married life. If that's what you have in mind. Not that you necessarily do. Not that there aren't married sops, of course."

"Hadn't thought you were going into counseling," Evan said, a little drily.

Joss waved his hands in a negative gesture. "Don't be an idiot." And he fell silent.

Evan looked at him and shook his head. "Joss," he said, "I don't know what I'm going to do. Really I don't. I just want to know where she is. I just want—"

Joss nodded and picked up the book again. "Right," he said, in the voice of one man who was desperately sorry he had brought the whole thing up.

One of the alarms at the control console went off and Joss jumped up to see to it, much more quickly than usual. He had hooked various proximity alarms to the radar and the mass scanners, just on general principle. Though they were well above the plane of the Belts proper, there was still a chance that some random rock might come drifting into them. And there were more immediate dangers which might find them and poke holes in them with missiles or something even more destructive.

Joss stood over the holograph, which he had hyped up to the best view they could get from that distance without waking up someone's targeting radar. "Just a couple more ships popping out of the inside of the asteroid,'' he said. ''Probably another patrol.''

''Does it seem to you that they're getting a bit more active?'' Evan said.

Joss shrugged. ''Hard to say. Our statistical sample is on the sparse side.''

''So what else is new?'' Evan looked over at the holograph, then said, ''Wait a minute. Was that another one?''

''Yes,'' Joss said, and sat down to watch the holograph for a moment or so. Another small bright dot—another ship—popped suddenly into existence. And one more.

''That's the most we've seen formating at once,'' Evan said.

''And here come a few more. What is this?'' Joss said.

They watched ship after ship suddenly appear around the asteroid. ''Ten of them now,'' Evan said.

''Look at that,'' Joss said. ''They're doing a real formation.''

There was no more movement for a few minutes. Then an eleventh ship appeared, took its place at the front of the formation of ten, and slowly they moved off together.

Sunward.

Joss and Evan looked at each other.

''What's the total we've counted there so far?'' Evan said.

''I make it about fifteen total,'' Joss said. ''At least, there are fifteen sets of signatures I recognize, including five sets of signatures that belong to ships we were investigating as reported missing.'' He sat down at the comms console and began tapping at it. ''Which is something I want to look at. Keep an eye on that for me, if you would.''

''Right,'' Evan said, and did so. But there were no changes, really; the formated ships simply continued to head away from the asteroid.

''Where are they going?'' Evan said.

''Tell you in a minute,'' Joss said. ''I'm working on something else right now. They still all together?''

''Yes, they are.''

"Good."

There was no more sound for several minutes, as Joss worked on his console. "There now," he said, and in the holographic display there appeared the black box signatures of each ship in the group, the broadcast ID number and name of each.

"They're splitting up," Evan said.

"I thought they might," Joss said. "Keep an eye on them."

He tapped at his console again. The course of the group as a whole appeared in the holograph; a long line reaching straight out of the display, ever so slightly curved. Joss tapped at the console and increased the scale. The line reached out, up above the Belt, heading inward.

"There," Joss said. "I thought they might do that. Look at the IDs."

They were changing. One by one, the patterns of letters and numbers were replaced by new ones. "Fake transponders." Joss said. "Stolen. Look at them."

Evan looked at the annotation Joss brought up in the bottom on the holograph. "Some of those," he said, thinking a bit, "are out of Willans, aren't they?"

Joss nodded. "And some of them are ships that haven't been reported as missing. Yet. See that one on the left? *Lark?* That's the ship that belongs to the people who passed us as we first came in. You remember: the ones who spat at us, and told us to move *Nosey* out of the way." He looked grim. "Want to bet the pilots are dead?"

"I wouldn't take your money," Evan said softly, looking at the other IDs changing one by one. "So now they're heading into the inner system—all separately. The country cousins, in to look at the bright lights. And that's not a course for Mars; they'd be heading way over this other side. This bunch is going to Earth." He looked at Joss. "What's going on near Earth over the next few days?"

Joss looked at him with an expression that Evan couldn't decipher. "You truly don't remember? Well, we *have* been busy."

Evan stared at Joss. "What am I, then, a bloody social calendar?" he asked.

And then got quiet.

"Oh, heaven," he said. "The HighLands L5 is opening. Is it not? All those VIPs in one place, all that investment capital, all that cooperation. What a lovely target for a terrorist. To hold for ransom-" HIs breath caught in his chest again. "Or to blow up—"

"Seems likely, doesn't it?" Joss said. "God only knows the why of it. But we have a little time to find out. They can't go faster than ships of their kind normally would, or they'll blow their cover. At best, they might be in Earth orbit, oh, in thirty-six hours. If I can get Lucretia to come out of her hole—!"

But Evan had other thoughts in his mind. "Listen to me, Joss," he said. "There are other concerns for the moment. Just about all the firepower in that place has emptied out right in front of us."

Joss looked at Evan with dawning horror. "What are you thinking of? Don't tell me. You've been watching too many of my vids—that's the problem. You've got some damn death-or-glory stand in mind."

"Death strikes me as an interference with my plans for the moment," Evan said, "and glory is usually overrated, so you keep telling me. Hush now. Joss, almost all their ships are gone! What do we need the Space Forces for?"

"Phrased that way," Joss said, "the question practically answers itself. But there are other considerations, you dumb Taff. We can't be absolutely sure those guys are going to Earth. Courses can be changed. These guys have been doing that kind of thing for days, on their patrols."

"That wasn't a patrol leaving," Evan said, "and perfectly well you know it. That was a combat group. I know you're going to suggest following them, but there's no point in it! If they notice us—and the further we follow them, the greater the odds of our being noticed—then we're dead. They will chop us up like the garlic in your spaghetti sauce. And at this point, which one would we try to follow, anyway? They've all split up. Hyperbolic orbits, I should think. Do a plot on them and see what you can make of it, fine, but don't waste your time following.''

"You," Joss said, "want to get into your suit and trash that base.''

"Of course not," Evan said. And grinned all over his face.

Joss looked hard at him. "And what am I supposed to be doing while you're playing soldier?"

Evan took a breath, choosing his words carefully. "Neutralization," he said.

Joss eyed him narrowly. Inside Evan rejoiced; he knew from that still look that he had caught Joss's attention perfectly. "I can't go in there without proper cover, after all," he said. "You're going to have to do a little trashing yourself. We could completely ruin this place in a matter of minutes. Kill its radars, mess over the main exit airlocks inside those holes, seal up the people who are there inside. Then I go in and deal with them.''

"Out of the question," Joss said. But he was thinking, and Evan knew it.

"I have to admit," Joss said, "that following them seems futile just now.''

"I'll get my suit," said Evan.

"Now just you wait one goddam minute, you dim-bulb Taff!" Joss shouted after him. "Has something occurred to you?"

"What?"

"If the people who have just left," Joss said, with the exaggerated patience of a man explaining a rainbow to the blind, "get wind of what we're doing, they will come back and trash us. And there goes everything. Your romantic life, my crossword puzzles, the great novel I haven't finished writing yet—"

"I read the first chapter," Evan said. "It's not half bad.''

"What??!"

"Yes," Evan said, "and I found the bug you put on me four days ago, too."

Joss looked stricken.

" 'We don't have a closet,' indeed," said Evan. "So let's hear no more of *that,* you bloody little keyhole-peeping crypto-Irish voyeur!"

Joss actually hung his head. Evan had never seen anyone do that before, and he just stood and enjoyed it for a moment. "And anyway," Evan said, "if you in your great cleverness have in good time managed to kill these people's communications, then no one is going to find out *anything.* And what you can't subvert with your clever machinery, I can blow up."

"My cable," Joss said sadly. But there was a sort of gleam in his eye.

Evan pressed his advantage. "Weren't you talking to me the other week about how easy it was to jam selected frequencies from short range? Eh? You and your jargon, your superheterodyning and all. Well *do* something with it! Check their frequencies and jam them solid. And then I'll find their transmitter masts and dishes, and blow them. Or you will. And with no way to yell for help, and three-fifths of their force gone—"

"Leaving me with five ships to blow by myself?"

"Na na na na na na na na naaaaaaaa," Evan said softly, in exact imitation of Joss.

Joss looked at him, eight-tenths convinced, with his eyes saying yes and his mouth saying no. "You don't even know who Bill Cosby is," he said.

Evan said, "I should very much like to find out. But if we sit here much longer, and some one of those lads comes out to do a patrol, I may not have the chance. Make up your mind, Joss *bwri.*"

Joss knit his brows together, then abruptly let them loose. "Fortune favors the brave," he said. "Or something like that. But plainly we can't wait for HQ to get off their butts." He shook his head. "What is going *on* with them?"

"With luck, this will all be over by the time we need to find out. Meanwhile, let's make our preparations. Think a moment."

"Yes," Joss said. He gazed thoughtfully at the radar image of the asteroid. "It looks to me as if a lot of the inside of that is gone. Slagged out and being used for service and so forth."

"And hiding their ships."

"So the actual population is probably pretty small."

"I would think so. Mostly ship's crews and maintenance people. You couldn't afford to have a large population here when you had some big paramilitary operation preparing. It's not even a question of cost. There's the matter of security as well, of too many people knowing too much."

Joss nodded. "All right. So there won't be twelve million storm troopers with guns in there. How long do you think it'll take you to get at the vital parts? You want to take the main power out, I suppose, and the hardware of the radar. I won't be able to target that, though the masts and dishes and so forth will be no problem. But the hardware has to go. Otherwise an emergency setup could be rigged, and our friends could be called back to save the day."

"I couldn't give you an estimate as yet. I think we need to make one close pass," Evan said, "in to about twenty kilometers, to get a good look with our own radar, and with the mass detectors and your RF-detecting equipment. After that I'll know, and I can drop right away."

"Drop?" said Joss.

"Drop, of course; did you think I was going to ask you to land on that rock, you fool? You stay wingloose and do as much damage as you can, and then guard the upper echelon. I'll just bail out the airlock and make my own way down. You'll want the dropping pass to be closer."

"I should think so," Joss said. "Otherwise you'd take a week to get down, with those titchy little jets of yours."

"I'll have you know that I can make twenty mips when I'm in the mood."

"And your mileage is crap," Joss said. "Never mind that. I'll start plotting the recon sweep. You had better send a note to Lucretia, and make sure you tell the pad to scramble and pack it before it squirts. I don't want those clowns with their braided lasers hearing anything but a burp from this direction. And we're not going to start the blowing-up part of the operation before another three hours or so have passed. I want a good safety cushion between me and them, thanks."

"That seems fair," Evan said; and truly there was no arguing it.

It took Joss some time to set up his reconnaisance sweep; and then they went back to waiting again. Evan found this hard, even with his suit waiting for him, even with crossword puzzles to keep him busy. And images of Mell kept intruding. He spent a while writing the message to Lucretia, describing what they were going to be doing, and approximately when; he checked his suit over and over again, paying especial attention to the weapons systems. His beamers in particular were overcharged, which suited him well, and he was well stocked with the little Dart missiles that loaded from his backpack. All his electronics were in order.

There was nothing to do but wait.

And then two hours had passed.

There was still no word from Lucretia. Joss glanced over at him from the command console and said, "Time."

Evan went and got into the suit.

He was twitching slightly as he did so. Usually when he was working in the suit, he was in atmosphere of some kind or another. It was, of course, perfectly spaceworthy. But it was also vulnerable to exactly the same kinds of accidents that less well-armored pressure suits suffered. He could blow a gasket as easily as anyone else, when the suit was in strenuous use.

As far as he knew, though, it was in perfect condition. He would shortly be finding out.

Joss was already adjusting controls at the command console. "All right," he said. "Going to start swinging in now. You might want to lock yourself down. This is going to be tight and fast. I've been monitoring the frequencies they're using, mostly UHF, and I'll jam all of them that I can on the first pass, and pick up the rest on the second. But the less chance we give them to notice that anything untoward is happening, the better, Ready?"

Evan climbed into the seat next to Joss's. He had already spent some time readjusting the straps, "Let's go," he said.

Joss kicked in the iondrivers.

It was a wild ride, even faster than when they had been running from the altered mining ship, and Joss apparently had no concern for what rapid shifts in gee forces might do to a man's stomach. Evan was beginning to regret the late morning's Spaghetti Carbonara, and said as much.

"Shouldn't eat food that goes down so easy," Joss said, and grinned.

Evan rolled his eyes at him—not hard, since they were in the tightest part of the sweep around the asteroid, the top of the hyperbola. He turned his attention to the holograph. It was filling in with added detail of the asteroid; he could see the masts at either end of it now, like those at Willans, the tight-beam transmittal dishes, and the domes containing the power plants that maintained them. "Those are for you, I think," Joss said. "Here's my business."

He pointed in at the artificially enlarged holes in three places on the asteroid's surface. "The airlocks are down in each of those," he said. "If the correlation I'm doing between the radar and the mass-readers is correct, there's a hangar cave behind each one. Blow the doors off, and it's going to make repairs a lot harder for these people to do in the future. If they have a future. Any ships inside them won't, if I have my way. At the same time, there should be pressure-lockable doors inside, so I think we can count on not killing everybody in the place with explosive decompression.''

"Good," Evan said. "I'll try not to take too long about the sweep, through, after you've blown the doors.''

"Yes, well, you'd better not," Joss said, "because it's going to be difficult for me to make pickup on you if you get in trouble. If I ram this ship into the side of an asteroid, Lucretia is going to cancel *both* our expense accounts.''

"She's such a cheapskate," Evan said, letting loose his grip on his seat slightly, as the gee forces declined somewhat with Joss's easing up on the hyperbolic orbit.

"Now, while you're in there," Joss said, "you're going to have to find out if the place has computers for me. And if it does, you take this.'' He rummaged around down beside the command console, and handed Evan a small black box about three inches square, with a shiny metal contact panel on one side.

"This," Joss said, "is a comms pack and latchkey for recalcitrant machinery. Odds are I can get access into their computers, if you can get this onto any contact pad or exposed wiring that the computer has. Make a hole, if you have to. I just wish we still had my cable.''

"You'd need a much longer one," Evan said, tucking the access box into one of the pressure-tight bays on his forearm, the one that held spare grenades.

"Too damn true, but I still miss it. Those alligator clips were useful. If you can get this thing in the right spot, I should be able to dump their whole computer memory, at least everything that's presently running in the machine, into ours. And there ought to be something in it that will explain where our friends just went in such a hurry, and why. And who knows what other happy information we'll find at the same time? Do that first if you can. Then run around and wreak some random damage to keep people from interfering with my download.''

"I think I can manage something of that kind," Evan said.

"I just bet you can. All right," Joss said. "Take a good look at that holo. You want to copy it into your armpad?"

"I have it stored as a sketch already."

"Good. So shout for pickup when you're ready. And stay away from those airlocks until I'm finished with them."

"I'll do that."

"Good. Evan—"

With a look of mild embarrassment, Joss held out a hand. Evan took it.

"Break a leg, you dumb Taff," Joss said.

"Godspeed to you too," Evan said, and headed for the airlock.

He felt the gee forces beginning to pile up again as Joss started the second pass, the really close one. "I'm going to be firing," Joss shouted at him, "so for pity's sake, don't get in my way!"

"The first thing they taught us in Para was to jump backwards," Evan said, as he climbed into the airlock and sealed his helm.

"Oh? What was the second?"

Evan told him. Joss laughed so hard he started to choke.

"All set," Evan said.

Joss finished his choking and said, "Are your comms on scramble?"

"Yes, they are."

"Good. Never hurts to check. Fifteen seconds."

Evan sealed the inner door of *Nosey*'s airlock, waited for the air to exhaust, and opened the outer. Stars wheeled past it; Joss was turning hard.

"Ten seconds. Backward and to your left as you're facing the lock," Joss said. "That's the far end of the asteroid, and the first mast."

"Right you are."

"Five seconds. Three, two, one, jump!"

Evan pushed himself out the lock, hard, and kicked his

jets in downward and leftward. The ship slipped silently by behind him; he saw the gleam of dim sunlight off the broad silvery parabolic scoop of the iondriver. Evan tucked himself into a ball, gave himself another push of the leg jets, and "fell" toward the asteroid's surface as quickly as he could.

Off to his right, he could see *Nosey* diving around toward the first of the huge airlock apertures, not intending to go straight in, but to pass over low. As she did, two bright streaks leapt away from her, down into the hole. A moment later, a huge bloom of blue fire and dust came billowing out. The fire only lasted a second, but the dust kept rising from where the missiles had fallen, a plume already a quarter-kilometer long and still growing. Evan uncurled a bit, eyeing his first target, the comms mast at the narrow end of the asteroid. There was no point in waiting; he could manage a precision strike very well from here, and not have to wait around.

He turned one arm forearm-up, pointed it at the base of the mast, and curled a finger back to hit the patterned release in his palm. The missile kicked out of his arm, pushing him back a little with the recoil. Without thinking, he bent his knees as he fell, corrected with his leg jets, and fired off another, just to be sure. *You can never tell, sometimes the cable that serves things like this is armored. . . .*

Evan counted silently. On five, the mast blew off the end of the satellite in a rain of splinters of metal and stone. The second missile hit the place where the mast had been anchored, dug a two-meter-deep hole in it, and revealed a thick buried cable, now snapped off short.

Good, Evan thought, and turned his attention to the business of landing. The surface of the asteroid was some three hundred meters below him now and coming up fast. This was no problem; landings in zero gee were something a suited sop was trained in until they presented no more problems than jumping off a bottom step. He landed, bounced hard; the suit's restringing had been a good job, and he got much more bounce out of the landing than usual. The first leap bounce was fifty meters long at least, and carried him almost to the next set of antennaes, a dish grouping.

What is it about architects that makes them put all the antennae together in the same place? Evan thought absently, as he pointed another small missile at the middle of the grouping. *Sure, the cabling is simpler, but people can come in the middle of the night and do stuff like— this—* The dish antennas shattered, leaping off the surface of the asteroid and flying in all directions.

That's the VHF and UHF done, then, and any tight-beam micro they may have. As soon as I get the other one— He bounced faster, concerned that no one had even come out to shoot at him yet. What were they all doing in there? Playing pinochle?

A shudder ran all through the surface of the asteroid when Evan next touched ground. *Here comes Joss,* he thought, and sure enough in less than thirty seconds the sleek long shape of *Nosey* came swooping around again, in a tighter approach even than last time, barely fifty meters above the surface, and heading straight for another of the big airlock apertures. Evan saw the bombs rocket down into it, saw the dust and flame come streaming out again, as Joss skimmed past around the other side of the asteroid and was gone.

Diw, but he can fly that thing, Evan thought admiringly as he made his way swiftly across the grey-brown surface to the second mast. He got another missile ready for it. Odds were he wouldn't need them inside the station; for doors and walls he had grenades, and for anything else, his beamer was charged.

"News in from Lucretia," said a voice in his helmet. "You're not going to like it. Details later. Meanwhile, just got the third big hole, and all five of the chicks in the nest. She's all yours."

"Right-o," Evan said, and let his missile loose at the

second mast. The missile hit it hard, at the base, and the whole thing toppled.

He bounced over to the base just to make sure. The cable had in fact not been severed. He beamed it; it split in a brief haze of smoke and sparks. Then he turned and headed for the nearest of the shattered airlocks.

The hole itself was still intact. Evan swan dived off the edge of it, using his jets to give him some extra push. The airlock doors below had been massive semicircles. They were now a ruin, the thick metal bent back inward. He continued his dive down through them, through the second set of doors—which Joss's bombs had also taken out—and down into what had been the hanger.

The hangar was a spherical area which had been slagged out of the rock; ships had been tethered to its walls and floor. There were hulks there that had been miners' ships once. Joss had beamed them. How he managed it, Evan wasn't sure. He hadn't seen it happening. The hangar had airlocked pressure doors in several of its walls. Evan chose the middle one, opened it, ducked inside.

There were still lights here, and power; Joss had not yet found the power plant, which was all right with Evan. Alarms were howling all over the place. Well, it could hardly be avoided, with Joss blowing the doors in, and five ships dead in their hangars. *No matter.* Inside his helm, Evan did the pattern of eyelid-flickers that brought down the radiation-sensitive filter. It was RF he was looking for: computers of the kind Joss was after still tended to leak it. There was a dim glow to his left.

He started off that way, looking around him as he bounced through the corridors. This place was everything that Willans should have been and wasn't: neat, clean, new. Surprisingly new; these hallways could hardly be more than a year old.

He was distracted by a man coming out in front of him, with a gun. The man shot at him.

Slugs? Evan thought with surprise, as the stream of high-velocity bullets piled into him. Normally one didn't use slugs in an airtight environment, preferring beams. At any rate, the servos took the difference, helping him keep his balance. He staggered slightly, walked straight into the stream of bullets. The man looked at him in shock and his ammunition clip abruptly ran out. He turned to run away and change it.

Evan lifted his right arm and let the built-in machine gun do the talking for him. The man fell twitching to the floor in a spray of red.

Evan headed past him and looked at a sign on the wall of the T-junction of the corridor. It was in Japanese, both *kanji* and *katakana*.

So much for the classical education, Evan thought sadly. He didn't understand Japanese. He consulted his RF detector: it still said left. Experimentally, he tilted his head first up, then down, to see if there was a variation of reading. *A little more on the up side,* he thought. *All right: I want a lift, then.*

He jogged along the corridor, warily watching the doorways. No one came out of them, which slightly surprised him. *This place must have really emptied out.* But that suited him, too.

From around a corner ahead of him, a group of men burst out, all armed. Evan noticed that they were each wearing a sort of coverall that amounted to a uniform; there were what seemed to be rank tags on the sleeves, and possibly name tags as well. But then he had other things to think about, as they opened fire on him.

It was beams as well as slugs this time, and relatively high-powered ones at that. But that was one of the things reflective armor was for, and Evan hadn't kept polishing it for his health. The shine was as much a part of the defense as the ablative coating underneath. He walked right into the stream of fire, the bullets bouncing off all around him, the reflected beams glancing harmlessly off. *All right,* he thought, *let's see if I can't leave one of you lads alive.*

He began shooting, with care and resolution: head shots.

One by one he picked them off with short bursts of the machine gun, wanting to conserve his own ammunition, until there was only one man standing. The look of panic in that man's face was awful, and Evan could understand it perfectly; the horror of the faceless, invulnerable suit bearing down on you was a weapon he had learned to exploit a long time back. The man fired his gun uselessly until it was empty, then turned to run. With great care Evan swept his beamer across the backs of the man's knees, effectively hamstringing him. Screaming, the man fell down.

Evan bounced over to him, grabbed him by the back of his coverall, and jerked him to his feet, shaking him to keep him from going into shock. "Where are the master computers?" he said.

The man stared at him in utter terror. "Where are the computers?" Evan repeated, and for good measure put his hands around the man's neck and began to squeeze. That was something most people understood, especially when they knew something of the power inherent in a suit. Nobody wanted his head twisted off like a chicken's.

"Uh-uh-up one," the man said, "far end."

"Thank you," Evan said. He clouted the man on the side of the head hard enough to keep him asleep for about a day, and dropped him. It was always nice to know that your equipment was giving you the right information.

He turned down what looked like a major corridor and ran into some more people, about ten of them this time. They all had high-intensity beamers, and Evan walked into them firing, not wanting to let too many of them get to work on his armor at the same time. It might have gotten hot inside. *And I just had this foam replaced, after all,* he thought. *No use smelling it up.* One by one they fell, not being armored against the beams of his Winchester as he was against their guns.

As he started walking through the bodies, he paused to pick up one of the guns, curious. It was of very good make, a Toshiba by the looks of it, though it didn't have the usual brand name flash on the barrel. *Private manufacture?* he wondered. *Very, very interesting. If I didn't know there was a lot of money involved in this venture, I'd know now.*

He came to a lift. Generally, Evan preferred stairs, but this would do for the moment. The lift was still sitting at this floor, probably having been ridden down here by the group of people who had just attacked him. He got in, looked at the controls-in Japanese again, but this time with Arabic numerals as well. This floor was six, to judge by the number that was presently lit. He punched for seven, and waited.

The doors closed, and the elevator hummed quietly to itself. Then it stopped, and its doors opened.

Someone threw a grenade in.

That's antisocial, Evan thought. He picked up the grenade and walked out of the elevator.

The small group of men in coveralls standing there looked at Evan in tremendous shock, then in worse shock at the grenade he flipped back at them. It went off.

When the smoke had cleared a bit, he checked his RF detector and went on, to his right this time, stepping over the shredded meat. He paused, looking down at what remained of one of the bodies. It was mostly trunk, with an arm and shoulder still attached by a few strings of muscle and ligament. On the shoulder was one of the rank tabs he had seen before, and below it, an insignia. Evan bent close to look. It was a stylized blue dragon.

He straightened up, frowning. He had seen that insignia—that logo—many times, as had everybody else who lived on Earth: hundreds of products wore it somewhere in their packaging, from cars to food. Evan hunted in his mind for a moment, then came up with the umbrella corporation's name: TKB International, it was. One of the multinationals. Japanese-run, he thought.

He thought of the Japanese signage on the walls, frowned, and went on.

No one else came to meet him for a while, which suited

him. *Somehow I would have thought there were fewer people here,* he thought. *But it argues the presence of a large support force. What have they been building here besides weapons, I wonder? Or what have they been preparing for? They're certainly well-enough armed.*

As he came around the curve in the corridor, he was met by a stream of bullets. *Now, this really is annoying,* he thought, as he actively had to fight against the stream to keep upright. Someone down there was using a fixed-mount gun instead of the little portable stuff they had been using on him. He waded into the bullets, pushing harder and harder as he got closer to the gun, and slowly raising one arm as he got nearer. It was one of those machine guns that hit you with six hundred slugs a second, and there was a large shield behind it to keep you from picking off the person who was doing the firing.

I must be getting close to something good, he thought, and came up to the front of the gun. Bullets splattered off him in normally impossible ricochet angles as he picked up the gun by its muzzle, made sure of his grip, and then heaved it over.

The man on the other side of the shield sprawled over backwards. Evan shot him and moved on, pausing only a moment to look at his uniform. It, too, had the blue dragon insignia. Then he turned his attention back to the RF detector. The incidence of RF in the area was getting quite strong.

Evan walked on, seeing and hearing no one further for the time being. *It didn't take very long to mobilize when we came in,* he thought. *Definitely a paramilitary organization of some kind. Filing clerks would hardly respond that quickly to an armed incursion. And their aim is pretty good. Not that it's been helping them.*

He paused at a T-junction, and looked both ways to see what the RF detector suggested. It suggested that he go right. He did, and as he passed one doorway, the reading peaked, then began to fall off a bit.

Aha, Evan thought, and tried the door. Locked. Well,

there were remedies for that. He leaned against it and gave it a good push. It didn't give right away. *Armored,* he thought. *Excellent. So there is something sensitive in there. But I'd really rather not take the chance of damaging any of the equipment in there—Joss would have my head.*

Evan set himself squarely in front of the door, found his balance point, and pushed, really leaning into it this time. The door groaned, resisting him. *Reinforced hinges,* he thought, *inside right—* He administered a few focused blows to that side of the door with one gauntlet, then pushed again. His servos whined in protest.

He ignored them and kept pushing.

And the door fell inward, off its hinges, Evan fell in with it.

He bounced to his feet, expecting more shooting, and annoyed by the prospect; he didn't want this equipment hurt. But there was no one else in the room. *All right,* he thought, and looked around the place. The room had that same sort of tidy sterility that computer rooms had had for some centuries now; empty space, with low black cabinets lined up around the walls, and a central table for the people who worked at the computer and tended it.

He picked one of the black boxes, out of the way in a corner, and noted approvingly that it was a little way away from the wall. He reached down, felt around for a ventilating panel, found one, and carefully tugged it off. He tapped open the fairing on his arm and came up with Joss's widget; then looked around to see if he could find a contact pad inside the machine. Fortunately it was one of those that took plug-in modules, and the contact seats that those used would work just fine. Evan snugged Joss's little black box down against one of them and broke radio silence for the first time. "Need a check from you," he said.

There was a pause. "Reading you quite clearly," Joss said, "and I confirm that twice. Don't worry about it; you take care of business there, and I'll take care of it here."

"Right," Evan said. He replaced the ventilating cover

on the back of the machine, pushed it exactly into place, and headed out to see what else he could see. There was something itching him, a hunch, a feeling that there was something he ought to look into. Evan tended to trust his hunches. Outside the door he paused and said to the hunch, *All right, ride me. Where do you want to go?*

For a moment there was simply nothing. Then he thought he might go off to the right a bit further.

He went.

JOSS SAT AT HIS COMMS CONSOLE, SWEATING. He had six kinds of alarm set up for the detection of any kind of radio traffic, for abnormal radiation, for motion outside the ship. They were all on the job, but at a moment like this he could never quite bring himself to trust them.

The little black box he had given to Evan was in place and was doing its job—or at least, it would start to, as soon as Joss could figure out what to tell it to do. Evan had been canny enough to install it in what was apparently one of the machine's processing cores. *Or he was lucky. We'll find out later.* But in the meantime, all Joss was seeing on his readout screen was a flow of hexadecimal gibberish. The machine was in the middle of executing some program, and not one that he could understand just by reading it.

He instructed his logic probe to feel around a bit and see what else it could find. Its eye slid into another area of memory, found it static, not executing. All very well, but no use to Joss at the moment. It was files he wanted, not programs. He instructed the box to look for simple storage files.

The search came up with a long stream of more gibberish. In the whole system, the black box didn't see a single type of file name that it recognized.

Garbage, Joss thought. *No one has that much security*

in a machine. Someone's probably encoded the file allocation tables, mixing descriptions of files together with sizes and dates and so forth. That would be a good way to produce this result.

He told the black box to break off, then set it to send data through to *Nosey*'s own computer, and started it reading the encoded file allocation table again. Once he had it all, he woke up the cryptoanalysis program that he had been working on sporadically for all these months with the ladies in Crypto on the Moon. Code had been a hobby of Joss's since his father had given him an antique Commander Bleep decoder ring when he was eight. It had turned out to be a useful hobby when he was older; maybe it would be more useful today than it had been for a long time.

The computer naturally made no sound while it worked. Sometimes he wished it would; tape carrels that went around and around, or lights that flashed on and off, would have added to the effect. But it didn't really matter. He preferred fast function to any amounts of lights, especially on a day like this.

Nothing seemed to happen for a shockingly long time. Joss sweated. Without the evidence about goings-on here that these files would provide, he and Evan would be in shit of a depths and smelliness such as they had never experienced before. Or would again, since they would certainly both be thrown out of the SP in short order. *Come on, machine,* he said, *get you act in gear here!*

The machine sat and thought to itself, and didn't say a thing.

Oh, come on, come on—

EVAN WAS STALKING.

He had been in a corridor one level down from where the computer was, moving quietly and looking down toward a T–junction about a hundred yards away. Hearing footsteps, he had tucked himself into a doorway, out of sight. There he had stayed for a moment.

Down at the end of the corridor, at the *T,* a man with a large package under his arm had paused, looked down the corridor, then hurried on again.

Evan's curiosity was piqued. He had waited about three seconds, then gone loping down the corridor in silence. He had had to dive sideways again; another figure in a coverall and a baseball cap had been fairly close behind the first man, and was hurrying after him.

Evan waited another second or so, then hurried up the corridor himself and paused at the corner of it to see where the two of them were going.

Straight on down. Evan paused, then very softly followed them.

They did not use a lift; they took a stairwell some distance down the corridor, first the tall figure with the package, then the smaller one with the cap. Evan waited a decent interval, and stepped down softly after them.

They went down a fair distance, four levels. Evan had been keeping a map in the helmet's memory of the places where he had been so far, and this put him and the people he was pursuing not too far from the airlock at which he had made his entry. This was good enough news; if he had to get out fast, he could.

Suddenly, about two levels down, the sound of their footsteps stopped. Evan hurried down as quietly as he could, getting rid of the RF detector and putting up an infrared detector instead. He could see the traces of their bodies' passage in the air, now, and be sure of not missing where they went.

No one but they had been down this stairwell for some time, so the track was clear. One taller, cooler shape, one smaller and hotter were both exiting this doorway. Evan pulled it open silently, looked out. Both traces went to the right. Visually, both people were already gone, around the next corner. He followed.

And he knew he was onto something hot, literally, when

he saw the yellow trefoil on black on the wall, and an arrow pointing down the hallway, and both of the traces headed that way. *Hot dog,* Evan thought, *the reactor!*

He began to hurry. The thought occurred to him that there might be something nasty in the package under that guy's arm.

He paused at a bend in the corridor, looked around. There was a door open in the next bend of the hall, and the second figure, the smaller one, was just slipping inside it. Evan made a small tossing motion with his arm, triggering the autoloader that would flip another magazine into his machine gun. He stepped forward.

A man's scream came from inside the room with the open door.

Evan ran forward, his gun ready, and as he reached the doorway he saw the two shapes in their coveralls struggling fiercely on the floor. The package was cast off to one side. The baseball cap fell off one of the fighting figures as it struggled to get to its feet—

—and long, long, black hair spilled out from under it.

Evan's breath stuck just under his sternum, and his heart skipped several beats it didn't particularly need. He dashed in, picked up the package, and tossed it out into the hall so hard that it threatened to dent the wall. There was a muffled *boom* as it hit, and debris came raining in the doorway a second later.

That done, Evan went over to the man on the floor, who was launching himself at Mell, caught the guy by the front of his coverall, and side swiped him so hard that his head came off, flew across the room, and fetched up against a control console with a very audible crack.

Evan turned and put up his visor, just for the moment. "Mell," he said.

She stared at him in utter shock, then ran to him and threw her arms around his suit. Evan made a silent resolution to get it off as soon as possible.

"Where the bloody devil have you been?" he said. "What are you doing here?"

"They brought me. They were people from Willans, Evan, people I knew! Some of them stopped by my place, said they had a repair job for me. But they wouldn't quite say what it was, and I got suspicious and told them I was busy. So they upped the ante." She shrugged, "I like money, but not that much, not if I'm not happy with the job. So they snatched me. Dragged me off here, wherever here is, and gave me this great useless heap of scrap metal, old ships, and told me to start mating the engine shells and the cargo pods together." She wiped her hair out of her face, the old familiar gesture. "I think they were adding some equipment to them afterwards—"

"I *know* they were, *cariad*. Listen, we can't take time for this now. We have to get you a P-suit and get you out of here." Evan looked around him in mild annoyance and added, "They were going to blow up their reactor's control room? Surely they knew the whole thing would go supercritical and blow—"

"To destroy the evidence, I thought. I knew someone was busting into this station, and I thought it might be you, and I didn't want the evidence destroyed. You'll need it. Evan, these are some kind of crazy people. They were going on about splitting the world up, splitting up the Planets. Getting the world back to the way it used to be before the Union."

"Separate countries?" Evan said, repulsed. "All that fighting again—are you crazy?"

"They probably think it's a good idea," Mell said. "I think they're arms manufacturers on the side. But a whole lot of these people are just plain raving loonies, Evan. Just fanatics. I heard them talking all the time, and it gave me the creeps. All this victory-or-death stuff."

"Wonderful," Evan said. "Come on, though."

Together they went out into the corridor. It was full of debris from the packed charge that Evan had tossed out there, and there was a good big hole in the wall. "Excellent," Evan said, and grabbed the wall by the wire reinforcing in it. "Let's see. Stand back a bit, Mell, if you would."

Eyeing him suspiciously, she did. Evan made sure of his grip and pulled a ten-foot section of the wall away, with reinforcement and some plascrete still sticking to it. "Shut that door for me, will you?" he said.

Mell slapped the door's closer panel. Evan pointed his arm beamer at it and fused it solid. Then he leaned the section of wall against the door, tamping it into place.

"That should keep anyone who's still alive from trying that little trick," he said. "at least until Joss has what he needs. After that, it won't matter. But I don't think there's anyone left alive here. Anyway, come on—let's find you a suit, and I'll tow you out to the ship. I don't want to linger here."

JOSS SAT AT HIS CONSOLE, MUTTERING. THE cryptography program was sitting there thinking to itself, doing nothing in particular, or so it seemed. "Come on, you dumb pile of code," Joss said, "let's get on with it."

Nothing.

Perhaps it had hung up. It *was* a privately written program, after all. There were always bugs lurking in such—

The screen began to fill with file names.

"Aha," Joss said with vast relief. "That's what I wanted to see." He had no idea what all the files meant. That would take hours to tell, perhaps days, as he started sifting through them. But he had to get them first, and the home system would certainly object.

Or it would try to. Joss grinned.

He tapped a set of commands into the console. Down on the asteroid his little black box woke up and sent a small, tight burst of code into the station computer's main processor. This was perhaps the easiest part: injecting the virus. The question was how long it would take to work.

Joss thought he recognized the software systems the machine was using—off-the-shelf stuff, not custom. That helped a bit. But a clever programmer could do quite a lot of customizing in the area of security, if he was feeling paranoid, or merely playful.

And there was really no way to tell what was going on, at least not while the virus itself was replicating. When it had control of the central processor, it would let him know. Meanwhile he had to leave it to its own devices. It was a clever enough virus; it did a very sophisticated job of copying itself into numerous places, too quickly for whatever flu-shot programs were already resident to do anything about it. Once it was established, it would take about ten minutes to copy the entire contents of that computer into *Nosey*'s data banks.

It would be faster, though, if I still had my cable, Joss thought mournfully.

There was a noise in the airlock. Joss didn't bother being startled; the lock was voiceprinted, and he knew perfectly well who it would be. Though Evan was a bit early, by his reckoning.

"We have company," Evan's voice said cheerfully.

"Oh?" Joss turned to see Mell come in behind Joss. "Well, well! So that's where you were!"

"I caught her," Evan said, "in the act of trying to kill the guy who was trying to blow the station up, so *you* wouldn't find out what was going on."

Joss smiled slightly. "Mell," he said, "if I've misjudged you, apologies. You just seem to have a gift for looking as if you might be on the other side of the argument."

"How are we doing?" Evan said.

Joss glowered at the screen. "Nothing yet. I'm still infecting the computer. Or trying to. But I know all the file names I want. There's a pile of stuff in there, Evan. Text files mostly."

"Good," Evan said. "Everybody in there was heavily

armed—no suits, though. It's a paramilitary group, well financed, from at least one Japanese corporation.''

"TKB, they said,'' said Mell. "Evan, they were proud of it, they were bragging about it. I saw some of their execs touring the place a couple of days ago, when they brought me in to fix their miserable ships.'' She looked angrily at Evan. "Some of those belonged to people I know. Or knew!''

"I know,'' Evan said.

"Aha!'' Joss said, almost singing. "Got it!''

"Good,'' Evan said. "Get the goodies down, and let's run. What was the message from Lucretia, by the way?''

Joss grimaced. "She understands what we think is happening, and agrees with us. There's only one problem. Security is being kept very low key for this event. The publicity buildup has been concentrating on the peace and brotherhood aspects of the project. Having the Space forces around is deemed—'' Joss made a face "—inappropriate for the PR that's been conducted. So we can expect no help from them. And there will be no overt rollout of SP forces, either. It would be noticed, Lucretia says. And unfortunately, orders have come down from the Commissioner, that brass-plated loon, that the security arrangements are to remain exactly as has been previously announced to the public.''

"So we *are* going to have to handle this by ourselves,'' Evan said, in a voice rich with disgust. "Joss, they don't pay us enough!''

"They never have,'' Joss said mildly. "But by Lucretia's reckoning, this is still the same riot. Any help we get will be strictly covert. And no big guns involved.''

Evan sighed. "That's that, then. Mell, you have your choices. Come with us? Or stay? I think you should stay, myself.''

She looked at Evan coolly. "Think I can't take it with the big boys?''

"I would prefer,'' he said, "that you were in a place

where the odds of your being killed were rather lower than they will be with us. If you didn't mind terribly, that is."

"Of course you would."

"Now, Mell, listen, you know I know you better than that—"

"You just think you do! I think you—"

"Mell," Joss said, "think of the salvage."

Both Evan and Mell turned to look at him.

Joss shrugged, keeping one eye on the instruments that were watching on the intruders, and another on the ongoing download. "It just occurs to me that no one owns that station, you see. At least, there's no one alive on it now. Is there?"

Evan and Mell looked at each other.

"Sensors don't reveal any movement in the aboveground parts," Joss said. "You would know better about the below-ground bits than I would."

"There were never more than forty or fifty people in the place, even when it was full," Mell said.

"I did for about twenty-five or so myself," said Evan.

"Well, then. Mell, if you go back there, you can spend a little while rigging one of the leftover ships to run. I saw a couple of them there that were obviously unfinished."

"I wasn't hurrying," Mell said with a slight smile. "I resent being made to work on a job without a contract."

"If you even want to leave," Joss said. "I mean, if there's no one on that station now, the first person on it, owns it."

Mell looked at Evan.

He raised his eyebrows at her.

"Right," she said. "When are you two leaving?"

"Now, wait a moment!" Evan said, sounding slightly hurt.

"I was just asking," she said.

"We ought to be out of here in a couple of hours," Joss said. "One more message to Lucretia, to tell her what's happening. Then off we go. I'm almost through here. When you're there, Mell, you might want to seal off that computer room. The computers themselves may be needed as evidence.''

"No problem with that," she said.

"In the meantime," Evan said, "will you stay to dinner?" And he smiled most beatifically at Joss. "My partner makes a wonderful Spaghetti Carbonara.''

Joss rolled his eyes and said, "Unfortunately, we can't offer you any wine.''

"I can bring a bottle," Mell said. "They've got lots of it over there." She paused and smiled and said, "I've got lots of it.''

"Good Lord," Joss said, looking at Evan in shock. "They *must* have money. Importing wine to the Belts?!''

"I shan't complain at the moment," Evan said.

"You're sure this doesn't come under drinking on duty?" Joss said.

Evan pointedly took his helm off and tossed it onto the command seat.

"Right," Mell said. "This suit's maneuvering pack is charged. I'll just run over and get a couple of bottles.''

"One will do," Joss said. "We have to save the universe in the morning.''

"Joss!''

"Oh, all right," Joss said, seeing the look in Evan's eye. "Two, then.''

"Don't be long," Evan said to Mell, as she put her helmet back on.

It was an excellent red. Joss sat nursing a glass of it, after dinner, while looking over some of the files from the base.

These are sick people, he thought.

There was a click as Evan's stateroom door unlatched. Evan and Mell came out, looking only slightly tousled. Evan grinned at Joss, a totally unrepentant look.

Joss just twitched an eyebrow at him. Then he said, "Why don't you crack that other bottle, you two, and pull up a couple of data pads. We have some interesting reading here.''

Evan saw to the wine and filled glasses all around, while Joss hunted up the extra pad and gave it to Mell. She fiddled with the controls for a few seconds until she got the feel of them, and then said, "Goodness. All this?"

"There's a fair amount of material. But I've excerpted out the best of it for you."

Evan settled down beside Mell and pulled his own pad over, and a companionable silence fell as they started to read.

"TKB," said Evan after a little while.

"Yes. And some others: but I think the board of TKB, and one man on it in particular, are the leading lights. There are a lot of memos in here, interoffice stuff—all very casual-looking. Copies of material on Earth, with the routing numbers still on it. Should make things convenient for us," Joss said.

Mell was scanning down through some of this material. "It looks like so much executive talk," she said in mild wonderment. "Until they start talking about the guns and the missiles. And not just selling them, either. Using them."

Evan said, "TKB took quite a lot of losses after Union, didn't it? They were almost more powerful than some governments on Earth, while they had all those different governments to play off each other. And then all of a sudden, all the power bases were changed, they didn't have the influence they had before."

Mell nodded. "Fewer wars, too. They made an awful lot of money out of munitions before Union."

"They diversified, of course," Joss said. "They weren't stupid. But the family that ran the company have to have felt they had lost a lot of ground, and Union was the cause of it. And this particular family was never the kind to sit around and be resigned about things. There are some interesting files in here with records of industrial dirty tricks going back a century."

Mell's mouth was hanging open at something she was reading. "Get this," she said. "At present, profit projections are sufficiently poor in terms of past years' performance to suggest moderately radical measures. Destabilization of political structures as below should cause the usual positive speculation in the markets, consonant with the 'greed and fear' principle.'' She looked at Joss in confusion.

Joss sighed. "Yes. The stockbroker's motto. People invest out of greed, or fear. When things are scary, or politically uncertain, the market goes up. When things are stable, it goes down."

She shook her head. "That's awful. And it's a great rationalization, too. But it's not the kind of thing I was hearing on the station. That was more sort of—'' her face screwed up with distaste "—racist stuff. Nationalist. Separate countries, and one of them better than all the others.''

Joss nodded. "Yes, that's in here too. I did some context-sensitive scans when I first ran across it. The board of TKB—several members of the same family are on it—are very interested in seeing Japan restored as a nation. And all the other remade countries subjected to it, in fact if not actually in name.''

"They're completely around the bend," Evan said, almost in awe.

"They're busy hating the way the world is now, and blaming it for their problems," Joss said. "And wanting to change it back to the way it used to be. Or the way they think it used to be—or should have been. That's crazy by *my* definition," Joss said. "But they also have lots of money, enough to do crazy things on a very big scale. Like 'destabilizing' the Union. Can you imagine the results if these loons managed to actually blow up High-Lands? It wouldn't start a war, I don't think, but a lot of trust that has been a good while forging would be shattered. Destabilized is the word for it, at the very least. And almost certainly the damned stock market *would* go up. I can't stand the thought of these bastards profiting from terrorism—since you can see from some of these reports that they've covered their tracks very efficiently.''

"They can afford to,'' Evan said softly. "This one report you tagged—very sweet. A lot of money spent in the Belts, here—paying off miners to avoid certain areas, killing others who would not avoid them, paying off station personnel to look the other way and not notice things. The money nicely laundered through several different accounts.'' He peered at the pad. "And the signatures are all people on the TKB board. Takawabara—one or another of the family.''

Joss nodded. "Something else interesting there, by the way. Look at the next file list—no, the next one. That one there: the manifest list for the base. Recent shipments.''

Evan looked at the list, and sucked breath in appreciatively. "Goodness. Someone had a suit delivered. And not a cheap one, either. A Krupp-Tonagawa.''

"Is that good?'' Mell said.

Evan laughed, a quick harsh sound. "Just about the best. They sell to the earthbound military, mostly. Space Forces are on too tight a budget to afford Krupp-Tonagawa suits. Pity,'' he added a little wistfully. "This suit has a lot of goodies on it.''

"And you will have noticed the name of the person to take delivery.''

Evan nodded. "Takawabara,'' he said, and frowned.

Joss sighed and pushed his own pad away. "I've sent this stuff off to Lucretia by squirt,'' he said. "But I don't think it's going to change her mind, and even if it did, we have no guarantee it would change the Commissioner's. We have to proceed as if there is going to be no help. If you look at that 'action plan' that's tagged on the third list in, you'll see what they're doing. At lease we know, which is a help. There are already bombs in place on Highlands, in case the armed attack fails. Lucretia will have to do something about that, no matter what. But as for the rest of it . . .''

Evan made a face. "Please, Evan and Joss,'' he said,

"blow up eleven ships better armed than you are, and possibly all stuffed with explosives, possibly nukes, to judge from that one we hit the other day; and don't make a fuss about it, and don't get noticed. And here's a pea-shooter to do it with."

"Well, we're a *little* better armed than with peashooters," Joss said, patting *Nosey*'s console apologetically. "But the situation is still pretty . . . uh, unbalanced."

Evan laughed softly, then sighed and turned to Mell. "We're going to have to get started," he said.

She just looked at him for a moment, then said, "I'll get my suit on."

Joss busied himself with other things for a while, purposely keeping his attention away from the other end of the ship. After a while Mell came out, in her suit, and Evan with her.

"Does your maneuvering pack need a recharge?" Joss said.

"No, I'm in good shape."

"Then go home safely," Joss said, "and for God's sake don't drink all that wine! We'll want some when we get back."

She nodded vigorously. Without another word she grabbed Evan by the head and planted a kiss on him that would have curled up a bulkhead. Evan dealt with it the best he could, and came up smiling.

"Nine point four," Joss said.

Mell chuckled. "Later for you. Evan—keep him out of trouble."

"I've been trying," Evan said. "It seems a life's work."

Mell smiled at that, locked her helmet down, and got into the airlock.

Evan closed it for her, and waved out the little porthole. A few moments later she was gone, and he closed the outer lock door as well.

Joss reached over to the command console and began hitting the controls to wake up the iondrivers. "We'll see her safely inside," he said, "and then get the hell out of there. We need to take a different course home, and still beat those people into Earth orbit.''

Evan said, ''Can we do it?''

''We'll find out,'' Joss said, and busied himself at the console.

SEVEN
★

"FINESSE," JOSS SAID, AND SNORTED.

"Stop complaining," said the voice in his ear. "Gosh, it feels great to tell you that! It's been days."

"Has been a little quiet," Joss said to Talya. They were in Earth orbit again, and once more she, and Lucretia, and all the rest of the SP, were just a half-second away.

Unfortunately, they weren't being any help.

"Look," he said. "I gave you no less than five possible locations for the damn bomb on the L5. What's keeping them, up there? We can't start our operation until that's handled."

"Last I heard," Talya said, from safe in the data center under the Moon, "they had found bombs in every one of those places. They're combing the rest of the station now, as best they can. No one's supposed to notice, you see."

Joss drummed his fingers. Behind him, in his stateroom, Evan was climbing into his suit. "When will we know?"

"Twenty minutes, they say."

Joss groaned. "The ceremony starts in twenty minutes!"

"So I hear."

"Joss," Evan said, "stop complaining. I've got your dinky toys right here, and they'll never have a chance against them."

"Always assuming you can get the contraptions up against them in the first place," Joss said gloomily. It was a plan of his that he had never tried before, and as usual, when trying something for the first time, he was twitching.

Evan came out with the little front pack of black boxes, eleven of them, each with its own magnet. He strapped the front pack on. "Look," he said. "I told you I can do twenty mps or so when I get going."

"I just hope it's enough." The black boxes had two things inside them: a powerful comm link, that should be able to break into a ship's comms network from outside the skin; and a derivative of the virus that killed the computer on the clandestine base. Comms on any small ship had to live in the master computer, otherwise, nothing got done. The virus would get into the ship's computer via comms, and freeze everything it touched, including the guidance and navigation computers, and the weapons systems, and the non-remote guidance systems of any bomb the computer was managing. A passing patrol vessel could then shoot out the ship's engines at its leisure. But there were complications. "I mean," Joss said, "What if one of those sons of bitches has fired a missile or something, and it's on remote? It'll just keep going."

"Don't let them fire, then," Evan said. "Finesse it."

"I keep hearing this."

"You shouldn't worry so much," Evan said. "I'll blow anything that I can locally. Just keep those bloody braided lasers off me."

Joss looked unhappy. The best way to do that was by drawing their fire himself. A ship with one of his black boxes on it wouldn't be able to fire; the laser wouldn't braid without computer control. It was getting the boxes on that was going to be interesting.

"You're talking about pulling a lot of gee out there," Joss said to Evan, as he headed for the airlock. He was looking at the holograph, which had shown some of the enemy ships already in position, seemingly lounging through the area at low speeds, on other business. "Are you sure you're going to be all right?"

"I'll be fine."

Evan climbed into the airlock. "You know the course we want?" he said.

Joss nodded. "I'm swinging past the first two boys now. You should be able to hit them one after another. Just stay away from the fronts of them, if you can. Don't want you microwaved by their radars."

"I'll try to avoid it." And the door closed behind him.

"You do that," Joss said.

He kicked in the iondrivers, on low. His business at the moment was to seem to be a Patrol vessel ambling about its business. He had gone to some trouble, on the way out here, to change his registration numbers and to tinker with his own ID broadcast; he didn't want any of these raiders suddenly recognizing the sop vessel that had been hanging around Willans Station. These people were not dumb.

One of the panels on his console was monitoring the process and positioning of the little black boxes. There were eleven little lists of data, all quiescent at the moment.

Mostly what Joss wanted was to see Evan get them quietly placed. He would then activate them all at once, and every ship would find its comms jammed, its engines no longer under its control; but most specifically, those horrible braided lasers wouldn't be working.

That would be if everything worked.

"We have our course," Joss said to Evan. "This is where you get off, buddy."

"Right," Evan said, and he was gone.

"Tee, anything more from the bomb squad?"

"Nothing new," Talya said. "I'll call you. By the way, how were the restaurants out there?"

Joss started to laugh. "I'll tell you later. Michelin has some surprises in store."

Very suddenly, the data readout from one of the black boxes came alive. *Oh good,* Joss thought. And, *What kind of gee is he taking out there?*

He waited, silent. Out the plex, if he cared to look at it, HighLands glittered in the sunlight. It was an extremely beautiful station, one of the new designs with extended pods; it looked like an elegant, silvery glass water-strider, balancing (at the moment) on the blue water of the curvature of the Earth. And if things went well, it would not shortly be a mass of fragments of glass and metal and frozen air.

Another of the little blocks of data on his console woke up. *Two out of eleven. Better than nothing. Evan, what are you doing to yourself that you can move so fast?* For Evan had refused to take a remote pusher, saying that it would attract too much attention, whereas a suit was usually too small to show well on radar, or to be noticed visually. The only precaution he had taken was to spray himself with the dead-black lampblack spray that suited people used for stealth work in space. Joss looked at the smudges on the walls, and smiled slightly.

A third block of data came up, wobbled a little, settled. *Good solid contact,* Joss thought. *Nice clear data. But the next ones won't be so easy. They're further away—*

"There's some scrambled communication going on out there." Tee said, "on the marked frequency."

"Hope they're not getting suspicious," Joss said softly.

One more block of data came up on the board. Wavered a little, steadied down.

"Four," Joss said. "Tee, I don't know how he does that. He really must not have been kidding about the twenty mips."

And another block came up, settled. And then, suddenly, there was concerted movement in the holograph.

"Oh no," Joss said. "Evan? This is it."

"Do it," Evan said.

Joss slapped his hand down on the comms console and woke up the five black boxes that were settled in place. Under each set of readouts, a wild little storm of hexadecimals began to stream by as the boxes both jammed external communications and started subverting the internal ones in the raiders' ships. Five of the ships in the display coasted on, began to lose speed.

The others began to pick it up.

"Trouble, Evan," Joss said. "They know. Number eleven, the kingpin ship, is dropping back. The others are swinging in. Two kilometers now."

"So I see," Evan said.

He hung there is space with his little bag of goodies only half distributed. It was most annoying. Not far away from HighLands, he could see the glint of metal from the little mining ships, swinging in; more to the point, he could see their course predictions on the inside of his helm. All orbits were designed to swoop low around High-Lands—or to crash into it if necessary.

One of them was barely a kilometer from him, and would pass him by at about three hundred meters if he held still. He didn't hold still. It was passing him left to right and above; he turned his leg jets on, and left them on, not minding the feel of blood piling away from his head. He was in a hurry, and besides, the neural foam in the suit had squeeze pads in the legs for such an eventuality.

He drew close to the ship from the underside. It was one of the VW Boxes again, mostly box and only a little pilot compartment; its iondriver dish was the perfect target, and a mile wide from this angle. Evan scooted up behind it, at a slight angle, to miss the ion spillover, and from one of the suit's leg fairings, pulled out a grenade.

It was a charming combination of high and low tech: it had an ionchaser chip in it, and a little attitude jet of its very own, and it was filled with concentrated plastique. It flew into the iondriver like a baby bird to its nest, and blew up in a way that baby birds usually don't.

Half the back of the ship simply fell off; the rest explosively decompressed. One of the pieces of one of the corpses missed Evan by about twenty meters, its arm waving a rather forlorn hello, or in this case, goodbye. Evan ignored it, being more concerned with the way the ship had fallen apart. *No wonder they needed Mell*, he thought. *I wonder . . .*

Some distance away, another of the ships changed

course, toward him. It seemed unlikely that he had been seen, but he made himself small for the moment, curling up into a fetal position and watching. It coasted quickly closer.

Evan held quite still. His previous course was carrying him along at about fifteen mips, and it occurred to him that if he restrained himself from looking manlike for as long as possible, he might be able to fool these people into thinking he was a piece of debris. He stayed tucked up, and thought beautiful thoughts, as much as possible.

Mell was one of them.

"This was kind of dumb, on both our parts, wasn't it? she said. Still is, on yours."

"Yes," he had said.

"What do we do now?"

"I'm none too sure. Neither of us wants to marry. Neither of us wants to live the way the other does, particularly. But neither of us wants to lose the other, either."

"That would seem to about sum it up."

"So what do we do?"

"For the moment, our work. Later . . ."

"Later."

THE SECOND SHIP WAS GETTING QUITE CLOSE. *Five are paralyzed,* Evan thought, *one is gone, that's six not to worry about. Five more to go. Like this one.*

The second ship was no more than two hundred meters away now, slowing, nosing through the debris of the first one. Evan could see the gunport in the front as it passed over him, and was determined not to have that pointed at him on any account. He straightened, gave himself a hard push with the jets, and reached out to see what he could catch.

It took almost ten seconds, but he finally managed to grab hold of a strut and haul himself onto the chassis of the ship. This was a Lada, a box in front and a sphere in back, with a sort of wasp waist in between. He clambered carefully forward, not particularly caring how it sounded to anyone inside, and braced himself against the front cabin, grabbing hold of the cargo pod so hard his gauntlet's fingers sank into the steel.

He began to push.

And pushed harder.

And one more time.

The ship came apart at the center seam. Not even Evan's suit could hang on in the face of an explosive decompression a foot and a half away. He was blown off the surface of the ship like a cork out of a bottle of champagne, and he tumbled for a good thirty seconds before he could get enough control over his motion to start slowing himself down. But when he managed to see where he was again, the pieces of the enemy ship were going happily in two different directions, and he was pleased. *Saves ammo*, he thought.

And a bolt of blue fire went by him so close that it almost caught his outflung arm. Impossibly, in vacuum, he could actually feel the heat.

The bolt came from over his shoulder. He curled himself up and used the leg jets to kick himself sideways. The ship passed a hundred meters away, still firing, but it was useless; as Joss had said, the weapon was fixed. It might actually have to be mounted down the center of the craft, Evan thought, which would account for it. He went after the ship, praying he could get at it before it turned.

Then again, it was certainly convenient that they were hunting him down, rather than the other way around. It would save leg juice.

Lucretia is getting to me, he thought. He pushed his jets, pushed until he felt faint. The ship *was* turning, but he was more flexible; he could turn more quickly, and did. He came down on its underside, where the struts were. It was another VW, not a Box this time, but one of the slightly more upmarket Passat ore haulers. It was a little more solidly built. Evan sighed and got out another of the grenades, slipped it down into the iondriver, and pushed off hurriedly.

The ship blew behind him. He curled up small to take as little of the force, or the debris, as possible; then straightened up and looked around him.

Off past HighLands there was a silent bloom of fire.

"That you?" Joss's voice said hurriedly in his ear.

"Not me. I was doing something else."

"One of my frozen ones blew. They must be pretty well stocked with bombs, too," Joss said, slightly admiring. "There's junk all over. How many did you get?"

"Three. But I'm kind of over on the far side of things at the moment."

"I wish I were," Joss said.

Come on, *Nosey*, honey. We can do it.

And if we don't, we're dead ducks!

There were two of them after him. The kingpin ship was not one of them. The problem with these ships was, they were engined to cope with the weaponry they were carrying; and they were shooting at Joss, and they were plainly not interested in merely crippling him and then going back about their business. He had them mad.

It might be wise to make them madder yet—but, for the moment, it seemed smart to just concentrate on staying alive. For one thing, if his ship were destroyed, control over the five frozen ships would lapse, and Evan would suddenly have them to worry about as well. He had sounded a little tired; it seemed like a good idea, Joss thought, to keep his own baddies to himself.

Also, staying alive had its points.

The two ships were quite close behind him, but though they might have engines twice the size of *Nosey*'s, they weren't as maneuverable. He had been ducking and dodging all around them, which was one of the reasons they were so pissed off at him. He had also been letting them have the occasional shot at him, which was perhaps foolish, but every time they missed, they were convinced that they would hit him the next time.

That would be all he'd need, sooner or later.

One of them was shooting at him again, right now, but he had seen it lining up on him and was already fifty meters sideways from that spot. The ship behind him started turning; the other started to try to pull ahead, to catch him in crossfire.

That was something he desperately did not want. He hammered at the console, diving down out of their plane and toward the Earth. This was officially a no-no, but he wanted them as far from HighLands as possible, and perhaps their own logic might suggest that it was safer to be away from the L5, at the moment, than near it. Though, on the other hand, some of their ships were suddenly mysteriously nonfunctional, and several others were scrap and frozen air. Surely this should suggest to them that someone knew what they were up to at this point. *If I were a suicidal fanatic*, Joss wondered, *what would I do?*

Phrased that way he dismissed the question. Joss kept diving toward Earth, but slowed a little bit. Behind him the others slowed too, but still followed. If he could manage to suggest that he were running out of steam, or was otherwise in trouble—

They were closing on him. For a few more seconds, he let them. "Tee," he said, "this might be it."

"Luck," she said.

"Come on now, honey," he said to *Nosey,* and swung her over hard on her side, harder than he had ever tried to before. She groaned with gees, the first time he had ever heard the ship make a noise like that. The ships behind him tried to turn, but couldn't do it sharply enough. Joss threw *Nosey* back again, a sharp curve in the other direction, up and over, and kicked a missile loose.

It hit the ship that had been closest to him. The other one flew through its wreckage, scattering debris in all directions, and started to curve away.

Oh, no, you don't, Joss thought, and headed after him.

He would much rather have a suicidal fanatic chasing him than one heading back toward HighLands. And the problem was, there was still that eleventh ship out there, the group leader, just hanging there. *Am I being allowed to do my worst,* Joss thought, *while that bozo waits for both me and Evan to be out of the way, and then gets ready to nail the L5? Dammit, Lucretia, are you just going to sit there and assume we're going to save your little five-billion-credit propaganda piece for you?*

That question, too, was answered by the lack of any other SP vessels in the area. Joss swore, and said "Sorry, *Nosey,* I didn't mean you," and kept heading after the second bandit.

It ran. It ran fast, and didn't try to turn toward Joss. It did try to head toward Earth again, though. *Maybe not so suicidal as I thought,* Joss said to himself. *Doubtless they have a bolt-hole down there. And they know I can't follow.*

Joss smiled.

In front of him, curving around and down toward the Earth, the bandit mining ship fled. He tore after it. Joss did what he had always wanted to do, kicked the iondrivers up to maximum output. They were responding better than he would have thought—Mell's doing—he thought, and smiled harder.

Slowly he crept up behind the fleeing ship. The plex in front of him began to haze up with heat from the outside. *Atmosphere,* Joss thought, and pressed harder, running right up the bandit's tail. He couldn't shoot: on sensing atmosphere, his weaponry locked down. He was barely fifty meters away, barely thirty—

This was too much for the bandit. He turned tail, skimmed up and out of atmosphere, and headed out toward space again, faster yet.

Nice engines, Joss thought, *but not as nice as mine.* "Go, Nosey! Go, honey!" he shouted, pushing at the console as if that would help somehow. He was only a few meters away from having his missiles back. The ship in front of him put on another desperate burst and pulled ahead, just enough to break the lock again.

Joss could not possibly go any faster, and maneuverability was no use to him here. "Come on, *Nosey*," he begged the ship, "come *on!!*"

Its speed suddenly jumped by about five meters per second. It wasn't much but it was enough. The missile lock came on. Joss slammed the firing button, and threw *Nosey* sideways as sharply as he dared.

The ship in front of him blew up in three large explosions, its own and, Joss thought, those of the two bombs it was carrying.

He was panting as if he had been running a race.

"Got him," he said to Evan. "That's all but the head honcho."

But there was no answer.

"Evan?" said Joss.

Nothing.

"Evan??"

"Don't shout at him," Tee said in his ear. "He's busy. I'll patch you in."

EVAN'S HELM WAS TELLING HIM DISTURBING things about the condition of his suit. He didn't have time for them at the moment.

He was staring down the nose cannon of the last ship, the only one that had not been a mining vessel, but was new and shiny, a fine, sleek, small custom job. It was a ship that had money behind it—and money *in* it, Evan thought. He had headed for it, to see what could be done about it. It had seen him coming, which surprised him slightly, for he had been as careful as he knew how, and it had come for him, straight and slow, without firing. It had been hanging here, now, looking at him, for a couple of minutes.

He was tired of waiting. The conduit of the braided

laser was looking straight at him, glowing slightly, in standby mode. He looked up past it, at the plex of the pilot's cabin, and kicked his helm radio on, wide-frequency.

"This is the Solar Police," he said. "Surrender immediately, and it will affect your treatment when you come to trial."

There was a pause, and then laughter came back.

"Officer," said the voice, "at this late date you cannot expect us to take you seriously."

"You might do me the courtesy," Evan said, "since I have so far done you that courtesy."

Another pause. "Officer—I did not catch your name."

"Glyndower," Evan said. "Owen Glyndower."

"Officer Glyndower. You will have to understand that we are going to carry out our operation whether you continue attempting to affect it or not."

"You would equally have to understand that I can hardly just let you sail away from here." Evan said. "But you in particular, the leader of this group—Mr. Takawabara, is it not? That would have been the name that appears most often in your records back at your base; the name of the present head of the family. Of you, I would have expected better things."

There was a pause. Evan felt the sweat trickling down his forehead, past the telltale that was saying how little maneuvering fuel he had left to work with.

There was another silence. "You are surprisingly well informed, Officer Glyndower."

Evan smiled, and kept his voice hard. "Yes," he said. "What I don't understand is why you don't believe enough in what you're fighting for to come out and fight for yourself."

"The wise general," said the cool voice, "is not ruled by his passions, but by logic and the rules of battle."

"So Lao Tzu said. He also said, 'There is no joy in a victory won by the counsel of underlings and moneylenders.'"

"Officer Glyndower, you cannot possibly know—"

"I know that the economic aspects of terrorism are not why *you're* interested in starting this massacre," Evan said. "You may fool your subordinates and your business partners with such talk, but not me. Even without having read through some of the more interesting manifestos in your computers, I know an old-fashioned rabid nationalist when I see one."

"Glyndower," said the voice, musing. "Yes, perhaps you might."

"None better," Evan said. "But I also know which parts of nationalism to reject. The hate, the fear. One can be Welsh, or Japanese, without having to waste time servicing the old grudges and killing the old enemies, economic or otherwise. You, however, seem to prefer your nationalism whole and entire, with the useless old hates and prides retained."

"Why not?" said the voice, and its coolness was beginning to ebb away. "We have always been best, *known* that we were best; our craftsmanship has ruled the world for centuries now. But what are we? Less than a house, less than a power, in something now much less than a country."

"First among equals, surely."

"Who would be first among such equals?" The voice was full of scorn. "Nations of shopkeepers, races of power brokers and peasants who think themselves as good as everyone else. An etiolated world. Better to see them about their old business, squabbling and scrambling for power. It suited them better. And us."

"So you think," Evan said. "For all your proud words, though, you still won't fight. You're afraid. And your honor is lost to you. But you've fooled yourself into not even missing it."

"You have no knowledge of these matters."

"I have the *only* knowledge that matters. I went into your place, and ransacked it, when I had evidence of the murders your people were doing. I left those of your people who contested me lying in their blood. I took back the captive you took from me. I ripped two of your ships apart with my bare hands. I *am* the 'etiolated world', the pale imitation, the new order, everything you most hate and fear. And you sit inside, protected by your guns, and don't dare confront me to find out whether your words are true."

Evan let his scorn show in his voice now. "You are not worth as much as the least of the poor fools I killed today, who had given their word they'd fight for you—and died doing it, died believing in the vision that you showed them—and won't fight for. You are despicable, and if you were here before me, I would take your sword from you, and break it in front of your eyes."

"You would try," said the soft voice.

"Ask the men I killed today," said Evan, "how I tried."

There was a long, long pause.

"And when I kill you," said the voice, "what will you have gained?"

"When we fight," Evan said, "we'll both find where the real strength lies."

"If you know this much about me," said the voice, "you know how I am armed."

"I know what you wear, and what weapons come with it. How you're *armed* is another matter."

"Even if you should by some bizarre chance kill me," said Takawabara, "my people will not stop fighting. And I will not tell them to. They will destroy your precious station yet, and with it your all your nervous mock alliances."

"We can take care of your people," Evan said, quite calmly, more calmly than he had a right to be perhaps, since he had no idea how the station security people were doing. But this was not a time to betray any uncertainty. "Nothing is left, now, but this ship. And the man hiding inside it, behind the big gun."

He paused, a bit out of breath. *Thank you, debating society,* he thought; *thank you, Classics 101. And thank you, Evelyn Wood.* His speed-reading course had been one of the best things ever to happen to him, next to the ability to declaim the phone book and make it sound good. A trained voice with a Welsh accent had its uses.

"Well?" Evan said. "Is the Blue Dragon man enough to take on the Red? Or are you going to shoot me, and make my partner hunt you down? A man with honor rather differently shaped from yours," Evan added. "He would hunt you down and trick you to your death, and afterwards he would feel sorry about it."

A long, long pause.

"Officer Glyndower," said the voice, "I will be out shortly."

He did not keep Evan waiting long.

He came out of an airlock that had its own elevator, and magnetic locks for the boots, so that he ascended into view, like a stage magician or an aspiring god with a new pedestal. The suit was dead black, and it gleamed in the light reflected from HighLands. The faired-in hump on the back was huge. For all Evan knew, there was a nuke in there that was twice as big as the one he had carried in the service. *At least he won't be using it in close combat,* Evan thought. *Must make sure he doesn't try to lob it at the station, if that's what it is. But heaven only knows what else he might have in there.* There were certainly two slug cannons in the arms—the Krupp specialty—and paired tuned beamers, and a flamethrower, perhaps two. There were also the missiles; eight in the arm packs, two heatseekers in the backpack in the normal configuration. Not that they were much use on a man. But on a space station . . .

Evan checked his own specs, and looked at what he knew the other man's to be, and sighed. *I teased him into this. What am I going to do now? Hit him with a stick?*

And for evidence's sake, I really should try to avoid killing him. Maybe now I can taunt him into turning himself in.

And maybe pigs will fly. . . .

Tactically, it was a nasty situation. Mostly preventive, the hardest kind to manage. Keep the enemy from using the long range weapons, make him concentrate on the short range . . . on *you*. Always easier said than done.

And Joss had his hands full elsewhere, and was in no position to clean up any spills, as it were. *No, Evan my lad,* he thought, *this one you save or screw over by your own self.*

Evan checked his specs again. He was low on maneuvering fuel, but that couldn't be helped at this point. *I much doubt I'll have to chase this lad all over the place, anyway,* he thought. He turned all his alert systems on, gave himself a slight boost of jet towards Takawabara, and for the moment just listened to what the audio outputs of the alert system had to say to him.

They were picking up a disturbing hum of power from the other man's suit, much higher than would be accounted for by the suit's basic power rating. *No surprise there,* Evan thought. *The head of the company can damned well afford to put a few extras in his custom job. But what sucks power like that? And what needs that kind of power plant to run it?*

There seemed to be no point in speculating. The thing now was to close in, try a few initial moves to feel the other combatant out, and see what his weaknesses were.

If any, said some tremulous, traitor part of Evan's mind. That suit looked meaner than most—but then, it had been engineered to. Most of the design that went into a given suit had nothing to do with weapon engineering; it was psychological. It was more cost-effective, after all, to get an enemy to run away at the sight of you. It saved ammunition, and lives. Takawabara's suit had been designed to provoke the runaway response with a vengeance. The blackness of it, the blankness of the helm, missing even the slight facial-shape cues that Evan's had; the huge bulk of the forearm and leg fairings—you were meant to see a giant, looking at it; a monster, an ogre that would twist your head off and crunch it up like an hors d'oeuvre. Next to it, Evan felt rather like a midget, like David going up against Goliath.

He smiled slightly. The smile was a useful one.

He was closer, about fifty meters away now. That blank helm studied him. One arm moved slightly, a gesture that swept off to one side.

Something small and dark leapt from the arm fairing. Evan reacted without thinking, waking up his arm cannon, which he had gratefully reloaded with slugs as soon as they had left the pressure-sensitive environment of Willans. The reaction of his own firing slowed his own forward movement, which was just as well, as his slugs met the mini-missile halfway and exploded it.

His helm polarized and depolarized, sparing him the flash without bothering him with the details. But the scream of his audio alarms told him that two more missiles were coming at him while the first one was in the act of exploding. His helm was dark, but Evan wasn't blind. Tactical projection on the inside helm surface gave him heads-up display, the tracks of the incoming missiles, one from each side. He brought both arms up, and fired the slug cannons again, in a broad pattern, the way a hunter lets a pattern of shot take down several birds at once. Both missiles exploded.

Then a blast of heat went past his left leg, and Evan cut in every jet he had, and moved sideways in a hurry, firing some slugs as well to help the process alone. The alert system screamed in his ears of massive energy output; head-up display showed him a line of light streaking past him, broader than any normal laser beam. His helm depolarized in time to show him Takawabara turning again to follow him. Evan pointed straight up over his head, fired another burst to knock himself downward, and the braided laser went by over his head.

"Take that sword," Takawabara said, "if you can."

He stepped up off his pedestal, floating free, and fired again. *It's impossible,* Evan thought. *He can't possibly be carrying the onboard computer power necessary to get the damn thing to braid!* For the lasing crystals had to have their structure agitated by precisely tuned and fired radiation outputs, and the firing of the output radiation was managed by a modulation algorithm that assessed the lasing crystals' shifting energy states millisecond by millisecond. Such delicate control could only be managed by a computer with huge processing speed, and gigs and gigs of memory. There was no way to fit any such thing onto a chip, or even a pack, portable enough to fit into a suit.

Evan's mouth was dry. He did his best to ignore it, and thought, *Bloody hell with this; time to get cranky.* He picked one of his optional heatseekers, killed the heatseeking option, pointed his left arm at Takawabara, and fired. And fired a second, and a third, and then pointed his other arm at the man's own lifting right arm, adjusted his stream to minimum, and fired a long burst, about four breaths' worth.

Takawabara's left arm pointed, fired the braided laser again, taking out the first missile, the second. The third was a close miss, and it almost took off the end of the right arm, which Evan had driven back by sheer pressure of slugs ramming into it. He smiled slightly. That was all it would take: one small mistake. The man was heavily armed, yes, but possibly for that very reason, he was somewhat slow with the tricks well known to someone with a suit with fewer options.

Then the world spilled sideways as slugs began pounding into Evan's armor, tumbling him over and over. Gyros groaned as his suit strained to find its own stability again, and Evan's inertial tracking systems went crazy as the hail of slugs rammed into him harder than any lead would have done. *Exhausted uranium,* he thought, somewhat admiringly, even as he spun and wobbled out of control, and fought to stop himself. *Very nice. A bit pricy, though.*

He tried firing his jets to take him out of the stream. They were very low, too slow to do much good. At the same time, his alert system began screaming in his ear again, about another burst of energy being used. A different sound from the pre-laser scream, this: more of a series of spaced howls. Evan swallowed, keyed another of the heatseekers loose, turned its heat sensitivity down, told it to watch for chemical output as well, and turned it loose.

The missile went, and for several long, long moments there was no response. Evan was still tumbling in a hail of slugs from Takawabara's guns. The braided laser raked by him, missing again. *On purpose?* Evan thought. *Or is he just too mad to shoot straight?*

Then the missile found its target. Evan saw the initial impact, twisted his face away, not trusting even the polarization of the helm (though he ordered it as black as it would go), and made himself into a small tight ball. The flash like a sun flare came a second later, and then the shock wave. They were still close enough to Earth for the vacuum to be not nearly complete, and every free molecule in the area went rushing out in a common shock wave as the low-yield pressured nuke that Takawabara had fired went off. *About a kiloton,* Evan thought, with some professional interest, as the horrible storm of slugs stopped suddenly. *We'll see how well his armor takes it.* For himself, he just hung on, doubled over his knees and holding onto them, as the mushroom expanded out and out. His heads-up showed him the spread as a vague bloom of rose-colored fog; not very hot, but potentially quite destructive, had it hit anything physical. Evan as he watched, the fireball was collapsing in on itself. *Wonder how his radiation shielding is?* Evan thought. He was going to check his own dosimeter pretty carefully when he got home. There was no use trying to sneak up on baddies in the middle of the night if you glowed in the dark. But if Lucretia was hoping for a quiet end to all this, it's blown now. Half the station has to be hanging out the windows at this point, wondering what's happening—

—and then something hit him hard, in the back, that his heads-up display had not shown him. Evan uncurled in shock, gasping for air for a moment, briefly unsure that this armor hadn't cracked in back. Unlikely as it seemed, he was being grappled. *What kind of jets has that man got?* Evan wondered, as he felt Takawabara's arms around his, pinning him, and realized that the nuke's output must have blinded his close-in detection for the moment. *Something else to talk to the mechanics about*— he thought, as he struggled. In gravity he would have pitched his enemy over his head, but there was no way to do that here; no leverage. The other had more jets than he did, more fuel in any case, so trying to confuse Takawabara's gyros was out of the question. *Got to get turned,* he thought, desperately wriggling, straining any way he could; *got to face him*— For without facing him, there was no telling where that damned braided laser was pointed. And at this range, the man couldn't possibly miss.

Neither can I, Evan thought, and turned his attention downward. Every suit had an Achilles heel, literally. No one had yet been able to convince the suit manufacturers that feet needed much in the way of armoring, and to the cognoscenti of suit warfare, it was *the* preferred target, a great place to shoot people and give them something else to think about. The problem was that Evan was still being grappled from behind, by someone in a suit with perhaps twice the crush and tear ratings that his had. And the pressure was building up. *Maybe I shouldn't have bragged so much about tearing his ships up with my bare hands,* Evan thought, as he did the only thing he could against the increasing pressure. He flexed everything he had outward; arms, legs. Then all at once he stopped struggling—

A foot kicked forward from behind him, in reaction. The man had too little zero-gee experience, didn't know how to handle himself. *Right,* Evan thought, and pointed his left-hand slugfirer at that foot, narrowed the stream, and fired at the foot full-speed. Slugs—not exhausted uranium, but they would do—tore down in a stream of almost-solid metal, at about 500 kph. Someone might as well have grabbed Takawabara by the foot and pulled him off Evan's back; at any rate he let go, pushed hard down by the stream of slug fire, unable to react with jets just yet.

And this was the bad moment, for the minute he recovered himself at all, he would certainly fire. Evan turned hard, grabbed whatever he could catch—one arm—hauled Takawabara up by it, and made it his business to keep that arm pointed away from him. *Damn it all, anyway*, he thought, *it's still impossible. He can't be firing that thing—*

From the wrist of the flailing arm, it went off in front of his nose, and his helm blacked; the wash of heat was palpable, and it made Evan shudder with the strangeness of being able to feel *any* heat at all through his suit in space. *Doesn't matter*, he thought, kicking Takawabara in the stomach to buy himself a moment, and some motion; *he's firing it anyway—*

It went off again. Evan was getting annoyed, not so much by his own situation, of holding a tiger by the tail and not daring to let go, but by the sheer impossibility of it all. He kicked Takawabara's other arm out of the way, hard enough to break something inside the armor, he hoped. He kicked it again, and again, and set them both spinning. *It's just not fair, him and his fancy suit and all, and breaking the rules in ways that don't even make sense—*

Then he had the idea. And at the same time, Takawabara's other flailing hand reached out and clamped onto the front pack that Evan was wearing, and started to rip it off.

Oh, no, you don't! Evan thought, and grabbed at the other arm. Two-handed they grappled, and the situation was not a good one for Evan. Slugs came tearing out of the arm that didn't have the braided laser, and rattled and howled against Evan's breastplate and helm. He gasped for breath, unable to hear himself think, if thinking had made any noise, and praying silently that the chest and helm wouldn't give at such close range. They weren't really designed for such impacts. But they seemed to be holding for the moment.

Something kicked him in the shins. He ignored the pain

and concentrated on keeping the front pack on, forcing his hand between Takawabara's clutching fingers and the woven fabric of the bag. It was Kevlon, theoretically un-tearable, but no one seemed to have told Takawabara's suit-makers about this. The stuff was ripping. *He must have a hint of what's in there;* Evan thought, in a rush of angry pleasure. *And if he's reacting this way, then I must be right!*

Abruptly he let go the man's hand, instead shoving his own into what remained of the bag and managing to grab two of Joss's little black boxes. Now there was only one problem; to keep that damned laser off his case for a few seconds, just a few—

He was still hanging onto the other arm, the one with the laser. It fired another time or two into the emptiness, but Evan was almost past being scared of it now. *As long as it doesn't hit me from behind—* He flipped himself end-for-end, kicked away Takawabara's other wildly waving arm, and positioned himself with some care; then he kicked Takawabara's helm hard, twice, once more for good luck. He shoved away from the man and kicked his jets in one last time, heading toward the ship.

Only the slightest result—the gauges in his heads-up dis-play—showed the fuel gauges to his jets empty. He threw an anxious glance back at Takawabara. The man was mov-ing slightly, whether from Evan's kick or under his own power was hard to tell. Evan didn't waste time wondering. Not even the best-cushioned helm could protect well against heavy close-up "mechanical" impacts like that. Evan had had some internal bracing added to his own, so that he had mostly to deal with noise rather than impact. Takawabara's armor, though, seemed to have been built on the concept that no one would ever get close enough to do anything so crude or low-tech as to merely strike. Its bracing was not what it might have been.

Evan pointed his own slug-firer behind him, gave it sev-eral short bursts. They pushed him in the direction he needed to go, a little more quickly than the jets would have. He resisted the urge to make small running motions. Everyone did that, when they were terrified, and something nasty was behind them. His breathing was loud in his ears. He looked with some anxiety at his oxygen mix; it was getting a bit on the low side. He kicked the suit over onto rebreathing mode, and hoped that all this wouldn't take him too much longer. The rebreather was only good for half an hour or so before it needed to be recharged.

He glanced over his shoulder. A little feeble motion. *Didn't kick him hard enough,* Evan thought regretfully. *Too concerned about evidence. For all my warrior's talk, they've made a sop of me at last.* He laughed shortly. *Hope they don't have to write that on my memorial. Won't be anything left to put under a tombstone—*

The ship was no more than ten meters from him. He was approaching it from its blind side, down below. Doubtless Takawabara's people had orders not to fire. He had probably been quite sure he would be able to finish Evan off by himself. Hubris, Evan thought, as he reached the ship. He hauled himself along by the convenient handholds, found a service power port, pried it open, and slapped Joss's baby into the contacts.

In his helm he could hear that scream of building power again. He turned, looked at Takawabara. He was floating there, pointing the arm that had the braided laser with great care at his own ship, and Evan. Evan had no doubt whatever that he would fire. He had thrown his own people's lives away easily enough elsewhere.

The scream built. Evan hung on, hung there, staring his enemy down.

It built in his ears, deafening. Built—

—And cut off.

Nothing happened. No heat, no blast of braided blue fire. Takawabara hung there pointing, to no effect.

Evan smiled. *Commlink to the ship's computers,* he thought; *it was the only way that made sense. No way that suit had enough processing. Now, then—*

He clambered up over the body of the ship. Takawabara was jetting toward him, but slowly. Either he hadn't noticed Evan's trick with the guns, or thought it beneath him. *Never make a real suit jockey out of the man,* Evan thought, as he made his way up to where Takawabara's elevator was, his little pedestal. It was retracting as he came to it, for though the people in the ship were at no angle at the moment to shoot at him, it had certainly occurred to them that he was in a position to get inside. That, however, was far from Evan's mind. He put a hand out, grabbed the elevator platform just before it sank level with the hull; and held it there. Through his feet, braced against the hull, he could feel the groaning of resisting machinery. Evan smiled, and pulled harder.

The groaning stopped. Then, with a wrench, the platform came off in his hand. He held it for a moment, watching the approaching Takawabara, watching the man fighting his jets, trying to stop as he realized he couldn't get back into his ship, that he was stuck out here, with Evan.

Evan hefted the platform thoughtfully. He had been good with discus at University. He wondered whether Takawabara's helm would just come right off at the neck, or whether the neck would break and the helm stay on. The thought of the experiment was tempting.

But Lucretia would be frightfully annoyed. She was probably annoyed already, what with the nuke and all. Filling out the environmental impact statement was going to be enough of a nuisance, without an investigation into why Evan had killed someone wanted for questioning. He tossed the platform away.

And then the explosion hit him.

It was bad. He was sure he blacked out several times in succession: the world came and went like a slideshow, in fragment-images of billowing light and coaldust smoke, and somewhere above it all, HighLands gleamed like a glass toy. When consciousness came back to stay, he found that his feet hurt; and that suggested what had saved him:

he had been standing on something explosive when it went off, and so was offering the least possible surface area for the blast to work on. He was sailing through the dark at a fair clip, and underneath him was a roiling cloud with most of the fire gone out of it. Hanging not too far away was *Nosey,* shining a searchlight through the cloud.

"You've *got* to stop just shooting everything you see!" Evan said.

"Sorry," said Joss's voice in his ear, rather tinnily; it sounded as if the audio circuitry had taken some damage. "But I could hear their comms, thanks to you getting my little widget onto their hull. They were preparing to launch missiles and then blow themselves right there, with everything they were carrying, to get rid of both you and their boss. Apparently he had left orders not to be taken."

"No surprise," Evan said. "You might have let me know you were coming."

"Too much chance they might have heard," Joss said. "Besides, I was concentrating on the best place to hit them to involve as little of the HE they were carrying. You wouldn't have wanted to be there if the whole load had gone off, boyo, indeed you wouldn't."

"Where's Takawabara?"

"Looking for him now. Getting some faint signals. His suit's still with us, I think, even if he isn't. You'd better hope he is, though."

"Tell me about it," Evan said. "Lucretia the Terrible will be after us both. You should have let me work on him a little more."

"I prefer you in one piece, thanks," Joss said.

"Me, too," said Talya. "You were terrific!"

Evan smiled. "A woman who knows when to keep quiet," he said, "is worth more than gold."

"Thank you. I think."

"There he is," Joss said suddenly. "Still in one piece, and still alive. I'll get him. Come on home, why don't you?"

"Glad to," Evan said, and pointed his slug-firer away from the ship. "My feet hurt."

"What cop's don't?" said Joss.

THE DEBRIEFINGS TOOK THEM ONLY A COUPLE of days on the Moon. Joss and Evan had the satisfaction of knowing that miners and their ships would not be disappearing nearly as often any more. The data they had found was being sorted through with the finest of fine tooth combs by both the SP and the judiciaries of various countries on Earth, and the nationalist terrorist groups Takawabara and his companies had founded, or funded, would not be able to pull anything clandestine for a long time. Takawabara's machinations had been suspected by numerous jurisdictions on Earth, but none of them had been able to do anything without evidence. They had it now, in plenty. He was under arrest, in the hospital on (ironically) HighLands, which had the equipment best suited for saving the life of a man suffering from hypoxia, marginal brain damage, systemic shock, renal failure, and numerous bruises and contusions that suggested someone had kicked him in the head, and elsewhere, very hard.

In areas of concern closer to home, the pirate base had been confirmed as Mell's. And to Evan's considerable surprise, expense accounts were not mentioned during their briefings, nor were environmental impact statements. But neither were they given medals, which he and Joss both thought they deserved.

Lucretia looked at them unbelievingly at the end of the last debriefing. "What do you think you are?" she said. "Some kind of special cases? We sent you out on a job. You did it. I ought to get a medal for every piece of paper that crosses this damned desk, if that's the way we're going to run things."

Joss and Evan looked at each other. "We did a nearly impossible job," Joss said, "without anything like the men or material we needed. You'd think that would be worth some recognition.''

Lucretia gave them the gentle look that Evan suspected she usually reserved for the chronically insane. ''You are both people of surprising intelligence and resourcefulness,'' she said, ''even if you do spend entirely too many of those valuable brain cells drinking stuff that even yeasts refuse to admit is alcohol after they're through with it, they're so ashamed. And you did exactly what I thought you would do, which is turn a nasty situation to your advantage somehow and make it pay off. When you do something that *surprises* me, I'll give you medals. Meanwhile, clear the hell out of here before I change my mind about the two weeks' leave. And I want your final written reports by tomorrow noon.'' Whereupon Lucretia began rummaging about on her desk in a way that suggested she was looking for something to throw at them.

Therefore they did the wise thing, and got out.

''No gratitude,'' Joss said. ''None. I think we should show them how upset we are.''

''What did you have in mind?'' said Evan.

Joss looked thoughtful. ''We could always go see if the yeasts are really that ashamed.''

Evan smiled slightly. They headed off for the hanger domes.

FOUR DAYS LATER THEY WERE ON WILLANS. Seven days later they were still on Willans, and the party that had started when they got there had not really stopped yet, though it had changed venues from bar to bar, and Evan had lost count of exactly how many establishments he had been in at all. Joss had been making hopeful notes for the *Guide Michelin* in between times. The Thai food on Willans was extremely good.

The atmosphere of the community toward them had changed a great deal since the news got out of what Joss and Evan had found, and what they had been up to. No one, even Leif the Turk, seemed content to greet them without also buying them a drink. Leif did start a fight with Evan, just for old time's sake, and was sat on by nearly half the population of one bar, while sincere apologies were made by those not actually on the pile at the moment. Later on, Leif was fine again, and joined Evan (to his utter astonishment) in a rendition of "We'll Keep A Welcome in the Valleys," in flawless northern-accented Welsh. Evan spent a long while wondering about this, until someone abruptly produced a barrel of homemade mead. He forgot to wonder about Leif, or anything else, for a day or so.

On the seventh day was the naming party for *Nosey*, and her new paint job was sorely tested, as large amounts of newly-minted ethanol were poured over every square inch of the hull, and her name or an approximation of it was pronounced in every language then current on Willans.

Mell and Evan stood off to one side of this, watching, while Joss toured with the christening crew, himself armed with a squirt-bottle of hooch, making sure nothing was missed. "Can't let our ship have any weak spots," he was saying to the rest of the reeking crew, as they worked their way around.

Evan smiled a bit at that. "Finally," he said.

"Hmm?"

"Our ship."

Mell nodded. Her smile was slightly somber. "So it is," she said.

Evan glanced at her; together they walked off a little way, toward the hangar's inner doors. "So," he said. "What about you, now that you're a rich lady who owns a space station?"

"Now I have to keep it," Mell said. She smiled a bit. "Not that anyone here would try to take it from me. But there are others elsewhere who might think it was an easy grab." She looked ruefully at Evan. "You boys did a job on the defense systems, I can tell you that. Going to cost me a million or so to put them back."

"You can always lease out computer time," Evan said.

She nodded. "I already have a broker on Mars looking over a few contracts. There aren't that many computer installations out this way that have that kind of power. It's a valuable resource. And the SP are paying me a finder's fee on the Takawabara data, so that's a help too. It shouldn't be too long before the station is fully operational as a repair and infoprocessing facility. Give me a year or so."

She looked at him sidewise. "And what about you?" she said. "Now that you're famous all over the solar system for breaking up a dangerous nationalist ring?"

He laughed, but the laugh wasn't entirely happy. "Famous. Never mind that. The SP takes the credit; and that's our agreement with them, so it's no matter." He shrugged. "But after another week, we're back to work. Heaven knows where."

"Is there a way of finding out in advance whether it'll take you out this way?" Mell said.

Evan looked at her, a bit sadly, "Should there be?"

She breathed in, then sighed. "I don't know. Really, I don't. Right now things are a bit hectic. Have been, anyway."

"For me, too," Evan said. "But regardless of everything else, you ought to know . . . it was splendid."

She glanced up, and smiled, just that slight smile that had made the breath catch in his chest before. It did so now. But then it came loose again, and Evan knew the truth, and smiled back. "For me, too," she said. "Maybe someday again."

"Maybe," Evan said. It was, after all, a big universe: the words "impossible" and "never" tended to backfire on you. . . .

They looked back at the mad crew still pouring potheen over the ship. "I suppose," Evan said, "if we don't get some of that on us, the smell of everyone else is going to drive us nuts for the next week.''

"Seems likely.'' She looked around, and down, and picked something up from beside the sprawling form of Leif the Turk. "Spray-bottle, sir?''

"Don't mind if I do,'' Evan said, and took it.

"And then I know this little Nepalese place—''

"You're on,'' Evan said, "but first things first.''

Together they headed over to the ship and started spraying.